The Unfortunate Isles

M.C. MUIR

By M.C. Muir

Under Admiralty Orders - The Oliver Quintrell Series
Book 1 - Floating Gold
Book 2 -The Tainted Prize
Book 3 - Admiralty Orders

King Richard and the Mountain Goat (Young adult)

By Margaret Muir

Sea Dust
Through Glass Eyes
The Black Thread
The Condor's Feather
Words on a Crumpled Page (Poetry)

The Unfortunate Isles

Under Admiralty Orders – The Oliver Quintrell Series
Book 4

M.C. MUIR

Chapter 1

Gibraltar Bay - December 1804

A gentle wave curled from the ship's bow and rippled along the hull. Another followed. Aloft, the masts creaked when the yards were hauled around. Staysails, hardened by sun and salt-air, luffed then clapped loudly, as if applauding the breeze and announcing the fact the British Royal Navy's frigate *Perpetual* was under-way.

Having lost count of the number of circles their feet had trudged around the capstan's drum, the crews' efforts had raised the best bower from the seabed. Draped in weed, the vessel's largest anchor now hung suspended from the starboard cathead. Mr Hanson, the youngest midshipman aboard, had watched the cable as it had slithered through the hawse-hole and flopped onto the deck slippery as an eel.

The stout hempen line, almost double the thickness of a man's forearm glistened, not from the seawater saturating it but from the coat of slime, pitted with sand and dotted with barnacles, covering it. Also decorating it were growths of bright green weed. It bore little resemblance to the cable that had followed the anchor to the bottom and settled there over three months ago.

Having concluded his business with the garrison and come aboard only half an hour earlier, Captain Oliver Quintrell was anxious to get underway. From the quarterdeck, he observed the ship's company and was satisfied with their performance, but the state of the anchor cable concerned him. It raised a disturbing question in his mind: *What is the condition of Perpetual's hull?*

While copper plating partially protected the frigate's hull from attack by the hungry Teredo worm, the sheathing failed to prevent slime, weed and barnacles attaching themselves to it. According to the captain, it would take a maelstrom or a spell of hard manual work in dry dock to clean the ship's bottom. As neither was immediately available, for the present, he had no alternative but to accept the drag the weed would create with the resulting reduction in speed. Like his men, he did not wish to delay his departure from Gibraltar any longer than necessary.

The explosive thunder from one of the frigate's 12-pounders sent a shudder through every timber in the ship. It attracted the attention of those on board and prompted the flocks of gulls bobbing on the bay to take to the air. Though the tongue of orange flame that poked out from the gun port was visible for only a few seconds, the acrid smoke that filled the waist lingered a while before slowly floating skywards.

A spontaneous round of *huzzas* rang from the deck as the crew considered the port they were farewelling. Not a soul aboard the frigate was sorry to be leaving. Unlike a shot fired in anger during close action, the gun salute, signalling their departure, was music to the seamen's ears.

On the quarterdeck, Captain Oliver Quintrell was conscious of the sound hitting the Rock of Gibraltar and echoing across the bay to the ships anchored at the Spanish mainland port of Algeciras only five miles away. A few minutes later, one of Gibraltar's big guns responded. The grey smoke, accompanying the deafening discharge, drifted from the stone ramparts of the Parson's Lodge Battery, the largest of the garrison's defensive battlements overlooking Rosia Bay. It raised a second round of *huzzas* from the crew and put a further furrow in the captain's brow. No doubt a thousand ears in the Spanish port would have heard it and a thousand eyes would now be observing the frigate's departure.

Mid-way across the bay, a single dhow with its lateen sail furled loosely to the yard, rocked on the water. On board, a pair of white-clad Moroccan fishermen hauled in their net paying not the slightest attention to the British ship or the gun salutes.

With the necessary formalities duly completed and satisfied his vessel was safely underway, Captain Quintrell turned to his first lieutenant. 'Take us into the Strait, Mr Parry. Let us pray the wind holds and carries us through to the Atlantic. The deck is yours.'

With the northern Pillar of Hercules on its larboard side and the entrance to the Gibraltar Strait less than two miles away, *Perpetual* proceeded slowly across the bay. Not a single man aboard was going to miss the landmark. They had watched the sun rise over it every morning for the past three months and observed the ominous tear-drop shaped cloud swirling around its summit. They had smelt the miasmic mist that rolled down the mountain's flank and engulfed the town with its deadly vapours delivering death to the residents and claiming the lives of half the population of the colony in a matter of weeks. Fortunately very few of the frigate's crew had fallen victim to the malignant fever.

With the quarantine declared over, the lassitude, the sailors had worn like a cloak, was cast off. The sooner the frigate was heading for the open sea the better. But when the frigate made its turn into the Gibraltar Strait, the Levanter, which had them carried from the bay, showed little inclination to follow, giving precedence to a stronger north-westerly blowing down from the Iberian Peninsula and making their onward passage arduous. Any remaining cobwebs on the staysails were swept away as *Perpetual* was obliged to tack back and forth between the southern coast of Spain and the north coast of Africa.

An hour later, when the ship's bell indicated time for the watches to change, several of the sailors remained on deck. After months of breathing stagnant air, they had little desire to go below. They preferred to relax in the fo'c'sle, sleep under one of the boats or hang in the rigging where they could fill their lungs with fresh air and appreciate the fact they were at sea again.

William Ethridge nudged alongside the old cooper who was leaning his shoulder against the hammock netting above the cap rail. 'Are you glad to be sailing?' the young shipwright asked.

'What sort of daft question is that?' Bungs snorted. 'Every man-Jack of the crew, from ship's boy to lieutenant, is glad to see the back of that place. Or haven't you noticed? Gibraltar? A waste of time and lives, to my mind. Stuck like pigs in a cesspit, we were. Beats me how more men didn't die.'

Will knew better than to argue with the cooper. For the next few minutes, he contented himself with watching the sea as it slid by.

'Remember the Muffin-man?' Bungs asked. 'He was one of your mess-mates when you last sailed with the captain.'

Will nodded. 'Of course, I remember him.'

'The fever took him. The doctor did all he could to fix him and I tried to cheer him up. But he never pulled through.'

Will shook his head. 'I remember Muffin. He never said much, but he was a good mate. I'm sorry.'

'What's for you to be sorry about?' Bungs said. 'You didn't give him the fever, did you? Anyway, you were in yonder navy-yard at the same time. How come you didn't cop a dose?'

Will shrugged his shoulders. 'Just lucky, I guess. There were some in the yard that did.'

'Well,' the cooper said, his tone mellowing. 'That's over and done with now and best forgotten.' He changed the subject. 'So what became of you after you jumped ship at Greenwich and left us with a sinking hulk?'

'I didn't jump ship,' William said indignantly. 'I was one of the last to leave. It weren't my fault she was sinking. I did what I could to keep her afloat. I got you safely back to England in her, didn't I?'

The cooper winked. 'Too right, you did, lad. She was a good ship.'

'*Elusive*,' Will mused, thinking about the frigate he'd been dragged onto against his will. It was the ship he'd served on for over a year; the vessel on which he'd honed his craft and where he'd formed true friendships. It was where his life had changed and he had grown from boy to man, but not without enduring some pain. 'Do you know what became of her?'

'The frigate? Do you think the Navy Board would have told me?' Bungs asked cynically.

'But you always know what's going on.'

'Well, between you and me and the keelson, I heard she had her hull patched up, had her innards ripped out and was towed into the Thames to serve as a coal hulk. The Admiralty hasn't got time or money to waste on rotten old frigates. It's a crying shame, but that's how it is these days.'

William shrugged.

Mr Hanson interrupted the pair pointing to the bunt-lines and clew-garnets hanging loosely at the fife rail. 'Make yourself useful. Tidy those lines.'

The cooper looked up to the sweep of the sails and ambled over to the rail. After taking up the slack, he coiled the lines, placed them on the belaying pins and returned to his conversation.

'Has Captain Quintrell spoken with you yet?' the cooper asked.

'Why would he want to talk to me? I doubt he even knows I've come aboard.'

'You'd be surprised. There's not much goes on he don't know about. But, I'll tell you this, the captain ain't been himself recently. Hardly seen hide or hair of him this last week.'

A pair of seagulls wheeled and dived only twenty yards from the rail. Their cries caught the men's attention. 'Do you know where we're bound?' Will asked.

Bungs shook his head. 'That way,' he said with a straight face, pointing his finger towards the ship's bow. Will punched him on the arm.

'Another thing I can tell you for certain, we won't be going far. We're almost out of water and provisions is low. I reckon we'll bear off for the coast of Portugal and fill some casks like we did when we sailed out.'

'Then Portsmouth?'

'You best chew the captain's ear if you want an answer to that. All I knows is that most of the barrels is empty and the captain knows it. And the bellies of everyman aboard will be too if we don't pick up some victuals before long.'

'The crew seem happy enough.'

The old cooper shrugged his shoulders. 'Aye, the crew's in good spirits. You heard them whooping when we left the Bay. But watch their faces lengthen, quick as a flash, when the rations are cut in half. It'll be frowns, not smiles, that'll crease their fizzogs, and moans and complaints not *huzzas* you'll hear. You mark my words, but I don't need to tell you that, you've seen it before.'

Will nodded. It was true. He had witnessed the rapid change in a crew's temperament whenever the word *rationing* was mentioned. It appeared to him that hunger affected sailors' brains more than it affected their bellies.

'Enough of that,' Bungs went on. 'This talk of food makes me hungry.' He poked his elbow into the young man's side. 'You'll sit by me in the mess, like you used to. I've got a spot saved for you and two new mess-mates for you to meet.' Then he stopped abruptly and pointed to the Spanish coast. 'That's Terifa over there and, if you take a gander over the larboard side, you can see the coast of Africa. The captain'll be happy we cleared the Strait without meeting any other ships.'

William scanned the sea. 'Frogs, you mean?'

'Aye.'

'Are there many of them about?'

'How in Hell's name am I supposed to know? Boney don't tell me where he sends his ships.'

An involuntary smile lit Will's face. The cooper's bark hadn't changed.

'All I know is they steered clear of Gibraltar Bay when the fever was at its worst. Not only them, but the bloody British, too. No one was allowed in and we weren't allowed out. Then his face broke into an involuntary smile. 'But we sent two of them Frenchies to the bottom of the Mediterranean. They got the surprise of their lives, when we showered 'em with shot from the top of the Rock.'

'I heard the guns,' William Ethridge said. 'Everyone in the colony heard them. It must have been quite a sight. I wish I'd been there to see it.'

The smile on the cooper's face faded as quickly as it had formed. 'It'll be a while before we see another fight. If we stay with this heading, it'll take us across the Atlantic. With most of the Frogs bottled up in Brest and Toulon, it's not likely we'll meet any action out there.'

'No prizes then?'

'Not likely,' Bungs said.

Leaning against the hammock netting, the shipmates watched a pair of porpoises slicing through the waves before diving under the hull. Several others leapt clear then sped effortlessly along beside the frigate. For a full five minutes their antics entertained the two mates, then, as if orchestrated, they all dived together and never reappeared.

Standing upright and stretching his back, William Ethridge glanced to the south-east. The coast of Africa was but a hazy smudge in the distance. 'I best get back to the carpenter's shop,' he said. 'Mr Crosby will be wondering what has become of me.'

'Aye, piss off,' Bungs said. 'I don't have time to stand here blathering all day.' But just as the wright turned to go, the cooper grabbed him firmly by the arm. 'So what are you hiding in the carpenter's shop?'

Will was shocked. 'What do you mean, what am I hiding? I ain't hiding nothing.'

Bungs looked him straight in the eye. 'Come on, you can tell your old mate. I know something's going on in there. I ain't never known that door be closed all day. There must be a reason.'

'Beats me,' said Will, tugging his arm free. 'If you find out, let me know.'

When the broad Atlantic presented itself ahead of them, the order was given.

'West-north-west, helmsman,' Mr Parry called.

Standing beside the binnacle, the sailing master could not resist making an observation. 'That course will carry us out of the path of any French ships making for the Channel.'

'Thank you, Mr Mundy. I believe that is the captain's intention.'

The first lieutenant was satisfied they had cleared the Strait and cast his eyes over the top hamper. Apart from the studding sails, every stitch of canvas was flying but, because of the weed dragging on the hull, *Perpetual* was only making four knots. Unless the frigate was careened and the bottom scraped, it would be impossible to outrun an enemy ship. It was a fact everyone was aware of.

Chapter 2

Heading West

Will Ethridge descended the companion ladder to the galley hoping to slip quietly into the mess without being noticed, but sailors have keen eyes and are always on the lookout for any chance to deride some unfortunate fellow, especially if he is unable to defend himself.

'Well I'll be, if it ain't the fish we pulled out of the Solent!' Smithers yelled, drawing everyone's attention.

'Built any more boats lately?' another man called, to the encouragement of the mates sitting at his table. All eyes turned to see the new arrival and the banter continued.

'Have you learned how to steer a boat yet?' one asked.

Another cooed, 'I suggest you fit a rudder on the next one.'

'And how about a thwart to sit on?'

By now, the deck was vibrating from the stamping feet, and the tankards on the swinging tables danced to the slap of hands. Will's cheeks coloured slightly. He smiled and shrugged. For him, the well-meaning taunts meant he was back amongst friends.

'Stow it, you lot,' he said, making his way down the centre of the mess, unable to avoid a punch on the arm by one sailor, a poke in the ribs from another and several well-meaning thumps on the back. A leg shot out from under a table to trip him, but he was too canny for that and jumped over it. Then the jibes subsided as quickly as they had begun.

Of the faces that glanced up at him, there were those he didn't recognize, but there were a lot of mates he remembered from two years earlier. How could he forget the weeks spent in the high southern latitudes cooped up in the mess with the same faces day after day, while a blizzard raged outside and pendulous icicles hung like organ pipes from the yards threatening to spear a man's skull, if he happened to be standing beneath one when it fell? Those images were imprinted on his brain, but there were other memories of that cruise Will Ethridge preferred not to remember.

'Welcome back, Will,' one of the older hands said quietly. 'Cast adrift again, were you?'

Will smiled again.

'Let the lad alone,' Bungs growled.

'It don't worry me,' the young shipwright murmured. 'I'm thankful to be back. I couldn't have wished for anything better.'

'Just as well, because that's the only favour you'll be getting on this ship. We'll all be living off rations of fresh air before long.' Sliding out from the mess table and indicating for his mate to join him on the sea chest. 'Stop your jabbering and sit your body down next to me.'

Will ignored the remark and nodded to the Negro sitting opposite Bungs, and the young lad perched next to him. They were both strangers to him.

'I suppose you'll want to know who this is,' the cooper said with a sigh.

'If it's not too much trouble,' Will said, winking at the lad opposite.

'You watch your tone, young fella. Don't you forget who's head of this mess table.

'You ain't changed much, have you, Bungs?' Then he turned to the two other sailors at the table. 'I'm Will,' he said. 'William Ethridge. I sailed with Bungs on *Elusive*.'

'Ekundayo,' the big West Indian announced, 'but I go by the name of Eku. And this scallywag is young Tom.'

'I'll warn you now,' Bungs said, 'don't be fooled by that leathery skin, there's half a brain between those black ears. And, be warned, there's no mischief this young imp ain't up for either.'

The boy smiled. 'Tommy Wainwright. That's me. I clean up after the surgeon in the cockpit.'

'Have you both sailed with Captain Quintrell afore?' Will asked, glancing from one to the other.

'Surely have,' Eku said. 'Doubled the Horn last cruise. Sailed north to Peru.'

'Did you take any prizes?'

'We did all right,' Eku said.

'Aye, a darned sight better than we did in Gibraltar,' Bungs added.

Will shook his head. 'There was plenty of talk in the naval yard about the British frigate anchored in the bay, but the name *Perpetual* didn't mean anything to me and I never heard mention of the captain's name. Not until I came aboard and heard it was Captain Quintrell. What a stroke of luck.'

'That's not what you said when we pulled you out of the Solent a couple of years back.'

Will ignored the cooper's quip. 'And where's the ship heading this time?'

'Azores, I heard,' Eku answered. 'The Western Islands.'

'How would you know that?' Bungs demanded.

'I keep me ears open.'

'Are you one of the new carpenters?' Tommy Wainwright asked Will, his accent straight from the grime of the north of England.

'I am that, lad. A shipwright by trade.'

Bungs turned to the new arrival. He still had questions for him. 'I guess you managed to find your way back to Buckler's Hard when you left *Elusive*.'

'I did. And I finished my time, like I said I would. But I didn't stay on the Hard after that, even though the master shipwright wanted me to.'

'What happened to that old grandfather of yours, the one who near chopped his leg off with his adze?' Bungs asked.

'You've got a good memory.'

'It don't pay to be forgetful. Did he recover?'

Will shook his head. 'Ma said he died not long after I'd gone. She said his leg swelled up and went black and the doctor wanted to cut it off, but Grandfather would have none of that. He argued that there was no place on the Hard for a one-legged shipwright. He was a stubborn old beggar. Ma said that after he was buried, the doctor told her he'd likely have died whether he'd taken the leg off or not, and the pain of the amputation would have been far worse than the blood poisoning.' Will sighed. 'The worst thing, for me, is that all the time I was gone, he thought I was dead. He thought I'd drowned in the boat I made and he blamed himself that he hadn't made sure it was watertight before I dropped it in the river. He carried the guilt to his grave.'

'Well, he was wrong, wasn't he? You didn't drown, did you? And you can't change that.'

Will shrugged. 'I suppose so.'

'But what about that mother of yours? I'm surprised you left her alone.'

'I didn't,' William said. 'Ma left first. That was a reason I didn't stay long at Buckler's Hard. After grandfather died, ma couldn't stay in the house on her own. It had to pass to another wright and his family so she went to live with her sister and husband. He owns his own cottage in Southampton. That was where I found her when I went back.'

'I bet she was surprised to see you.'

Will laughed. 'When she opened the door and saw me standing there with the lamp-light flickering on my face, she thought I was a ghost. For a full two days after that she wouldn't leave my side. And what a fuss the men made when I went back to Buckler's Hard. They couldn't believe their eyes either. What a story I had to tell. Some of the wrights accused me of telling tales. They said the things I spoke of just didn't happen.'

Bungs knew better. 'So what brought you to Gibraltar?'

'When we launched one of the ships and it was ready to be towed to Portsmouth to have its masts stepped, I asked Mr Adams if I might go with it. He agreed, but when I was at the naval dockyard, I was asked if I wanted a job there. By that time, the war with France was on again and there was more work than the men could cope with. I agreed to stay and worked there. One day, I heard they wanted a dozen carpenters to work at the yard in Gibraltar. Since leaving *Elusive*, I'd had a hankering to go to sea again.'

'So you signed for the colony and sailed,' Bungs said.

'Indeed. Me and eleven other wrights. We were all delighted. We were told there'd be plenty of work and there was no mention of fever at that time. But once the epidemic took hold and the quarantine regulations were enforced, that spelled an end to the work. The Mediterranean Fleet that usually came in for refits had to go elsewhere. And with no money to build new ships, there was nothing to do in the yard.' He shook his head. 'For the past month we were busy making coffins for them that could afford to buy wood, and find a patch of dirt big enough to put them in.'

'You didn't get the fever?' Bungs asked.

'No, I was lucky. Two carpenters died and several infants. I woke every morning wondering if I would be next.'

'Well, you're safe now,' Eku said.

'I hope so.'

A voice, yelling from the hatch, interrupted their conversation.'

'Bungs get up here.' Mr Tully's voice carried the length of the mess. 'The captain wants to speak with you.'

The cooper winked at young Tom. 'There you go,' he said, 'the captain wants me ear.'

'Like as not to chew it off,' Smithers scoffed from the next table.

'Shut your mouth, you old coot. What would you know about anything?'

Under a full press of sails, the 32-gun frigate was heading for the Portuguese islands situated nine hundred miles west of Lisbon, one thousand sea miles north-west of their current position. The voyage should take ten to twelve days providing they did not encounter any French ships.

Ahead, the western sky bloomed with the colours of autumn leaves—gold, rust and magenta, yet to the east, the curtain of night had already been drawn across the Strait behind them. With the winter solstice approaching, the days had become shorter, though not as noticeably as in England. It was anticipated that the coming year would herald change for all the ship's company and everyone was looking forward to that.

First Lieutenant Simon Parry wondered what 1805 would mean to Europe. With Bonaparte's army clawing its way east from France, no one knew where the fighting would end. From all that had been written about him, Emperor Napoleon was an ambitious man who thought nothing of erasing the boundaries of states, countries and empires that had existed unchanged for centuries. He had long since set his sights on invading England but, so far, the Sea Fencibles and the Channel Fleet had prevented him from running a single boat up on the beaches of southern England. The navy, too, under Admirals Nelson and Cornwallis had successfully kept the warmonger's fleets confined within their harbours, thus preventing the Frogs from wreaking any serious damage at sea.

The current concern for the Lords Commissioners in Whitehall was Napoleon's unrelenting efforts to seduce the Spanish Crown—to entice, force or blackmail the King of Spain into joining forces with him. If that occurred, the number of fighting ships in a combined Franco/Spanish fleet would outnumber all the ships of war Britain could muster. Besides which, while Britain had spent the lull during the Peace of Amiens breaking up its old vessels and relegating them to coal hulks or prison ships, Napoleon's ambitious schemes and plans had continued unabated. Despite the blockades, construction of new and faster vessels had continued in the French yards and, as a result, Britain's control of the seas was tenuous, to say the least.

According to Captain Quintrell's orders, *Perpetual* was heading away from the ongoing conflict. Its destination was Van Diemen's Land, part of the colony of New South Wales on the other side of the globe—the place where the dregs of England's jails, the thieves, frauds and murderers were being transported to since Britain could no longer use America as its dumping ground for felons. It was to be a long voyage, sailing via the coast of Brazil before heading south to gain the Roaring Forties that would carry them south of the Cape of Good Hope and across the Indian Ocean to New Holland.

While news of the frigate's latest destination had filtered down to some of the crew, Simon wondered if the length of the voyage had struck home. It was four months since they had sailed from Portsmouth and, no doubt, several were anxious to see the shores of England again, but that would not happen for more than a year. However, for the present, the fickle-minded seamen were happy to be sailing with nothing but sky on the horizon. What more could they wish for except, perhaps, the chance of prize money? Prizes of war were another commodity they had been deprived of in Gibraltar Bay. A sailor's pay alone would not line his pocket for very long when his ship was eventually paid off.

Mr Parry was not one to question the destination. He accepted the news and followed orders as required. As first lieutenant, he was responsible for the crew—the men whose sweat and skill worked the ship. He knew Oliver Quintrell was confident of his ability and, on most occasions, they worked well together anticipating and understanding something of how each other thought.

Despite that mutual respect, Simon Parry was troubled. Prior to *Perpetual* setting sail, he had made certain decisions that went directly against the captain's standing orders—decisions he knew would ruffle the captain's feathers, if not infuriate him. Being left in charge, he had been obliged to make them and now he would have to bear the consequences.

In retrospect, he questioned his own judgement, but what was done was done and could not be undone at this stage. He regretted not having spoken with the captain immediately prior to departure, but the opportunity had not arisen. No sooner had the captain stepped aboard than he had descended to his cabin and given strict orders that he was not to be disturbed. He had appeared on deck when the ship weighed, but did not linger long. Being obliged to remain on the quarterdeck, a suitable opportunity to inform the captain of his actions had not arisen until it was too late.

As first officer, he had detailed the decisions he had made in his daily report and forwarded it in the proper manner, but he'd received no response. Feeling a gnawing need to broach the subject personally, yet being aware of the captain's present sullen mood, he chose not to pursue it. If all went well, once they reached the Azores the problem would evaporate.

Turning his face into the wind, Simon Parry closed his eyes but only briefly. The luff of the mainsail chuckled to itself, then filled momentarily before flapping again. The helmsman observed the canvas and adjusted the rudder, but he had no control over the wind.

'Pray God it doesn't fail us now,' Jack Mundy said. 'Pray God the westerly does not come through or we'll be blown back to the Spanish Coast.'

Like every sailor who had ever passed through the Pillars of Hercules, Mr Parry was aware of the problem. In ancient times, the Phoenicians and Moors sailing from the Mediterranean Sea or the coast of North Africa had combatted the lack of wind with a hundred slaves bound to the oars of their immense galleys. The rowers had little choice but to respond to the beat of the drum and the crack of the whip. For the frigate, there was no such solution. Being becalmed at any stage of the voyage was something no one wanted, and the first lieutenant did not appreciate being reminded of the fact by the sailing master.

After twenty minutes of tacking, chasing the last zephyrs, no amount of adjustment of helm and rudder or bracing yards could prevent the air in the sails from expiring. With the courses furled and the flagging topsails showing no inclination to fill, *Perpetual* was left at the mercy of the currents lolling like a piece of flotsam south of Cape Trafalgar.

Joining the first lieutenant on the quarterdeck, Mr Tully enquired if there were any change in orders. 'Begging your pardon, Mr Parry, but did I hear tell that we were making for the Western Islands. They're to the north-west of our present position, aren't they?'

'I am well aware of the location of the Azores, Mr Tully. At the moment, however, I am more concerned with the loss of wind.' He glanced up to the flaccid canvas, aware his reply had sounded curt.

'I wonder why we are not heading for Madeira,' the second lieutenant said.

Mr Parry glanced at the officer standing beside him. 'Follow orders, Mr Tully. Do not question them.'

'Not questioning, sir, just wondering.'

Crossing to the lee side of the quarterdeck, Mr Parry cast a quizzical glance at the man who had once signed as a foremast Jack before entering the service as a midshipman and rising fairly rapidly up the ranks. Though he was no newcomer to the sea, *Perpetual*'s second lieutenant still had something of a brazen child-like impudence about him. Ben Tully knew the ropes as well as any seasoned sailor, he climbed the rigging as nimbly as a Barbary ape, he bore the marks of the cat across his back proving his right-of-passage in the fo'c'sle, and he had the papers to show he had passed the examination for lieutenant. He had proved himself worthy of the position he held and, though he lacked breeding, he had a brain between his ears—an attribute sadly lacking in some officers Simon Parry had served with in the past.

'I want a man in the foretop, Mr Hanson, and tell him to keep his eyes open.'

'Aye, aye, Mr Parry,' the midshipman said, before striding briskly along the gangway to pass the message along.

In the waist, on the deck below, the captain's steward was squatting beside a wooden pail, scrubbing some pots. Mr Parry excused himself from the quarterdeck and descended the steps. There was a question he wanted to put.

'Casson, do you have a moment?'

'Always plenty of time for you, Mr Parry, sir,' the steward said, wiping his hands on his apron.

'Is the captain available for me to speak with him?'

The steward shook his head. 'Gave me strict orders he does not want to be disturbed by anyone.'

'Anyone?' Simon sighed, tilting his head to one side. 'Is the captain all right? I mean, is he well? Would you know if he is unwell?' Then a thought struck him. *Pray to God the captain was not harbouring the malignant fever.*

'He's fine. You can take my word for it,' Casson said, 'I've been with him long enough to know him better than he knows himself. Wasn't I the only one to visit him when he suffered the brain fever, when he didn't know a stuns'l from a stays'l?'

'I trust you are not suggesting there is a problem with the captain's mental capacity?'

'Oh, no, Mr Parry, sir, don't get me wrong, he's all right. Just for the present, he's a little out of sorts. That's all. I just hope he ain't sickening for som'at.'

'What makes you say that?' Simon asked.

'Because he ain't eating no more than a sparrow. He just pecks at his food and leaves most of it untouched. I've told him more than once it ain't right to waste good food.'

'And what is the captain's response to that, pray?'

'Says if I don't want it to go to waste, then I should eat it myself.'

'And what is your reply to that?'

'I don't say nothing. I do what the captain says and finish it off myself.' Casson smacked his belly appreciatively with both hands. 'Mark my word though, it can't last for ever. Before long he's going to get mighty hungry, and then he'll soon forget whatever's eating away at his innards.'

The lieutenant didn't comment but thanked the steward and returned to the deck, though his concerns for the captain's well-being would not leave him. Since the ship had departed the colony, Oliver Quintrell had appeared on deck only when requested by the officer-of-the-watch, or if a sudden sound or movement disturbed him, or late in the evening when the ship was sailing smoothly with a following wind and demanding very little attendance by the watch.

In the pallor of the moon, as it slid back and forth behind the sails, his skin had appeared grey. His expressionless features reflected the morose nature of his disposition. Even when he stepped on deck in daylight, he had turned from the sun and fixed his gaze on the endless and empty far horizon. He had gazed into the distance, as if something in particular was holding his attention when, in fact, there was nothing to break the monotony of sea and sky.

In comparison with the captain's despondent state, he thought it fortunate the crew's spirits had remained high since departing the colony. But the first lieutenant had not been the only one to notice the change in the captain's demeanour. This was the first occasion he had not invited any of his officers to dine with him on leaving port.

Under normal circumstances, it was a ritual conducted on the first or second evening at sea. It allowed the captain the opportunity to share information about the forthcoming mission in an informal manner, and discuss the ports they would touch on during the voyage. In the past, Oliver Quintrell had always enjoyed the men's company over a meal sharing anecdotes or listening to the often exaggerated exploits of younger officers after downing several glasses of fine wine.

But, having heard the steward's comments, Simon Parry's concerns were heightened. He now reprimanded himself for not sharing his worries with one of the other senior officers or the ship's surgeon. He felt remiss for not doing so and wanted to rectify the situation.

Aware the officers were planning a celebratory meal in the wardroom that evening, he bid Casson convey a written invitation to Captain Quintrell to join the gathering for dinner. As the day slipped by and no word was received to say the captain had declined, Simon remained hopeful. At five in the afternoon, when two bells rang from the belfry, Casson delivered a verbal message saying Captain Quintrell thanked the wardroom for their cordial invitation, wished them a pleasant meal, but asked to be excused as he had papers to attend to and he would be taking dinner alone in his cabin.

'What papers?' Mr Parry asked the ship's surgeon in private, prior to their meal. 'What has happened aboard this vessel in the past few days that demands the captain's undivided attention that he cannot spare an hour or two to enjoy the company of his senior officers?'

Jonathon Whipple raised his eyebrows. It was unusual to hear Mr Parry's voice raised in such a manner, but even more unusual to hear him questioning the captain's behaviour.

'We crossed the yards, raised the anchor, departed the bay and cleared the Strait of Gibraltar. How much paperwork does that entail? I cannot fathom it. Is there anything you would suggest?'

'A dose of tonic perhaps to titillate his appetite.'

'But what, might I ask, will stimulate his brain?'

'Have a care with your choice of words,' the doctor warned.

'But I do care. I care a great deal. That is the problem.'

The ship's surgeon acknowledged the officer's feelings. 'Be patient, Simon. Give him time. I have not examined him but, from what I have seen, there is nothing physically wrong with him. The death of his dear friend, however, is smouldering within him like a slow-match and only he has the power to snuff it out.' He looked into the worried eyes of the naval officer, a fine-looking man only a few years older than himself. 'Be patient a little longer,' he advised.

Chapter 3

The Squall

Overnight, a breeze picked up and carried the frigate in a north-westerly direction. By morning the wind had freshened, but the strength of the sudden squall that hit in the afternoon was not predicted. The gathering clouds had hung ominously above the western horizon for more than two hours, but although they indicated a storm, they appeared distant enough to be of little concern. Then, with an unexpected wind change, black clouds swirled overhead and the thunder of a thousand galloping hooves bore down on the ship. Moving faster than any coach and six, the rain approached, bouncing off the sea's surface and cutting visibility to almost nothing. The efforts to reduce sail came too late.

With lightning streaking the sky, the first gusts struck *Perpetual* on the starboard quarter throwing the frigate onto her beam ends and almost dipping the tips of the larboard yardarms into the sea. It bowled two of the middies on the quarterdeck off their feet. They went down like a pair of wooden skittles. White water and foam rushed in through the scuppers and washed the deck, sending water cascading into the waist. It was fortunate the gunports had been secured. With no time to rig lifelines, the sailors grabbed onto any line or pin or rail that was fixed to the ship.

Of the men who had been sent aloft to reef tops'ls, when the most powerful gusts hit, their scramble inboard was desperate. Wrapping their arms around a stay, weaving their legs through the rungs of the ratlines, they clung on, watching helplessly as the main tops'l blew out of its boltropes. The topman, who hadn't made it off the yard in time, dropped like a stone into the churning sea.

The call of man-overboard went out, but at the time, preventing the ship from going over was all the crew could hope to achieve. Then, less than five minutes after it had arrived, the squall passed and the sun broke through the clouds. The deck gleamed white and the beams of light catching the metal plates shone like mirrors.

When the noise and wind subsided, the hull righted itself. The worst of the weather died as abruptly as it had blown in and the vessel was immediately worn around to face the rainbow that decorated the eastern sky. The missing topman, identified as Andreas Hutt, had been a popular hand. Aged in his forties, he had a family in Plymouth but, though the sea was scoured for half an hour, no sign of the man could be found.

Annoyed at the loss of a valued topman and frustrated at the lost opportunity to collect the tons of fresh water that had washed over the deck, the captain remained on deck while a new tops'l was bent and the frigate was returned to the course it had previously been on. With the rain falling steadily, though less heavily, Oliver shook the water from his hat and boat cloak, and wiped away the rain running into his eyes.

Glancing forward, the captain didn't expect to see a bucket appearing out of the forward companionway. It was followed by a figure obviously struggling to make it up the ladder. Wearing a dark coloured cloak, he decided it must be one of the middies in an over-sized cape, but when the wind whipped the cowl from the figure's head, he knew instantly it was a female.

In complete disbelief at what he was seeing, Oliver wasted no time, left the quarterdeck and headed for'ard. With the cloak billowing around her legs and her rain-soaked hair streaking across her face, the woman made two attempts to empty the contents of the bucket over the rail, unaware the captain was approaching.

'You there,' he yelled. 'Whosoever you are, stop what you are doing! Put that down!'

The woman turned abruptly, placed the bucket on the deck and, at the same time, dropped an awkward curtsy.

'What you are doing on my ship?' Oliver demanded.

'Begging your pardon, sir—'

But Captain Quintrell had no time to listen to her explanation. 'Believe me, I will find the person who brought you aboard without permission.'

'If I might—'

'Females aboard a ship augur bad luck. They distract the men and lead to nothing but mischief.'

'But, sir, if I could only—'

'If you could only step ashore this very instant, madam, that is the only thing you could do that would appease me.'

'Then what the men said about you is not true.'

The captain looked from the woman to the handful of seamen who had crawled from under the boats where they'd been sheltering from the storm. Each man turned his head away in an effort to appear uninterested in the conversation.

Teeth clenched and brow furrowed, he dashed the wet hair from his face. Inside, he was seething, but despite his exasperation, the woman's words had struck a chord with him. What had the men been saying? Not that mess talk concerned him unless there was some underlying resentment or sinister motive behind it. No captain could ignore murmurings that were the possible harbingers of mutiny. Complaints were nothing new, and being captain meant unpopular decisions had to be made. He put the ship on half-rations when supplies were short. He ordered punishments for crimes as set down by the *Articles of War*. He sent men aloft to shorten sail when a storm was about to hit. He never liked giving such orders, but that was what command entailed and issuing them would always make him unpopular with some members of the crew some of the time.

'I do not give a hoot what tittle-tattle you have been lending your ear to,' he stated after ordering a group of men back to work.

Being given no opportunity to explain herself, the woman politely asked if she might be excused.

'No, you will not be excused for being aboard my ship. Nor will the person or persons responsible for your presence here. You are, however, excused from this deck and I suggest you crawl back into whatever hidey-hole you emerged from and do not show your face again until we reach port. There, I guarantee, you will go over the side with all possible haste.'

'Captain, if I might—'

Mr Hanson climbed from the forward hatch. He was out of breath. The sailors standing nearby tried to make themselves look busy recoiling lines on the pin rail.

'Take this person below and return her to wherever she came from.'

The woman, of matronly age, was confused. While Mr Hanson was tugging on her cape in an attempt to draw her towards the waist, she was anxious to head for the forward companion ladder and return below by the same way she had come on deck.

The captain stormed aft, glancing around. 'Mr Parry!' he bellowed.

The officers on the quarterdeck exchanged glances. It was the first time they had heard the captain raise his voice when they were not engaged in action.

'Mr Nightingale, you are officer-of-the-watch are you not?'

'I am.'

'Locate Mr Parry and have him present himself in my cabin immediately.'

'I think he is resting.'

'Then wake him up, damn you.'

'Aye, aye, sir.'

The midshipmen needed no further instruction. One hurried forward while the other made for the companionway, almost colliding with the captain's steward who had just stepped up onto the quarterdeck balancing a tray in his hand with a cup and saucer on it.

'Can I tempt you with a cup of tea, Capt'n?' Casson asked.

'Damn your tea!' Oliver yelled, as he stormed past him almost knocking the tray out of his hands.

Casson turned, rolled his eyes and followed the captain down the ladder.

Less than two minutes later, footsteps stopped outside the door and there was a sharp *rat-a-tat*.

Oliver Quintrell was already seated at the table. Leaning forward with his elbows firmly fixed on the table, he faced the door and issued a response to whosoever was outside. 'Enter,' he called. Despite his aggressive pose, his voice was completely composed.

Simon Parry, with his hat pressed under his arm, stepped through the doorway bowing his head beneath the low beams. 'I understand you want to speak with me,' he said. There was no need to add an apology, the expression on his face was sufficient.

'Indeed I do,' Oliver said, tapping the table with his index finger and thumb, all that remained of his right hand. It was an indication for the lieutenant to sit.

'Casson,' he called and waited for the steward's head to appear at the door. 'I will have that drink now. Coffee, I think, and bring one of the bottles of fine French Brandy I received from the garrison commander.'

The steward knuckled his forehead and glanced at the first lieutenant, but Mr Parry's eyes were firmly fixed on the captain. A mischievous smile played on the corner of the steward's lips. 'Coming up in two ticks, Capt'n.'

For several slightly awkward moments the two men sat opposite each other, neither speaking. With the squall having cleared completely, there was only gentle movement as the frigate slid from one broad trough of ocean into another. The smooth motion was insufficient to draw any audible response from the tired timbers.

As if he had been interrupted in his work, Oliver looked at the chart rolled out on the table, appeared to study it for a moment, then pushed it aside. When he eventually spoke, his voice remained calm though his tone was cynical.

'I am hoping you will convince me that I have been seeing things. That I only imagined the presence of a female person on my deck.' He paused for breath but not long enough for the lieutenant to reply. 'This apparition was carrying a wooden pail and attempted to discharge the contents over the side—the windward side, I might add. Needless to say, the bulk of the bucket's contents was returned to the deck. This person then proceeded to scoop water from the scuttlebutt into the pail, swill it about and repeat the abortive effort of emptying it. If I am not wrong, the reflux from some person's stomach is now decorating the side of the hull, while in the meantime, at least one man on watch has been deprived of his ration of drinking water from the butt. Tell me this incident is a figment of my imagination or convince me that you were deceived in the manner I was.'

This time the captain waited for an answer, his eyes glaring at the officer.

'I can assure you,' Mr Parry said, 'there was no intention to deceive or withhold information. I wished above all else to consult with you prior to sailing, but your affairs at the garrison consumed all your attention, and when you returned with orders to depart the port, you immediately retired to your cabin and the opportunity to speak with you never arose. The matter has troubled me since we sailed, and I can only offer my apologies.'

Oliver leaned forward, his elbows still anchored to the table. 'My affairs in Gibraltar are irrelevant to this conversation. Did I or did I not see a female on my ship? Do the articles not specifically state that females shall not sail aboard Royal Navy ships? And are you not aware of my personal views on this regulation? By now you should know I abhor the presence of women aboard His Majesty's vessels, be they wives of petty officers, passengers, stowaways or dowager duchesses.'

The lieutenant could not argue.

'In God's name, where is this washer-woman hiding?'

'Beg pardon, sir, but she is not a washer-woman, and she is not hiding. She is the wife of one of the artisans who came aboard in Gibraltar. She is being housed in the carpenter's shop with another woman and a boy. I gave my permission for them to come aboard.'

'Another woman? And you did what?'

Entering unannounced, as was the prerogative of the captain's steward, Casson put on a cheery voice. 'Here's your coffee, sir. And I thought you might fancy a bit of cheese and some olives to go with it.'

Rolling up the chart, Oliver turned in his chair and placed it on top of the pile of papers on his desk. Then, concentrating his attention on the two cups, he waited until his steward returned with a bottle and two glasses and deposited them on the table. 'Now leave us and shut the door. I do not wish to be disturbed.'

Knuckling his forelocks, the steward hurried out.

After pouring two glasses, Oliver pushed one across the table to his first officer. 'I am still waiting for your explanation, Simon.'

'I had little choice, sir. I could not refuse to sign the carpenters as I knew *Perpetual* desperately needed skilled tradesmen. As to the women, may I explain?'

'I think you had better do so and quickly before my patience runs out completely. At the moment, I can see no earthly reason to account for such a blatant breach of my orders.'

'Captain, despite the directives—'

'The directives were revised in '49 and '57, and I call them naval regulations.'

'—many ships of the line carry women, often the wives of warrant officers, and though their names are not entered in the muster book, I understand many of them prove useful on long voyages, for example, filling cartridges or tending to the wounded.'

'And are these two females you are referring to particularly adept in such skills?'

'I don't know, though I don't doubt they could learn.'

The captain leaned back, waiting to hear the rest of the lieutenant's feeble explanation.

'Mrs Crosby is the wife of one of the carpenters who recently joined the ship. The other is the wife of a shipwright who died at the navy yard. Mrs Crosby begged me to allow them to sail with us. She feared they would both die if they remained in the colony. She assured me her husband had some money put aside and he was willing to pay for their passage. I might add that she has sailed with her husband before.'

'Huh! If they have money, why did they not depart the colony on another ship?'

'Might I remind you, Captain, that since the quarantine, no British ships were allowed in or out of Gibraltar Bay?'

'Enough! I have heard enough,' Oliver cried, shaking his head. 'At this point in time, there is little that can be done barring throwing the pair of floozies overboard. And I presume that would not be deemed acceptable.'

Mr Parry offered no comment.

Oliver sat for a moment, tapping his finger-nail on the table. He was conscious of his shortcomings and regretted his outburst of temper in full view of the men. It was uncharacteristic and it troubled him, though he was loath to admit it to anyone, even to himself. He also didn't need to be told he had been withdrawn of late and made himself unavailable to his men while pondering the events that had occurred in Gibraltar. He was well aware that a captain's moods and personal feelings had no place on a ship in His Majesty's service. But the fact he had been reminded of his failings by a woman, and a woman he had never ever met before, made him realize he must leave the past behind and move on.

His reply came slowly and deliberately, allowing the tension in the air to relax a little. 'I am prepared to make the following allowances,' he said. 'You will inform the women I am not happy that this situation was ever allowed to arise. However, as it appears we are stuck with them for the duration of this cruise, inform them I will permit them to air themselves on the deck for twenty minutes in the morning and a similar length of time in the afternoon, providing they do not so much as look at any of the crew.'

The lieutenant acknowledged the arrangements.

'As soon as we reach Ponta Delgada, they will be conveyed to the quay and deposited there. If the woman's husband intends to leave the ship with them, he will need to speak with me prior to that time so I can release him. Once the women are ashore, I take no responsibility for their welfare or for their onward passage to England. Do I make myself clear?'

The lieutenant agreed. 'I assure you, sir, the women will cause no disruptions in the time it takes for us to arrive there.'

'Unless we find some wind, it could take us a month to raise the Azores.' The vein of cynicism had ruptured again.

Simon Parry excused himself from the table and turned to leave, but hovered for a moment by the door.

Captain Quintrell was about to take a drink, but as the glass touched his bottom lip, he stopped. 'Is there something more I should know that you have not told me?'

The shadow of guilt that flashed across the first lieutenant's face provided the answer. Oliver raised one eyebrow and waited.

Without his face changing expression, Mr Parry added, 'A milking goat, four laying hens and a pair of piglets also came aboard in Gibraltar—courtesy of Mrs Crosby and Mrs Pilkington. The purser was notified and the livestock had been installed in the manger with the other animals. The carpenter's wife indicated that the eggs and milk, and the piglets would contribute to the cost of their accommodation.'

'Did she indeed? Is that the full extent?'

'I believe so, Captain. I thought it unreasonable to refuse fresh supplies, however, as the quantity is very minimal, when I spoke with the purser, I suggested those victuals would best be allocated to the women and if there was any excess it should be delivered to the sick berth. I should note that I included this information in my written report, which I believe you received the day after we departed Gibraltar.'

Mr Parry glanced to papers still awaiting the captain's perusal littered on his desk.

The captain noted the direction he was looking.

'What accommodation has been afforded to the women?' he asked.

'They were issued with hammocks and have slung them in the carpenter's workshop.'

'And what of the daylight hours?' he replied with a frown.

'It is my intention to find some occupation for them. I will speak with Dr Whipple, if that meets with your approval.'

Captain Quintrell shrugged. 'I shall leave the arrangement to you. What do you know of them? Have you spoken with them at length?'

'Only briefly. The younger woman is reserved and prone to tearful outbursts and, for the present, has no stomach for the ship's movement. Mrs Crosby, who you met briefly, is of a stronger character and disposition. However, both are polite and well-mannered and I gave them strict orders not to wander the decks, or venture into the mess, or to interfere with or distract the men through conversation or unseemly behaviour. Mrs Crosby politely reminded me she was a married woman travelling in the company of her husband and she thanked me not to remind her how to behave.'

'Did she indeed?'

Simon Parry repressed a smile. 'It is possible that, like yourself, many of the men are not even aware that these two women are aboard.

The captain huffed. 'I find that hard to believe. Seamen who had been confined in a ship for three months can smell a woman a mile off. I presume their names have not been entered in the muster book.

'Naturally not.'

'Of course, but I need their names for the log.'

'The carpenter's wife is Mary Crosby. The younger woman is Mrs Pilkington. Her husband and children perished in the epidemic. I believe that is the reason she is rather fragile at the moment. She is the younger of the two, but is caring for a ten-year-old boy who accompanied them—Charles Goodridge, an orphan from the naval dockyard.'

Oliver shook his head. 'I had hoped all reference to the epidemic had been left in the colony, but it appears we are carrying a reminder with us.' Deep creases furrowed his brow. He rubbed his finger along them, as if to smooth them out, but the creases remained. 'I pray to God none of these people still carry the infection with them. Perhaps the doctor should examine them.'

'I will arrange that.'

'And I will need to speak with the carpenter, also.'

Mr Parry nodded and with nothing more to say excused himself and closed the cabin door.

Shaking his head, Oliver Quintrell returned to his chair, picked up the glass and swallowed the contents in two large mouthfuls. He immediately refilled it, but sat contemplating whether to drink it or not. A few minutes later, he pushed the glass aside, though his eyes remained settled on the Waterford crystal. Beams of bright sunlight streaming in from the side window were glancing off the faceted glass reflecting the rich blue and gold tones of the cabin's soft furnishings. Concentrating on the bursts of brilliant colour, his eyes glazed and the images in front of him grew blurred. Slowly and without prompting, the tears he had never shed for Susanna rolled down his cheeks and dripped onto the polished wooden surface.

The slow-match that had been burning within him was finally extinguished.

Chapter 4

A Dilemma

'Mr Crosby, is it not?' the captain asked, as he scrutinized the carpenter.

'Aye, your servant, sir.'

'How long were you employed at the naval yard in Gibraltar?'

'Seven years, Captain. I arrived in '97.'

'What were you doing there?'

'Mainly doing refits. But it was a poor yard in those days. It employed few skilled men and, with no money for materials, it was not a good place to work. But Sir John Jervis spent two years on the station and left in ninety-nine.'

'Did conditions improve after that?'

'His Lordship recommended many changes to the port facilities, and Admiral Nelson, when he was commander of the Mediterranean Fleet, saw the situation for himself and agreed something needed to be done. Both sent reports to the Navy Board of what was wanted and, although it took some years, improvements came eventually. Then it all went bad again.'

The captain asked for an explanation.

'When malignant fever ran rampant and the quarantine regulations were in force, the ships of Nelson's fleet were ordered to stay away from Gibraltar and the work at the yard ground to a halt. Even before the people started dying in droves, I'd hoped for a chance to sign on a ship bound for England so I could get me and Mrs Crosby and my son away from the place.' He sighed. 'I can't thank you enough, Captain, for granting me and the other carpenters a berth and for allowing my missus and Mrs Pilkington to ship with us.'

Oliver grunted. 'I did not sanction your arrival on board. However, you and the other tradesmen are welcome. The frigate has been without a ship's carpenter for several weeks and I would not have put to sea without one. But be aware,' he added, 'I do not welcome females aboard my ship no matter what capacity they are travelling in.'

'I understand your feelings, Captain, but I had no choice. What should I have done? Left the womenfolk there in the colony with no one to support them, and with the shortage of food and fresh water as it was, they would have died. My only wish was to get them away from the Rock and see them shipped to England.'

'Then regard yourself fortunate that my first officer permitted them to come aboard. Had I been consulted, I would have refused. I have seen the disruption women cause at sea, from the frivolous antics of warrant officers' wives to the unbecoming behaviour of wives of senior officers. I have suffered the whining and wailing of sea-sick females from Plymouth to Port Royal.'

'I can assure you, Captain, Mrs Crosby has sailed with me before and she does not suffer sea-sickness. Nor does she recoil from the noise of battle or the sight of blood. I've known her stitch up an open wound quicker than you can sew on a button. I can promise you, my missus will give you nothing to complain of.'

'Mr Crosby,' the captain continued. 'My ruling is not founded on personal preferences. Need I remind you of Article 38 of the *Regulations and Instructions Relating to His Majesty's Service at Sea*, which clearly states that any captain or commander shall not carry any woman to sea without the instructions of the Admiralty?'

'But I came aboard under instructions from the Navy Board, which was aware of the situation existing in the colony.' He paused. 'I hear you are a married man, Captain. You must understand.'

Mr Crosby's brazen reference to his personal life rankled the captain.

'Let me remind you, mister, His Majesty's fighting ships are not run on the basis of whim or emotion. Special provisions or allowances cannot be made for a man's wife or any other female person when the ship is facing a broadside from enemy guns.'

The carpenter bowed his head but continued in a matter-of-fact tone. 'As for Mrs P,' he added, 'she lost her husband to the sickness. She and George Pilkington were married in Gibraltar near five years ago. He was a Portsmouth lad, but she was born and raised in the colony. Her forebears were Spanish, like many of the folk in Gibraltar. Her real name is Consuela, but my wife calls her Connie.'

'Huh. And what of the boy you mentioned—Charles Goodridge?'

'Orphan. Nice little lad. The son of one of the wrights—another good craftsman. He died two days before his wife. They were the first at the yard to perish, and before they went, they begged me to care for the lad if their lives were taken. I told him I would do what I could, but I made him no promise because I couldn't guarantee I would live through it myself. It was the same time Connie's two infants were taken. Less than two years old, the pair of them. So she took Charlie in and looked after him even when he got poorly. But she nursed him through it. Now, when you see the pair together, you would think they were family.'

The carpenter sniffed and screwed his woollen hat around in his hands. 'I buried my own son in the big ditch along with hundreds of other nameless souls. I'll never forget that scene as long as I live.'

The captain closed his eyes. He, too, had witnessed the horrors of the epidemic first-hand, and doubted the memory of Susanna's death would ever leave him. Pausing for a moment, he glanced through the stern window to the backdrop of blue. 'I am sorry for your loss,' he said, his expression of sympathy genuine. 'Thank you, Mr Crosby, you need say no more. However, I must advise we are not heading for England. My orders take me into the southern latitudes, far from Europe.'

The carpenter looked troubled.

'Do not worry. I intend to make landfall at St Michael, the main island in the Azores. The ship is in dire need of wood and water, and fresh supplies, which I can purchase at the victualling yard there. I will disembark your wife and her companion at Ponta Delgada. It is a busy port and many ships returning to England call in there. It will be your decision as to whether you accompany your wife or continue with the ship. Let me remind you, however, that when the Navy Board granted warrants to the wrights and carpenters transferring to *Perpetual*, it was with the intention those men would commit to service for at least the present voyage and not merely use it as a convenient means of escaping the colony. As captain of this vessel, I cannot sail without a good crew in the carpenter's shop. The role you play is one of the most important aboard. Very soon, I intend to careen the ship and, when that happens, I will be relying on the ship's carpenter and his mates to effect any repairs and oversee the scraping of the hull once it is out of the water.'

'Me and the lads can do that, sir.'

'That is well. I do not wish to linger in those waters any longer than necessary, but the work is unavoidable. Currently the ship is swimming like a fish wrapped in a woollen stocking. When we make the Western Islands, you have my permission to go ashore. I suggest you arrange suitable lodgings to accommodate the women in the town until a ship arrives to convey them to England.'

'Thank you kindly, Captain. Have no worries, I fully intend to stay with the ship.'

'Then we shall say no more on this matter. Providing we get some wind, we are less than two weeks sailing from our destination. In the meantime, the women must remain below. If they come on deck to take some exercise, they will be accompanied by a marine officer.'

The carpenter knuckled his forelocks and turned to leave but the captain interrupted him.

'One more thing, Crosby. From your papers, you are the most senior carpenter both in age and experience, therefore, I will have you rated as ship's carpenter. Are the other men fully skilled tradesmen?'

'Four skilled wrights with many years' experience between them, sir, and a lad who completed his time a year ago. He tells me he's sailed with you before. Goes by the name of William Ethridge.'

The captain showed sign of recognition. 'Indeed.'

'And I have an apprentice from the yard,' Mr Crosby added. 'He's served four years, but has the makings of a good tradesman.'

'Then I am satisfied the carpenter's shop is adequately served with mates. I will speak with you again when we raise the Azores.'

'Enter,' the captain called, not raising his eyes from the paper in his hand. Sitting at his desk, with his back to the door, he did not regard the man who entered, nor did he need to, the almost imperceptible footfall of his first lieutenant was familiar to him.

'Was there something, Simon?' Oliver asked, his tone much mellowed from their previous fractious encounter.

'Nothing to report, sir. We are making a little over two knots, and the sail sighted earlier is no longer visible. All the hands are in good health and spirits. Perhaps you would care to see for yourself.'

'Presently,' Oliver murmured, returning to the letter on his desk.

The lieutenant waited and watched as a pencil rolled back and forth on the polished table. The captain appeared oblivious to it.

'Was there something else?' he asked, without looking up.

'Indeed, there was not, I am pleased to say. But if you will pardon me for saying, you sound a little tired. Is there anything I can be of assistance with?'

'Perhaps there is,' the captain said. Leaving his desk, he turned and sat down at the table and indicated for his lieutenant to sit also. 'It is this,' he said, tapping his index finger on the paper he was holding. 'Article Eight. I have read the words so many times I know them by rote, but they no longer make sense to me.'

Like all serving seamen, both officers and common hands, Simon Parry was familiar with the *Articles of War*. The regulations, first set down in 1661 and revised only twice since that time, were the rules every man who served in the Royal Navy was obliged to adhere to. The set of regulations were relayed from the quarterdeck to the assembled company whenever a ship was commissioned and, after that, at least once a month, or every Sunday following the observation of worship of God Almighty.

But while most captains did not read the complete set of *Articles*, the ones that were most pertinent to the crew were regularly repeated. Punishments for crimes such as disobeying orders, abusive behaviour, murder or mutiny all carried severe sentences. The phrase, *shall suffer death* was rammed into every seaman's brain. But because the words were repeated so frequently throughout a sailor's time at sea made Oliver question whether they meant anything at all or were not worth the paper they were written on.

'Article Eight?' Simon quizzed.

Oliver frowned and glancing down at the page read:

'No person in or belonging to the fleet shall take out of any prize, or ship seized for prize, any money, plate, or goods...before the same be adjudged lawful prize in some admiralty court—'

He broke off and glanced at his lieutenant to make sure he was paying attention.

'As you are aware—and no doubt, every man-Jack aboard this ship is also aware, whilst anchored in the Bay of Gibraltar, I received on board *Perpetual* four wooden chests removed from a Spanish ship that had been attacked when returning home from South America. The action took place off Cape Saint Mary and was by a fleet of British frigates. On receipt of the chests, taken from one of those ships, I was informed they contained coins. I was further advised that this Spanish treasure had merely been *detained*. Huh!' he snorted, glancing behind him to the recently reinforced bulkhead near his desk. 'Four chests containing specie—coins of various types and, I understand, of considerable value.'

The lieutenant chose not to interrupt.

'I was assured that because Britain was not at war with Spain, the treasure had only been *detained* by the British fleet in order to prevent those funds finding their way into Napoleon's coffers. *Detained*,' he emphasized, 'with the proviso that the coins would be returned to Spain.'

Simon raised his eyebrows.

'I think you know as well as I, that such an eventuality is unlikely to happen. This confirms my original thoughts—the coins were never *adjudged lawful prize* as they were in fact *pirated* by the British squadron. *Pirated*!' he repeated, as he returned to the paper in front of him and continued reading: 'According to Article Eight:

'—*the full and entire account of the whole, without embezzlement, shall be brought in, and judgment passed entirely upon the whole without fraud, upon pain that every person offending herein shall forfeit and lose his share of the capture, and suffer such further punishment as shall be imposed by a court martial, or such court of admiralty, according to the nature and degree of the offense.*

'According to my interpretation of this *Article*, I have been made an unwitting third party to this blatant act of piracy and am, therefore, no less equally guilty of taking a portion of a prize illegally.'

'May I make a comment, Oliver?' Simon ventured.

'Go ahead.'

'Did you not receive a statement in writing from the Admiralty that the Treasury was to make good, to Spain, the equivalent value of the specie you received?'

'I did, but who is to convince my crew of that. Every man on board, even though he did not personally witness the transfer of the silver to the ship, is probably aware of what we are carrying.'

He slapped his hand on the pencil to stop it rolling off the table. 'When it came aboard, there were murmurs from the men that it would bring nothing but bad luck. I only hope their predictions are not correct.'

'If you are concerned that work of the treasure will be spread,' Simon said. 'I would beg to remind you we are heading across the Atlantic and the men will have no opportunity to share their knowledge, even if it was their intention to do so.'

Oliver laughed. 'Men do not need prompting to part with priceless snippets of gossip. Some would sell their soul for the whiff of a woman's purse, a gilded trinket, or even a twist of tobacco. Others have little control over their tongues once the taste of honeyed nectar loosens it and, given the opportunity in the Azores, they will no doubt consume their fill as soon as they step ashore.'

'Only if you allow them to do so.'

'The men have been cooped up in this ship for months, and once we have refurbished our supplies we have many months of sailing ahead with no ports to call into.' He looked at his first officer. 'If I do not permit the men to go ashore when we raise the islands, I will have a near mutiny on my hands.'

'If I might pose a question?'

The captain inclined his head.

Simon chose his words carefully. 'Would it be preferable that we headed for Madeira?'

For a second, a pained expression flashed across the captain's face.

Mr Parry failed to notice and continued. 'The men are familiar with that port, and it offers plenty of distractions. Plus, a south-westerly bearing from here would reduce our distance by two hundred sea miles, so the sailing master informs me.'

'Jack Mundy is a fine navigator, but he does not know what is in my mind. I have set my course, and I do not intend to change it.' Oliver's tone moderated as he looked directly at his first officer. 'I am certain when you had your own command, you were an excellent captain. And it is a travesty of justice that has destined you to serve as my subordinate. I appreciate your concern and value your opinion, Simon, but only I can resolve the concerns that trouble me.' He paused. 'You have been diplomatic in not reminding me of my personal reason for not wanting to visit Madeira.'

'I had no intention of doing that, sir.'

'Nevertheless, I am sure my relationship with a certain lady on that island and the circumstances surrounding her unfortunate death have been bandied around the mess and the wardroom.'

Simon Parry was adamant. 'I can assure you that is not the case.'

'Whatever,' Oliver replied, returning to the question in hand. 'Steering clear of Madeira for personal reasons is not why we are heading to the Western Islands. Apart from the need to take on provisions, the Portuguese islands of the Azores are many sea miles from the normal routes for shipping serving European ports. They are more frequently visited by ships sailing from Britain to the Cape of Good Hope, and by Nantucket whalers, West African slavers and Company ships heading east or west. If, by chance, word has been passed to Spain that we are transporting some of their plundered treasure and heading for the Southern Ocean, I guarantee the Spanish Navy would not search for us in the Azores. Madeira would be a much more likely place to expect to find us. Furthermore, the Azores is less likely to attract French ships of war.'

Simon Parry agreed. 'If it is our misfortune to encounter any enemy ships, you have a fine frigate, a loyal crew and a well-supplied magazine.'

'French frigates are built to make more speed than our ships, and with *Perpetual*'s hull in dire need of attention, we would be hard pressed to outrun them.'

Stretching his arms above his head, Oliver raked the single remaining finger on his right hand through his hair, and then adjusted the position of his queue. 'I have pondered over these aggravations long enough, and no amount of speculation will change the situation that exists. If I am stuck with the pirated treasure, I must make every effort not to lose it.'

While the brief conversation with his first officer had changed nothing, it had released the knot on the conundrums Oliver had been puzzling over for days.

'I think a modicum of fresh air is required. I shall join you on deck presently. Perhaps together we can raise some more wind.'

'Sail astern!'

The captain opened his telescope for the umpteenth time and put it to his eye. The sail reported two hours earlier had also been seen two hours prior to that. The lookout claimed it was a fully rigged ship, but with little more than its royals visible from the deck, the captain had not been convinced.

'What do you make of it, Mr Parry?' he asked.

'Can't rightly say, sir,' the lieutenant replied.

'A whaler, an Indiaman, a slave ship, a man-o'-war? What is it?' He shook his head. 'With no colours flying, it's impossible to tell friend from foe.'

'Perhaps it is a pirate or privateer,' the sailing master said. 'Perhaps its captain knows what we are carrying. Do you think she is following us by chance or chasing us, Captain?'

'I think many things, Mr Mundy, but I cannot predict the unpredictable. At best, I can only make sure I am well prepared. For the present, however, I suggest you pay attention to your duties and forget conjecture.' He paused. 'According to my calculations, we are only a few hours' sailing from the island of Saint Mary, the most southerly of the Western Isles. Let us put up every square inch of cloth we have,' he ordered. 'Let us raise the Azores before this stranger closes on us. If he wishes to speak with me, he is welcome to deliver his calling card when we are anchored in the harbour at Ponta Delgada.'

'Do you want the stuns'ls out, Captain?' the lieutenant asked.

'No, it takes too much time and we cannot rely on the wind holding. We cannot outrun this shadow, while dragging a stone anchor, therefore, let us continue to make what speed we can with the canvas we are flying. Keep her close to the wind, helmsman. Don't let her fall off.'

'It's like a ghost ship,' the sailing master said. 'It comes and goes like an illusion. One moment it's there and, the next, it's dropped below the horizon.'

Oliver Quintrell wondered if that was happening by accident, due to the fickle breeze, or if the following ship was deliberately spilling wind from its sails in order to reduce speed? The Barbary corsairs of the Mediterranean were known to follow a ship for days to ascertain if it was vulnerable before attacking it. While it was certainly not a ghost ship, it was an irritation. 'Let me know any change in its bearing immediately.'

'Aye, aye, sir.'

The captain was not happy and the concern was evident in his face.

'He'll be making for the Western Isles, like us,' the sailing master said, fully confident of his opinion. 'According to my reckoning, we'll be in Ponta Delgada in a day's time.

The captain was less enthusiastic. 'There is no immediate urgency for us to arrive. I have an uneasy feeling about that ship.'

Mr Mundy was oblivious to the captain's concern. 'It just happens to be heading in the same direction as us. There's no harm in that,' he insisted.

'I hope you are right, however, I have decided to extend its captain the courtesy of allowing him to enter the port before us.'

'But what of the victuals? We are running very low.'

'I am well aware of that, Mr Mundy, and a delay of a few more hours or days will make little difference. We are currently dragging a ton of weight on our hull, and until we rid ourselves of it, we will run from our enemies with the speed of a convict in a pair of leg irons. The needs of the ship must be attended to before the needs of men's bellies. I had planned to visit Ponta Delgada first and attend to the ship second, however, I have reconsidered. We will have no opportunity to clean the hull while anchored in the harbour.'

He explained his plans. 'I have decided to make for Santa Maria, the smaller island that is ahead of us. We will search out a sheltered cove to careen the ship and do whatever work is necessary to improve its speed on the water. While we are there, it will be an ideal opportunity to take on wood and water. After that, we sail for Ponta Delgada. Hopefully, by that time, the dog sniffing at our heels will have lost interest or satisfied himself that we have either sailed for England or headed out into the Atlantic.'

'With respect, sir,' the sailing master began, 'none of the anchorages on this island offer shelter and ships often have to put to sea at a short notice, especially at this time of the year.'

'All the more reason to find an isolated inlet sheltered from the prevailing winds.'

'But—'

'No buts, Mr Mundy. My mind is made up. While the barrels are empty and the provisions almost exhausted, the ship's burthen is considerably less than at any other time. With an empty hull, it will be easier to refloat the ship when the job is completed. I appreciate your observations, but I have no intention of sinking *Perpetual* on a beach of soft sand and being unable to haul her off. Do I make myself clear?'

'Aye, Capt'n. I'll have a look on the charts.'

'What I need may not be on the charts.'

'I'll have a look on the charts, anyway.'

'As you wish.'

'So when we find this beach, we run the frigate up on the beach?' the sailing master re-iterated.

'Isn't that what I just said? I should not have to repeat myself. As to the wood and water, those commodities can be collected and brought on board once we are afloat. There will be much to do. '

'That could take a while.'

'Did I not say three to four days? When all the jobs have been completed, then we head for the main port and its victualling store. Is that understood?'

'Aye, Captain. No problem.'

No Problem. Prophetic words indeed. Already the captain anticipated several problems.

First, the problem of locating a suitable beach. That was imperative. Next, there was the challenge of sailing the ship in safely, allowing the hull to carry far enough up the beach on the flow of the tide, but not too far. Then there was the question of the carpenters. He was dependant on a team of artisans who were all new to him. He must rely on them to careen the vessel using blocks and tackles, and to ensure it is well supported by struts and lines, so when it is leaned to one side it will not topple onto its beam ends. He was equally dependant on the bosun and riggers to further secure the hull with cables stretched out along the beach, fastened to anchors in the sand or to rocks or large trees. Finally, he would be dependent on Providence to forestall any storms or high seas for the period the ship was on the beach. It would be catastrophic if the frigate was carried further up the beach and left stranded. More importantly, when the time came to haul the ship back onto the water, he would need to call on every ounce of strength the boat crews could muster to pull the vessel from the sand, and pray for an obliging wind to back the sails to help carry *Perpetual* into deep water.

If only this work could have been done while they were biding their time in Gibraltar Bay, but that had not been the case. *No problem.* The sailing master's words echoed in Oliver Quintrell's brain. He hoped and prayed those words would prove to be true.

Chapter 5

Santa Maria

'Land ho!'

The call came from the forward masthead. All eyes scanned the sea ahead.

'Land, Captain,' the sailing master confirmed. 'The Western Islands. Two points off the larboard bow.'

Having stepped on deck only five minutes earlier, Oliver excused himself from his conversation with the doctor and strode across to the lee side of the quarterdeck.

With his hip leaned against the rail, Mr Mundy fixed his glass on the far horizon.

'That will be St Mary's. The most southerly island of the group,' he announced.

'Santa Maria or the Yellow Island, as the Portuguese say,' the captain commented.

'Aye, that's the one,' Jack Mundy acknowledged. 'Not much there for either man or beast, I hear.' He arched his back, exhaled heavily, then collapsed his telescope rather vigorously.

The captain frowned and took out his pocket watch. 'What of the sail to the south-east?'

'Lookout has reported it comes and goes and it appears to be following us to the islands.'

Oliver Quintrell didn't like the connotations of *following us*, but he concentrated his attention on the grey undulations emerging from the sea in the north-west. Glancing west, he shaded his eyes and considered the height of the sun as it was slowly descending from the heavens.

'How far to the island would you say?' he asked, looking at his watch.

'About eight or ten miles.'

'And two hours to sunset?'

The sailing master glanced at the horizon and nodded. 'From memory, it's a rugged coast with few people living there, so we'll have little hope of seeing any lights if we pass in the night. Best to steer well clear of it, if you ask me. In fact, I would suggest adding some sail so we can clear it before it's too dark. Do you want the stuns'ls out, Captain?'

'No,' Oliver replied bluntly, before turning to his first officer. 'Reduce sail, Mr Parry. Topsails only. Inform the lookout to report on the sail in our wake. I want to know what it is and where it is heading.'

Mr Mundy shrugged his shoulders, pulled open his telescope again and directed it towards the island.

It was obvious to Oliver that his sailing master did not always agree with his orders, and on this occasion, the seasoned seaman could see no sense in slowing the frigate when it was making a respectable four knots—a good speed considering the drag on its hull. In Oliver's eyes, Jack Mundy was a first-class navigator and was entitled to his opinions but, at times, he came perilously close to impertinence by pressing his views in a rather pointed fashion.

With the captain's orders conveyed along the ship, the hands eased the sheets and hauled away on clew-lines and bunt-lines, hauling the courses, topgallants and royals up to their yards. Balancing over the yardarms, the topmen gathered the huge squares canvas into loosely folded pleats before securing them to the yards with hempen gaskets. On deck, the reduction in sail was soon evident. The next time the log was heaved the speed registered two knots.

Over the next hour with the frigate approaching the easternmost point of the island of Santa Maria, the ship that had been running on the same course became fully visible and closed on them. With square sails crowded on all three masts, it was definitely a fully-rigged ship.

'Still no colours,' the lookout called.

'What do you think she is, sir?' Mr Mundy asked.

The captain studied the blurred image, but did not offer an opinion.

'She'll be a Portuguese trader bound for South America or an Indiaman returning home via the Cape. She'll break her passage at Ponta Delgada, like us, to pick up some cargo—wine or cattle perhaps.'

Again, Oliver did not respond to the sailing master's assessment. Now was not the time for guesses, beside which he had his own thoughts on the matter.

'What is your course, helmsman?'

'North-west, Capt'n.'

'North, if you please.'

'North it is,' the helmsman echoed, easing the wheel and waiting for the rudder to respond. Mr Parry's eyes concentrated on the set of the sails.

'We *are* heading for São Miguel, the main island, *aren't we*?' Mr Mundy enquired.

The captain turned to him. 'At the moment, we are heading into the night, which will be upon us in about half an hour. But before we dissolve into the blackness, I wish to convince that ship off our stern we are on course for Ponta Delgada. Then, with the assistance of night clouds and a late rising moon, all lights will be doused and we will bear west.'

'But we *must* make port on the main island to take on supplies and water. The leaguers and barrels are near empty.'

Oliver was very conscious of his ship's needs—the purser, the cooper and the sailing master made sure he could not forget. It was his intention to make port there—but not immediately.

As the day ended, a kaleidoscope of coloured clouds hung over the western horizon providing a spectacular aura of burnt orange and gold, but Oliver Quintrell's attention was on the hazy grey outline slightly west of north. It was the Portuguese island Santa Maria—the smallest and most southerly of the Azores group measuring a mere ten miles long from west to east by five miles in width.

Having made his decision, Captain Quintrell returned to the quarterdeck. 'If my assumption is correct, the ship following us will presume we are making for São Miguel. Hopefully, by daylight, we will have rid ourselves of him.'

As predicted, there was no moon and with the lights doused, including the lantern in the main cabin, *Perpetual* was quickly cloaked in darkness. Although he scanned the following sea at regular intervals, Oliver could detect no tell-tale pin-pricks of lights in the blackness. Word from the lookout confirmed that the final sighting of the unidentified sail had it maintaining a northerly heading.

Standing at the rail, swaying with the ship, he listened to the familiar sounds—the creak of the mizzen boom, the tap of a clay pipe as a sailor emptied its bowl, the flap of the flag to which he gave his allegiance and the occasional hiss from the frenetic wings of a flying fish. He watched the wavering line of wake trailing its aqua bloom on the sea and the black silhouettes of seabirds swooping down over it. When the sailor sucked on his pipe, the tobacco glowed red and, when the man exhaled, a stream of grey smoke trailed from the side of his mouth like the tail of pennant floating on the wind.

At midnight, the frigate changed from its northerly course and headed west.

According to the charts, Santa Maria's north coast was rugged with soaring cliffs and headlands with small coves and inlets cut between them. Being a hazardous lee shore, it could only be approached safely in daylight. Because of this, the captain opted to sail well clear of the island's western end then, with plenty of sea room around them, drop anchor for the night. At first light, they would weigh and head back to search for a suitable beach to run the ship up on.

Though nothing had been said to prompt his thinking, Oliver decided the men deserved a day of relaxation and despite rations being very low, considered that one more day's delay would make little difference. Christmas had come and gone on the previous Tuesday without service or celebration, and the coming Tuesday would be the first day of 1805. He knew that, once work began on the hull, there would be no respite for several days and, when that job was completed, they would have other duties to occupy them when they reached the port. He had already resolved to spend as little time as necessary in Ponta Delgada before heading for the coast of Brazil, so this was the last opportunity they would have.

To have a full day of leisure, free of all regular chores was usually a treat for the men but some soon became bored. They'd had a bellyful of deck-board leisure after three months rocking on Gibraltar Bay. What they clamoured for were taverns, women and traders hawking cheap trinkets they could barter for. The extra double tot of rum they received was soon swallowed and the effects did little to appease them.

Waking with clear heads the following morning, the crew was eager to make sail but a strong northerly had blown up during the night, threatening to dash the frigate on the rocks if they went anywhere near the coast. This meant wasting another day while waiting for the wind to change.

'It's only fifty miles to Ponta Delgada,' the sailing master reminded. 'We could have made it there and back in the time we're losing sitting here.'

'I have no intention of dragging a ton of barnacles any further than necessary,' Oliver growled.

'There are more facilities on the main island,' Mr Mundy insisted. 'It would be safer to do the work there.'

'Mr Mundy, If and when I require an opinion, I shall ask for one.' He turned away from his sailing master and returned to the helm where Mr Parry was talking with the quartermaster.

'Kindly ensure the men remain alert, Simon. I want no sudden surprises. Hopefully in the morning, the wind will have dropped enough for us to go about our search.'

The work the captain was contemplating was to be no easy task, but he had full confidence in his men. Two years earlier, he had careened *Elusive* within the volcanic island in the Southern Ocean, and as his present crew included many sailors who had served with him then, he was confident they were capable of performing the same task without damage being inflicted on the ship.

Throughout the night, the broad swell, whose troughs corrugated the Atlantic Ocean, rocked the seamen in their hammocks. Cocooned in canvas, each sleeping seaman swayed rhythmically from side to side without making contact with his neighbour. With one watch on deck while the other slept, each man's allocation of eighteen inches was extended to a comfortable thirty-six inches, allowing space for air to circulate between the rows. Despite this, the smells and sounds remained the same no matter how many men slung their hammocks above the tables in the mess.

At first light, the anchor was weighed and a course set to bring *Perpetual* to the western end of Santa Maria Island. The ship then headed east, following the coastline in search of a suitable bay.

Because its western end was arid and wore the sallow colour of a sickly child, Santa Maria had been called the Yellow Island. The other eight islands in the group, however, were renowned for their fertile soils which supported verdant forests and farms and produced all manner of fruits and vegetables, both tropical and Mediterranean.

Because the Azores had been raised by volcanoes from the seabed, all the islands, apart from Santa Maria, lived and breathed, exhaling sulphurous fumes and occasionally spewing lava from their peaks. The island of Santa Maria was old and dead.

Over the next two hours, several coves and inlets were sighted from the masthead and sail was further reduced to allow the captain and sailing master to consider each location from the deck. In section of the coast, where perpendicular cliffs rose to a considerable height and the sea creamed constantly around their crumbling bases, it was agreed even taking one of the ship's boats in would be dangerous. Of the inlets they sailed by, each in turn was considered before being discounted for various reasons—swirling currents, the surging waters funnelling fast though its entrance, the position of the inlet facing the prevailing winds or because of partly submerged boulders littering the entrance. For a few, the sole reason the location was discounted was because it gave Captain Quintrell an uneasy feeling.

A little before ten o'clock, a potential cove was sighted. After heaving to, the anchor splashed into the sea opposite the entrance. All eyes were focused on the beach. Facing north-east and almost hidden between the broad extended arms of two towering headlands, a strip of flat sand glistened white in the sunlight. The tide, on the make, was breaking on the rocks at the base of the cliffs, but little more than gentle wavelets washed the shore. With a soft breeze and a pleasantly warm day of sixty-five degrees, most of the sailors dispensed with their shirts and shoes. Spirits were high. The air was filled with anticipation. It was perfect.

'My boat, if you please, Mr Parry,' the captain called. 'I will go ashore. Have my boat crew ready and a dozen men besides, including some marines. While I am away, have the ship made ready to be sailed in.'

The sailing master was about to offer his opinion, but thought better of it and turned aside.

'Clear away the captain's boat,' Mr Parry ordered.

'Mr Mundy, I would like you to accompany me.'

Surprised, the sailing master raised his eyebrows, 'Indeed, Captain. I'm ready.'

With the captain sitting beside the coxswain in the stern sheets and the sailing master perched in the bow, nothing was said during the time it took the boat to swim across the stretch of ruffled sea before sliding onto the translucent water of the cove. The creak of the rowlocks and drip of water from the rising oars was the only sound until the bow crunched onto the sand. Mr Mundy was the first to jump ashore, followed by the sailors who heaved the boat a little further up the sand. Only then did the red-coated marines jump out followed by the captain.

How different the conditions were here, Oliver thought, to those his crew had been confronted with only two years earlier aboard His Majesty's frigate *Elusive*. In the freezing waters of the Antarctic at latitude 60°S, the inland sea they had entered had been surrounded by jagged snow-covered peaks covered with blue and white glaciers hanging from their summits. It was an eerie place where the icy wind blew daggers of sleet that sliced their cheeks, and where the water beneath the ship's keel was capable of freezing to solid ice or bubbling like a boiling caldron only a few yards away. And that was summer!

How idyllic the winter conditions in the Azores were. The sky was a continuous canvas of cerulean blue. The translucent sea in the bays was home to dolphins, grouper and numerous other fish and, further out on the fertile waters, were migrating whales. They attracted fleets of ships from Europe and North America anxious to fill their hulls with barrels of valuable oil before returning home. From the cliffs rising almost perpendicular from the sea, terns and other seabirds nested undisturbed on this little-visited stretch of coast. It is little wonder the French named the Azores, *Les Îsles Fortunées* along with the Canary Islands and Madeira.

After only a short time reconnoitring the beach and testing the firmness of the sand, Captain Quintrell returned to *Perpetual*. His main concern was to ensure all the empty barrels in the hold were stowed properly and the guns lashed tightly. He could not afford to have any heavy objects running loose when the ship was careened. He pondered on the fate of the *Royal George* a 100-gun ship of the line. Some years ago, the captain of the first rate had ordered the guns to be trundled across the deck in order to heel the vessel so repairs to the hull could be undertaken in Spithead. But, with the extra weight on the starboard side, the ship leaned too far and rolled over crushing or drowning at least eight hundred people. He would not make that mistake, nor would he allow the crew aboard once the frigate was on the sand. Only a few exceptions would be made.

Once satisfied all necessary eventualities had been considered and precautions taken, Oliver returned to the deck and, when the tide was on the make and almost at the full, he asked Mr Parry to sail her in.

Pacing the deck and anxiously looking over the side to check the depth of water beneath the hull, the first officer headed the ship into the cove. Spilling the wind from the foretopsail, a chain's length before the shore-line the frigate swam gracefully onto the beach, digging its keel into the sand and instantly coming to a stop.

Within minutes, a swarm of sailors climbed from the deck on rope ladders or slid down the lines and cables that were quickly run out on all quarters. These were attached to anchors that were half-buried in the sand. Although *Perpetual*'s slightly bulbous hull helped it to remain near upright, the carpenter made sure a line of props was placed on the larboard side to prevent it from toppling. With the preparations completed, the men watched and waited for the tide to turn and ebb away leaving the British frigate stranded on the sand in a pool of water.

Satisfied the hull would not move until it was righted and returned to the sea, the captain commended the men. Now there was work to be done. With the regular watches stood down, the sailors were split into groups and allocated to various tasks. As cleaning the hull was the most pressing and laborious job, the largest working party was allocated to it. The ship's carpenter, Mr Crosby, and his mates were given charge of that responsibility.

Supplied with hammers, chisels, buckets, brooms and ladders, their job was to brush, knock or scrape the barnacles from the ship's bottom. While the job was tedious and laborious, some care had to be taken to make sure the copper sheathing was not damaged. The protective layer of metal, intended to prevent worms chewing through the hull, had failed to prevent barnacles and other molluscs sucking onto it. Given the right conditions, the creatures reproduced in the thousands adding new layers on top of the old casings. The resulting layer was rock-hard and often razor sharp. The slime and weed was far easier to remove.

While this arduous work went on non-stop, a party of twenty strong young sailors headed off to cut firewood. The woodcutters left the beach in high spirits armed with axes, saws and rope baskets. They were charged with cutting seasoned wood suitable for the galley fire but because Santa Maria was arid in parts, they faced a long walk to find a suitable source of timber. In anticipation of an overnight camp, they carried water and a small ration of tea and ship's biscuits in their knapsacks.

Another group of a similar number headed from the bay. Some carried small casks on their shoulders, others rolled larger barrels along the ground. The captain said he would be satisfied if they could collect enough fresh water to tide the ship's company over for two or three days. This would avoid the necessity for strict rationing. Sufficient water to supply the ship for their voyage to South America would be collected at Ponta Delgada.

A small working party armed with palms and needles, led by the sail maker, selected a flat area at the edge of the beach above the high-tide mark to make and erect a large tent. Dragging several old sails and carrying spare spars across the sand, the men set about building a shelter in case of rain. It would serve as a mess for both sleeping and eating under if the weather turned bad. A separate tent would be rigged for the captain and his officers. Adjacent to that, cook set up a galley to prepare the meals. He was not permitted to light a fire in *Perpetual* while the deck was on an angle.

Finally, two pairs of topmen were ordered to scramble up the headlands on either side of the bay, where they would remain as lookouts. Four men, not allocated other tasks, were handed shovels and told to dig a long open ditch for the men to use as a privy.

'Mr Tully,' the captain called, turning to his second lieutenant. 'I have a job for you.'

'Aye, Capt'n.'

'I want you to go over the headland to the east and investigate the next few bays and inlets. I need to know if there is any activity on this coast, such as a fishing village.'

'Shall I take some men with me?'

'No, I need everyman here to complete these jobs as quickly as possible.'

'But I can't speak the language, Captain, and if I find anyone, I'll not be able to learn anything from them.'

Oliver thought for a moment. 'Ekundayo would be a good choice, but I can't spare him. His brawn is more useful here. Find the boy Charlie and take him along. Mr Crosby tells me the lad speaks Spanish like a native, so he should be capable of making himself understood to the Portuguese, if the need arises.'

'Aye, aye, Capt'n.' Ben Tully knuckled his forehead and turned on his heel.

'Take Tommy Wainwright out of the cockpit,' the captain added. 'The surgeon has enough hands assisting him. The fewer people aboard the ship while it is careened the better.'

The second lieutenant nodded and headed off to form his own small party.

After racing to the end of the short beach, the two lads dived headlong into the soft sand, sat up, looked at each other and burst out laughing. Then, after dusting themselves down, they got up, waited for the lieutenant to catch up to them then hared off again.

Surprisingly, though six years separated them in age there was little difference in their stature. Charles, only ten years old, was tall for his age. He had grown up in Gibraltar under a Mediterranean sun fed on a diet of exotic fruits, goat's milk and fish, chicken and fresh vegetables. Tommy Wainwright, at sixteen was still hoping to reach five feet tall. His lack of size could be blamed on working underground from the age of nine, inhaling fine coal dust into his lungs and never seeing the light of day through the long months of an English winter. His staple diet had included bread spread with mucky fat—salted pig or beef dripping. He had never seen an orange until he went to sea.

On the island of Santa Maria, the pair had not a care in the world. With boundless energy, they sped up the side of the dunes and rolled down the other side showering their hair and clothes in soft sand.

'Hey,' Mr Tully warned, 'you'll wear yourselves out before we even get started.' But the boys didn't hear or didn't want to hear. They laughed and joked together as if they had been mates for years. For them, being off the ship and heading over the hills and along the coast was a big adventure.

By two in the afternoon, the work on the hull was well underway, but progress was slower than expected. It was hard work knocking or scraping the shells from the hull, especially working with arms reaching above their heads for long periods. But the captain would not permit cradles to be slung from the side for fear it could add too much weight to the side and lean the hull further over. The sand also proved hazardous to work on with pieces of broken shell cutting into the bare feet of the men without shoes. Bleeding knuckles was another complaint when a chisel or hammer slipped on the razor sharp surface. The surgeon attended to the deep cuts while Mrs

Crosby and Connie remained in the sick berth tearing up strips of linen for bandages.

Shortly before dark, a large bonfire was lit on the beach and the men relaxed. A tune from a tin whistle encouraged a few voices to join in the shanties. A few danced but found the sand too soft. Most men were happy to rest after the day's hard toil. A few walked down to the water and dipped their feet. Others sprawled out on the beach, hands behind their heads, and gazed at the stars. The majority gathered around the fire or sat under the canvas awning and smoked or played games. With more than forty men absent collecting wood or water, the number of crew the cook had to feed was reduced.

It was the cries from the two young boys scrambling down the hillside that attracted everyone's attention. The captain in particular, was pleased to see them back. They had been gone longer than expected. Eager to know if there was any news, he ambled over the sand to speak with his lieutenant. But the expression on Ben Tully's face told him everything was not well.

'What is it?' the captain enquired.

The lieutenant kept his voice low. 'We found a gallows on a beach with six corpses hanging from it. Fresh corpses at that.'

Chapter 6

The Village

'The sight of dead bodies hanging from the gallows was a shock to the two lads, especially Tommy Wainwright. The younger boy, Charlie, said nothing. It was nothing new to him after seeing cartloads of carcasses wheeled through the streets in Gibraltar.'

'Describe what you saw when you reached that place,' the captain asked.

'I didn't see anything when I first stepped onto the beach,' Ben Tully replied. 'It was the sight of the buzzards wheeling overhead made me think something was amiss. The hawks were screeching and fighting each other and making a strange unholy noise—like a cat meowing. I'd never heard that sound before. But the boys didn't notice and ran ahead, racing up and down the sand hills. That's how they came across the gallows. Six poor beggars. Dead for not much more than a day or two, I'd say.'

'Was anyone about?'

Mr Tully nodded. 'An old woman was crouched at the feet of one of them. I think it was her husband. She was scared of us at first, until I got Charlie to speak to her. But because of her wailing and blubbering, he found it difficult to understand what she was saying. However, she told him of boats on the beach and men who had come to the village and done terrible things, and dragged the men away and hanged them.'

'Did she say for what reason?'

'No, and he couldn't find out.'

'Who were these men in boats? What nationality were they? What ship did they arrive in?' Oliver asked, anxious to know more.

'The boy tried his best, but it was impossible. She told him they were not Portuguese, and not whalers either. She understood about whaling ships and said American and British whalers had come to the island in the past. Charlie asked if the ship was a man-o'-war, but she told him she didn't see a ship, only the boats.'

'It's unlikely they were Barbary pirates,' Oliver murmured. 'Too far off course. More likely a slaver or rogue privateer—perhaps even the ship that was following us.'

'Is that possible?' Mr Tully asked.

Oliver shrugged. 'Anything is possible. But why would anyone stop at such an unlikely spot and do this?'

'Perhaps his ship was damaged, like ours, and they wanted to careen it.'

Oliver thought that was too unlikely a coincidence. 'Did you discover anything more?'

'No, sir. The woman was beyond talking. After Charlie had finished speaking with her, she didn't seem afraid of us, but she was anxious to get back to her village.'

'Did you go with her?'

'No,' the lieutenant replied. 'I didn't know how far it was or what reception we would receive when we arrived there. I thought it best to come back and tell you.'

'Very wise, Mr Tully, you did the right thing.'

It was too late to do anything that day, but early next morning while the men were eating breakfast, Captain Quintrell assembled his officers on the beach and advised them of his plans. He intended to see for himself the site where the hangings had taken place and speak with the locals in the woman's village. He wanted to know more about these unexpected and unwelcome foreigners in case they posed any threat to his ship.

'Mr Parry, you will take charge of everything here while I am away.'

'Yes, sir,' Simon said. 'I pray nothing unforseen will befall you.'

'I pray for that, also,' Oliver replied, before continuing. 'From what Mr Tully tells me, heading over the headland involves a long hard climb, therefore I have decided to take the cutter and raise the beach from the water. Mr Tully agrees it will be quicker.' He looked over the ocean glistening in the morning sun. 'The sea is calm. The wind fair. I trust it will remain that way. But, if a change in the weather blows in, we can take shelter on the beach and sleep under the boat if necessary. I will take a few provisions. We will not go hungry. I will require Ekundayo to accompany me and act as my translator. Kindly have him ready to leave when he has finished eating.'

'Anything else I can organise, Captain?'

'My boat crew and a few marines. Mr Tully will accompany me to indicate the correct bay. When we locate it, I will go ashore. I want the men armed. I intend to visit the village and talk with the woman he spoke of, if I can find her. I need to know more about this ship and its captain. From the evil he has done, I can only conclude he is a blackguard, devoid of all conscience. Who else would drag men from their homes and string them up like common criminals? While I am away, make sure the men continue working on the hull. The sooner we can put to sea and leave this cove the better. I have an uneasy feeling about this place.'

'I understand,' Simon said. 'Don't worry, I will take care of everything here.'

The captain considered the frigate, careened at a modest angle. But he saw no necessity to lean it any further.

'I was never more vulnerable than I am now with my ship lying on the sand like a beached whale,' Oliver said. 'My only hope is that it will not be seen from the sea. I caution you to keep a keen lookout at all times and, if a ship is sighted within five miles of here, despatch a messenger to me immediately.'

After dismissing the other officers, Oliver took his first lieutenant by the arm and walked down the beach to where the ship's boats had been hauled ashore. At that distance, their conversation could not be overheard.

'There is a pressing matter I must ask you to attend to while I am away. As you know, the cases of Spanish treasure hidden in my cabin have been bothering me since we left Gibraltar. Word of a ship visiting this coast delivering murder and mayhem, has heightened my concerns.

'I will let no one near,' Mr Parry said. 'You can trust the crew, but if you feel it necessary, I will place an extra guard on the cabin door.'

'It's not the crew that worries me, Simon, it's the possibility news of the treasure has leaked. If someone armed with that knowledge boarded the frigate and searched the great cabin, they would quickly identify the false bulwark and, in no time, the cache of coins would be gone. And along with it, the very purpose for my mission.'

'Do you sense that the ship which has been following us is bent on taking it from us?'

Oliver shook his head. 'I cannot answer that question. What I do know is that we have many months of sailing ahead, during which time every ship we encounter must be regarded as a potential threat. While that treasure is an enigma to me, it is my duty to defend it with my life. I am bound to follow Admiralty orders and convey it to the colony of New South Wales as instructed.'

'I understand but what can I do to safeguard it, other than carrying it ashore and burying it?'

'I think not,' Oliver said, 'for if we have to make a hasty departure from here, digging up heavy chests of silver is a chore we can well do without. However, I have an idea,' he said, glancing over his shoulder to make sure no one was around. 'I need you to speak with Bungs and one of the carpenters—William Ethridge would be a good choice. The two are mess-mates and I trust them both. While the leaguers and large barrels are empty, and before we take on water and victuals, the job should not be too difficult.'

He explained his plan. 'I want the cooper to select four empty barrels to rest on the shingle ballast in the hull. After the tops have been removed, I need the carpenter to rig up a thwart inside each for a heavy chest to rest on. Hopefully, this will prevent them from shifting about with the movement of the ship. As an added safeguard, the empty space inside them can be packed with old rope or teased oakum. It would not do for the cases to move or the barrels to collapse when the refurbished barrels are stacked on top of them.'

Mr Parry's mind jumped back to an earlier cruise. 'Perhaps young Will is not a good choice. Might I remind you of the incident with the barrel on *Elusive* in the Southern Ocean?'

Oliver's face showed no flicker of feeling. 'That event is in the past and work here must proceed with all haste. When the chests are in place, I want Bungs to re-organise the hold so it is impossible for anyone to locate the specific ones. Only you and I, the carpenter and the cooper are to know the exact location of the treasure.'

'Let us hope no one ever tries to find it,' Mr Parry said.

'Indeed,' Oliver replied. 'I leave that matter in your capable hands.'

Because of the captain's concern about placing any excess weight on the frigates larboard side, the job of reorganizing the barrels had to proceed with care. The ones that were still full of water or food were heavy and firmly set in the damp ballast. Trying to roll those was impossible. The empty barrels, however, appeared to have a will of their own, some threatening to roll across the ship and slam into the side of the hull.

Being in charge of the job, Bungs was in his element and, though he was known to dislike working with other tradesmen, on this occasion he held his tongue. As far as barrels were concerned, he was an old hand at making or breaking them and he knew he was a valuable asset to the ship. When he heard what had to be done, he knew exactly which barrels to select.

'Leave it to me,' he said, manoeuvring one of the empty containers to a standing position, then prising off two of the hoops in order to release the top. With his feet sinking into the damp shingles, he remembered the unusual ballast discovered in the hull of a brig they had taken off the coast of South America. The result was the prize money he had subsequently collected from that cruise. It was a tidy nest egg that was waiting for him in the bank in Portsmouth. One day, in not too many years, he would leave the sea and reap the rewards of his service to the Navy. But he had yet not decided when that would be or what he would do with it.

Leaving the careened ship and farewelling the crew on the beach, the cutter, with Captain Quintrell and his second lieutenant aboard, pushed off from the beach and raised the sail. It was mid-morning. But the intended short cruise took much longer than expected. Sailing easterly along the island's north coast, Mr Tully admitted it was difficult to recognize the inlet from the sea as he had descended to it from inland. After over an hour's sailing, he admitted they had come too far. Bottling his annoyance at being drawn far from his destination and from *Perpetual*, the captain was also frustrated by the amount of time they had wasted.

With the sails lowered and unbent, the crew manned the oars and headed back into the breeze in the direction from which they had come. Checking each cove and inlet thoroughly proved time consuming, but there was no other option. Eventually, the beach that Mr Tully and the boys had happened upon was located and the cutter was allowed to drift in on the breaking waves. Once it was hauled up on the beach beyond the high tide mark, the captain gathered his men around him and urged caution.

Towards the edge of the beach, coarse matted grasses held the sand in place, but beyond, the sandy hillside was overgrown with masses of huge fleshy plants. The long thick stems reached out like tentacles and carried sharp barbs along their edges. In parts, the masses of inhospitable growths formed a huge impenetrable barrier making access impossible. Oliver wondered how Mr Tully and the boys had travelled through the area without being torn to ribbons. Anxious that his boat should not be seen from the sea, Oliver ordered the men to drag it off the beach and hide it in the vegetation.

While the men collected branches to cover it, the captain scanned the beach expecting to see the gallows Mr Tully had described, but he could not.

'Follow me,' Mr Tully called, heading up the cove. Almost hidden behind a small rise of sand was a flat area. It was the site used for the executions. Even armed with the knowledge of what they were about to see did not prepare them for the scene awaiting them.

The gallows itself had been constructed from a ship's topmast balanced horizontally and lashed to upright struts at either end. Those supports also were formed from old spars. Along the length of the mast, the victims had been strung up twelve inches apart, each on a noose knotted from a length of old salt-hardened rope.

Though not long dead, the hawks, from which the islands got their name, had wasted no time in placing their mark on them. As the seamen drew closer the fearless birds swooped down, wings barely moving, then lifted on the warm air high into the sky and disappeared over the headland. There was no one else about.

'There is something not right here,' Oliver said.

His gross under-statement received quizzical attention.

'Perhaps there was a slave rebellion like those on the Caribbean islands,' one of the boat crew suggested.

Eku shook his head.

'Perhaps this is how they deal out justice in the Western Isles,' the coxswain said.

The captain disagreed. 'I think not, gentlemen. The people who live on these islands are peace-loving. These islands have long been known as the Islands of the Blessed.'

'Do you wish us to cut them down, Capt'n?' Ekundayo asked.

'No,' the captain replied. 'Sadly, it is too late for us to assist these men. Leave everything as is until we discover what really happened here.' He paused, looking up at the line of dead faces. 'I wonder what crime they committed to deserve such punishment.'

Gathering in a semicircle around the gallows, the sailors removed their hats in a gesture of reverence while Captain Quintrell offered a brief prayer. The well-worn clothing of the victims indicated they were local farmers or fishermen. They were not sailors.

'There is something odd here,' Oliver repeated. 'Do you notice anything particular about them?'

'Strikes me from the pain still creased on their faces and the mess they made, they didn't die quickly. Old rope is to blame. It doesn't slide through the knot,' Mr Tully explained, before questioning the captain. 'What is it you see, sir?'

Leaning down, the captain picked up a hand-stitched leather sandal that had fallen, or been kicked off the foot of one of the victims as he had struggled against the slow noose throttling the life from his body. Respectfully, he fitted it back onto the foot from which it had come.

'They are all old men,' he announced. 'See the white hair and bald heads. See the wrinkled necks, and twisted fingers. Apart from the gasping mouths and silent screams, these are the faces you see lining the wharfs at every port in England. Men too sick, too worn, or too feeble to be signed on a ship. These are weak old men who should be spending their days sucking on clay pipes and idling their days away. They are beyond the age of labouring.'

The crew agreed and gazed in disgust at the fate of the bodies hanging side-by-side.

'Let us not waste time,' Oliver said. 'We can do nothing for these poor souls.'

'What now, Captain?' Lieutenant Tully asked, looking to the sky and pointing to the ominous clouds that were rolling in. 'Shouldn't we be setting off back to the ship before the weather changes?'

'No, I came here to discover the truth. We head for the village. If I am not mistaken, there will be a path leading from the cove and, within a short distance, we shall find where the woman lives.'

'How do you know that, sir?'

'See the furrows in the sand. Those marks are from the keel of a small boat that has been brought to the beach and hauled to the water. See the pile of weed and dried jelly fish. I suggest they were discarded from a net when the boat was returned.'

For Oliver Quintrell, the sheltered bay, hidden from the sea by rugged cliffs, rekindled memories. There were many such coves in

Cornwall close to where he had grown up. Such inlets made ideal haunts for smugglers.

'There is no time to lose,' he said, casting his memories aside and heading up the beach. On reaching the path, his assumption proved correct. A track, trampled by the hoofs of mules or donkeys, led inland. Less than a hundred yards from the beach, a fresh-water spring rose from the bank at the side of the path. It delivered a natural fountain of clear but slightly rust-coloured water that trickled into a small pool before disappearing between the rocks. The water was cold, transparent and refreshing. Oliver waited while his men drank their fill and satisfied their thirst. Before the last man had finished drinking, he headed off again with the others following him.

Half-way up the hill, the prickly vegetation gave way to soft weeds and grasses, and dozens of plants and bushes flowering in profusion—hibiscus, lilies of Africa, camellias and azaleas. As the valley opened up, the hills rolled back to reveal fields surrounded by dry-stone walls, cattle and sheep grazing peacefully, winter crops growing and small vineyards.

Smoke was rising from the chimneys of the low stone houses, but it was the village square and the buildings around it that most interested the captain. With houses on three sides, a church dominated the fourth. Its white lime-washed walls were edged with black bevelled graphite creating a stark contrast. The old building boasted a square belfry. A large black cross rose from the highest point of the pitched roof.

The surface of the cobbled square was made up of thousands of tiny smooth white stones of identical size, while the border running around the outside formed a pathway decorated in mosaic patterns in white and black. Apart from a pair of idle dogs and cooing doves, the square was empty. There were no villagers to be seen, not even a child playing nearby. Captain Quintrell was cautious.

With his crew following only a few paces behind, the captain entered the square cautiously, his hand resting on the hilt of his sword and the pistol, lodged under his belt, pressing on his right hip. His men were armed and ready to draw their weapons if necessary. Stopping in the centre of the square, the sailors cast their eyes around watching for any movement from the windows or in the alleys leading between the houses.

'I am Captain Quintrell of His Britannic Majesty's Royal Navy,' Oliver called. 'Is anyone about?' After turning a full three hundred and sixty degrees, he repeated his question. A dog approached nervously, sniffed at the group of men, then ambled away and flopped down outside one of the closed doors.

'English,' he shouted, hoping the residents would understand that word, if no other.

Waiting for a response, he kicked the sand from his shoes and heard the church door creak open. A woman, her face half-hidden beneath a shawl, appeared in the arched doorway. A group of women was huddled behind her.

'Do not be afraid,' Oliver Quintrell said.

The woman replied in her native tongue. Ekundayo, the West Indian sailor, who spoke perfect Spanish and a little Portuguese, was able to interpret. 'What is your business here?' was the woman's question.

Oliver turned to the Negro. 'Tell her there are questions I must ask. Tell her I wish to speak with the priest or the mayor, or one of the menfolk. Tell her I am not here to harm them.'

With the message conveyed, the reply was translated.

'We have no menfolk,' the woman said. 'They are all gone, run away, taken or murdered.'

'She said they buried the priest in the graveyard only yesterday,' Ekundayo added.

Not wishing to alarm the women through any sudden movement, Oliver and his men did not move from where they were standing, but neither did the women venture beyond the church's entrance.

'With your permission, *Senhora*, I beg to speak with you.' The Negro translated the captain's request.

After a few whispered words shared within her group, the woman allowed the scarf to fall from her salt-white hair and took several tentative steps towards the man in naval uniform.

With Ekundayo shadowing him, Oliver stepped forward and bent his head and shoulders in a polite gesture.

Indicating to the stone trough next to the pump, the woman led the captain to it and sat down on the edge. Pointing a finger twisted with age and years of hard toil, she gestured to him to sit alongside her. After removing his sword belt and pistol and handing them to Mr Tully, the captain accepted her invitation and sat beside the matriarch.

'Madame,' he said through his translator, 'I landed my boat at the cove and witnessed with my own eyes a terrible injustice that has happened there. Those are your menfolk, I presume?'

After several deep breaths, she started to relate her story and the other women began filing from the sanctuary of the Church, but the fear in them was apparent as they clung tightly to each other's arms.

'The bad men came three days ago. They said they were Spanish, but my husband warned me they were not. He called them privateers or pirates. But they were neither—they were the hand servants of the Devil.'

'Why did they come here? What did they want? Meat? Wine? Bread?

Eku related the captain's questions word for word.

'They took whatever they wanted, but what they came for was men.'

'Were they slavers—white slavers from the Barbary Coast?'

The woman shook her head. 'No. My husband asked the same questions of the man who called himself their captain. He said he needed sailors to work his ship. He wanted young men. Strong men. All the men we had. He promised they would be rewarded for their work. My husband did not believe him, but the knives hanging from the men's belts and pistols in their hands were not to be argued with.'

'So the young men went with them?'

'How could they?' the woman replied.

Oliver was puzzled.

'We have no young men here.'

'Tell her I do not understand,' Oliver said politely, his words and tone being conveyed to the old woman.

She sighed and interlocked her crippled fingers in a gesture of praying. Closing her eyes for a second she explained. 'Since the Crown of Portugal ruled that all young men must serve the country's army, our young men have left the island by whatever means they could. Once they reach the age of sixteen years, they go. If they hear of a whale ship on this island or any other island, they leave in the hope of signing on or stowing away on it. The same happens if there is a word of a British ship or an Indiaman in Ponta Delgada, they take a boat and go. Those in the towns whose families have money pay for their sons to sail to England or America in the hope once they reach that destination, they will make their fortunes and return to collect their sisters and parents and deliver them to a new land. But that doesn't happen very often. Most boys are never heard of again.'

Oliver shook his head. 'That must be hard on the mothers.'

'Very hard. It breaks their hearts.'

Oliver paused.

'So how do you survive with no men to care for you?'

The woman straightened her back. 'We are strong and capable,' she said, her voice feeble, but her tone determined. 'Between us, we tend the fields, grow crops, fish, and care for the animals. We weave and sew, tan hides and fillet the fish we catch. We grind the grain and make out own bread, and we care for the old men who are too old or infirm to toil for us. But when this demon from the sea descended on us, he ordered all the men from their houses and lined them up. He cursed us because there were no young men amongst them and accused us of hiding our sons. The priest explained about the government's regulations, but he did not believe him, and even while the priest was explaining, he drew a curved blade and sliced it across his throat.'

Her words brought a sudden intake of breath and sobs from some of the women, but the expression on the wrinkled face remained steadfast.

'That is not the worst of it,' she said. 'The leader was a foreigner. He wore a long coat, like yours, in blue and red.' Then she shook her head and was unable to continue for a while.

The captain waited patiently.

Smearing the tears across her cheeks, she continued. 'This demon grabbed one of the girls—Antonia, my neighbour's granddaughter. He tied her hands to the pump behind you. "Where are your brothers and your father?" he asked in Spanish. When she didn't reply, he bellowed in her ear. The sound of his voice made her cry. From the fear and bewilderment on her face, it was obvious she did not understand his questions. Her mother, who was being held back by the other women, screamed at the man, "Her father is dead. Lost at sea. Her brother left the island on a ship". The man demanded to know the name of the ship, but she could not answer. While the villagers cursed and threatened him with sticks, Antonia begged for mercy. But he did not listen. He continued to demand men but when no one appeared, he took out his pistol and pointed it at the girl's head. He spoke in Spanish, and though it is not the language of the island, most understood what he was saying. But with no response to his call, he laughed. He accused us of defying him.' She caught her breath. 'He pulled the trigger.'

Ekundayo's face creased as he translated the woman's words. He felt her pain when she leaned down and touched the white stones at her feet crusted with blackened blood.

'It was a nightmare,' she continued. 'Like the demons of Hell had descended on us. The children screamed and grabbed their mother's skirts. The women whisked them into their arms and ran back to their houses. I did not move an inch from where I was standing because my legs would not carry me. My eyes would not leave the body of the young girl. She was only thirteen.'

'Dear God!' Oliver exclaimed. There was nothing more he could say.

'When my breath returned to me, I pointed my stick at him and cursed him with every ounce of my being. I spat at his feet and told him again and again that we had no young men, but the monster would not listen. He accused the men of being cowards hiding behind women's petticoats.'

'What happened next?'

'The captain was wild and ordered his men to search the houses. They took all the food they found, but they did not find anyone hiding from them, only six old men resting on their beds because they could hardly walk.'

'Could you not call on the local militia to help you?'

She explained that there were no soldiers or militia on Santa Maria. There was absolutely nothing they could do.

'While the old men were prepared to fight, we women knew it would be futile to try. What good are sticks against a mob of armed cut-throats?' Her body swayed back and forth on the cold stone trough. 'The six men he took were weak and infirm. Most of them could hardly walk. Yet he ordered them to march to the beach. I think by the time they reached there, he realized they were not fit enough to work on his ship. I think that is why he hung them.' The tears rolled freely down her cheeks. 'My husband was one of them.'

The captain was lost for words to express the depth of his sympathy.

'When this Devil departed the square he left one message. "I will return two days from now, and when I do, if you do no give me twenty strong men, I will blow the heads off twenty of your women and children right here in the village square."'

'God in Heaven,' Oliver cried, 'who is this devil? This son of Satan? Even our enemies would not behave in such a fiendish manner.'

'What can we do?' Eku begged. 'There must be something.'

The captain had no answer. He didn't even have his ship in the water to chase this pirate, so there was nothing more to be said. After thanking the Negro, who had translated the woman's words, he ordered his men back to the boat.

Before he left, Ekundayo talked quietly with women, speaking gently in a mixture of Spanish and broken Portuguese. Having witnessed the invasion of his home in the Caribbean, he understood their pain. He had watched the brutal murder of the plantation owner and could only imagine the fate suffered by his mother at the hands of the renegade black rebels. Though he had only been a boy at the time, those acts of butchery had never left him.

'Please, Captain,' the woman begged in faltering English. 'Do not leave us. This man is returning tomorrow. God only knows what will become of us then.'

'I am sorry, I must return to my ship,' he said sincerely. 'I am afraid there is nothing I can do.'

The old woman looked into his eyes and touched his arm. 'Then pray for us, *senhor*.'

In no mood to partake of the refreshments the villagers offered them, Captain Quintrell and his party left immediately and returned to the beach where it was apparent that, during their time in the village, the wind had freshened, whipping up the waves to a degree that would have made it near impossible to get the boat back out to sea safely. Furthermore, after what he had heard, the captain had no desire to encounter the foreign ship on the water. Therefore, he decided to leave the cutter and return to *Perpetual* on the track over the headland taken the previous day by Mr Tully and the two boys.

When the group of seamen hurried past the gallows, the beady gaze of the hawks perched along the spar followed them. This time, however, the birds were uninclined to leave their prey, and not a single feather fluttered in response to the seamen's presence.

Despite the captain's concerns about finding a suitable path, with numerous goats and pigs roaming wild on the island, there were plenty of well-used tracks to choose from. Following in single file, Mr Tully led the way. In parts, the uphill climb over steep uneven ground was difficult for men more adept at to climbing rigging. Scrambling down the intervening valleys was not easy either with vines hooking around their legs, and dry branches clawing their bare arms.

The captain estimated the journey on foot would take at least two hours with no time to rest along the way. After travelling for less than half that time, a noise in the bushes ahead of them alerted the captain. It was the sound of a cutlass blade slashing the undergrowth. Holding up his hand to halt his men, he put his finger to his mouth for silence.

Pray God it is not the band of cut-throats.

The crew immediately squatted down on the path or took cover in the bushes.

'Captain, is that you?' a familiar voice called. Then, after a moment of silence an officer showed himself. 'Thank the Lord, I have found you, sir.'

'Mr Nightingale, what brings you here?'

'I was sent to find you, Captain, I'm afraid all is not well,

Chapter 7

Careened

Within an hour of Captain Quintrell and his party being farewelled from the beach and the cutter disappearing from sight, Lieutenant Parry, who had been left in command, had allocated the hands to various groups. The woodcutters, armed with axes, saws and hatchets, were supplied with a day's rations and despatched to a woody headland that had been sighted from the frigate to the west. They would spend one day felling and sawing before the arduous job of transporting the wood back to the ship would begin.

Another party of twenty headed inland, following the course of the valley in the hope of finding a source of fresh water. Everyone knew it would be a frustratingly slow job to refill the empty leaguers in the hull from the small barrels the men were able to carry on their shoulders. But only enough water was needed to supply the ship for another week. By then, *Perpetual* would be refloated and would be heading for Ponta Delgada where supplies could be replenished from the reservoirs at the port.

With the cooper, carpenter and some of the carpenter's mates employed moving barrels in the hold under Mr Parry's orders, the keenest-eyed topmen were chosen as lookouts and despatched to the cliff tops.

For the rest of the crew, regular watches were discontinued and any man who could hold a chisel or swing a hammer or put a strong elbow behind a bristle brush was employed in scraping the crust of barnacles and weed from the frigate's hull. Being built in Bombay and constructed of Malabar teak, the oils in the wood had helped protect it from being bored into by the Teredo mollusc, and the copper plating had provided a further barrier to the worm, but nothing stopped barnacles from clinging to the hull. In parts the rock-hard layer was several inches thick. Had the frigate spent its recent months patrolling with the Channel Fleet or sailing in the North Sea, the constant pounding from the waves would have helped deter them, but sitting at anchor in the rich warm waters of Gibraltar Bay for several months had exacerbated the problem.

'I pity the poor souls who were keel-hauled,' Simon said, when examining the shells. 'Such a hull would have ripped a man's flesh from his bones. It would have been merciful for the man to drown.'

Sitting on the sand fifty paces from the careened ship with a drawing book propped on his knees, Jeremy Nightingale was happy to sketch the scene. Resting on the beach, leaning to her larboard side and well-supported with lines, anchor cable and struts, the naval frigate revealed to the artist its slightly bulbous curves usually hidden beneath the water. Mr Nightingale appreciated the lines and copied them accurately into his book.

With all precautions taken to prevent the vessel from rolling over, the waves of the incoming tide lapped the rudder and swirled around in the pool that had formed in the sand. But, otherwise, the sea had no effect on the hull. Everyone knew that when the time came to refloat the ship, it would take more than those transparent lapping wavelets to shift it.

Though the lieutenant enjoyed his art, today's sketching was not purely for pleasure. He had been charged with the task by the captain before he had departed in the cutter to investigate the gallows on the nearby beach. While the captain's log included adequate descriptive passages, he always appreciated a visual image to illustrate his entries. As was the artist's usual practice, he would make rough sketches on the beach and complete his drawings at the wardroom table when the frigate was back at sea.

The sound of hammers echoed around the ship's hull and, from the makeshift galley the smell of salt pork cooking wafted across the beach. It competed with the odour drifting from the bosun's pot of pitch bubbling on a brazier not far from the ship. The sounds and sights were reminiscent of any busy shipyard.

Turning his attention from the careened ship, Mr Nightingale turned to face the cove's entrance where the sea flowed in. Framed by two near-vertical headlands, it made a perfect picture. He watched the noisy terns diving into the water to catch fish and compared them with the larger gulls that appeared content to float on the water and wait for the fish to come to them.

Flipping the page, to commence his next sketch, he looked up and saw the image being sliced horizontally across by a long straight beam of timber. It was the bowsprit of a ship. Slowly and silently, it poked its nose from the point of the western headland and proceeded across the water half a mile from the cove's entrance.

Jumping to his feet and allowing his drawing book and pencil to drop to the sand, Mr Nightingale shouted for the first lieutenant. At the same time, a cry came from *Perpetual*'s deck. In answer to the urgent calls, Mr Parry emerged from behind the hull to a barrage of shouting and pointing fingers.

'What is it?' he called. But, by then, he could see the ship for himself. 'Bring me a glass,' he ordered one of the midshipmen.

'I see no flag,' Mr Nightingale said. 'Looks like a merchantman.' It was a ship, indeed. Square-rigged on all three masts. 'At least it's not a French man-o'-war.'

'Why was there no warning from the lookouts up on the cliffs?' Mr Parry quizzed, but no one answered.

From the beach, he followed the ship's progress as it swam across the azure sea. It was heading east in the direction of Portugal. But the half-smile disappeared from his face, when he heard the next call.

'She's heaving to!'

Grabbing the brass tube from the midshipman's hand, Mr Parry focused the lens on the passing ship. The lookout was right. As soon as the helm was thrown over, the wind backed the sails and the ship's progress slowed noticeably.

Mr Nightingale stepped up beside him. 'What are your orders, Mr Parry?'

'Tell the sergeant of marines to have his men armed and assembled on the beach and inform the men working below decks to be ready. Order the hands working on the hull on the starboard side to stand down and await my orders. Pass a message to the cockpit for the women to remain out of sight. Let us first ascertain the nationality and find out what the captain's intentions are. I want no firing.'

'Aye, aye, sir.' The third lieutenant quickly relayed the orders to two of the middies, who headed off to pass the orders to the others.

While the workers stopped what they were doing and watched from the beach, the visiting ship's anchor splashed into the sea. At the same time, they observed two boats being swayed out from the davits.

'Why doesn't he show his colours?' Mr Parry hissed.

Waiting was tedious, especially as little could be done from the beach or the gun deck. With *Perpetual*'s gunports closed and the muzzles pointing down to the sand from the larboard ports and at the sky on the opposite side, it would have been impossible to bring any gun to bear, even if there had been time permitting.

Mr Parry was uneasy. He had been instructed to send a message to Captain Quintrell should anything unusual eventuate, but the ship's arrival had happened without warning and he had been caught off-guard. He cursed the lookouts on the headland for not giving him prior warning.

Observing the ship carefully, he noted the men who descended into the boats. They were dressed neither as marines nor soldiers nor even as respectable sailors. But that was not unusual for traders or whalers. Of the two boats, each accommodated eight men besides the six sailors on the oars. After pushing off from the ship's side, the oars dipped rhythmically in the water as the sailors pulled towards the beach. Then two more boats emerged from around the far side of the vessel. Neither of the officers had noticed them being lowered.

With six red-coated marines standing at the cap rail on *Perpetual*'s deck and two in the shrouds, the remaining soldiers lined up in file in front of the frigate.

As if in answer to his earlier query, a large Danish flag was run up. Though it fell around the post, Mr Parry was familiar with that country's colours. Somewhat relieved, the first officer remained where he was and waited until the four approaching boats had been run up on the beach.

A short but solid man in a faded blue coat and wearing a bicorn hat was carried from the first boat in the arms of a mightily built African. It was evident this was the captain. Once his feet were placed on the sand, he lifted his hat and waved it in a friendly gesture in the direction of the group gathered on the beach.

Rolling down his shirt sleeves, Mr Parry fastened the shirt buttons across his chest. Wearing neither coat, nor hat, nor shoes, and without his sword, he was inadequately dressed to greet a visiting captain. But the visitor had arrived unannounced and there had been no time to prepare. With Lieutenant Nightingale beside him, Simon Parry stepped across the sand to welcome him. After rubbing the sand from his hands, he extended his hand to greet the foreigner.

The events that followed happened with the speed of lightning. The lieutenant's arm was grabbed and twisted behind his back and the point of a knife put to his throat. The third lieutenant received the same treatment. At the same time, the men who had manned the oars in the boats stood upright, but in place of oars, they levelled muskets at the marines and fired. The volley of shots hit two seamen, felled three of the marines on the beach and dropped two more from the shrouds. Their bodies thudded onto the sand beneath the hull.

Then a puff of tell-tale smoke and a tongue of orange flame shot out from the side of the ship. The blast of thunder from another three guns followed a moment later, the shots hissed across the cove. One landed in the coarse grass at the edge of the beach only fifty yards away. Another thumped into a dune startling the nesting birds. The third thudded into the foothills on the opposite side of the beach close to the track Mr Tully and the boys had taken.

With a firm grip on Mr Parry, the knife's blade pressing against his throat, the visitor spoke in good English with the hint of a Spanish accent. 'Order your men to drop their weapons and I will not spill your blood, otherwise, with one word from me, the next shot will turn your ship into matchwood.'

Mr Parry had little choice but to give the order and, when the crew complied, he was released from the foreigner's grip. It had taken less than three minutes for him to fail to comply with the promise he had made to Captain Quintrell. He had lost control of one of His Majesty's frigate's, had seen the lives of several marines and two seamen come to an end and, not least, had been made to forfeit his pride in front of the whole crew.

'What can we do?' Mr Nightingale whispered.

'We do as he says,' Mr Parry said reluctantly. 'We wait to discover what his intentions are.'

'At least he cannot take *Perpetual* while it is stuck in the sand,' Mr Nightingale said. 'And hopefully the captain will have heard the shots.'

'Silence!' The order was screamed into the faces of the two officers. 'Who is in charge here?'

'I am,' Simon Parry replied.

'Your name?'

'Simon Parry.'

'Ah, I have heard of you, Captain Parry.'

The first lieutenant did not correct the visitor's assumption.

'Let me introduce myself. My name is Fredrik Johannes van Zetten. My ship is the *San Nicola* recently arrived from Brazil and bound for—who knows where?'

'Then perhaps you would allow me to go to my cabin and attend to my dress.'

Van Zetten cast a disparaging look at the British officer. 'To alert your men and return with a weapon?' He laughed. 'I prefer you the way you are.'

'So be it,' Simon Parry said.

'I should advise you, Captain Parry, I have come here to take your ship, but it appears it is not ready to sail at this moment.'

'Your observations are correct. The frigate was taking water so there was no alternative but to run her up on the sand before she sank.'

The two midshipmen exchanged enquiring glances. Fortunately their puzzled expressions went unnoticed.

'And how long will these repairs take, might I ask?'

'A week perhaps, maybe more. It will depend on the extent of the rot. She is not a young ship and many of her timbers are tired. When the work has been completed, we shall have to wait for the full of the moon and a high tide to lift her from the beach. Even so, it will not be an easy task.'

'Do not concern me with such trivia,' Captain van Zetten said. 'If I relieve you of some of your cargo, I will make the job much easier for you.'

'Under what flag and authority?'

'Under my authority, Captain Parry. I sail under whichever flag I find convenient.'

'You are a pirate then?'

'You may call me what you wish. I can show Letters of Marque proving that I am a privateer, but I care little for slips of paper that can be forged or stolen. I am here to take your ship and its cargo.'

'Then I am afraid you will be disappointed on that score also. The ship is carrying no cargo and has virtually no supplies on board.'

The pirate laughed. 'You have been fighting the French in the Mediterranean. You must have amassed some plunder?'

'No, sir. We have been anchored in Gibraltar Bay for the past three months amidst the death and suffering of the malignant fever. It has claimed thousands of lives. I am sure you have heard about it. We only escaped the place a few weeks ago. We were desperate for water and food and our sails and cordage are in dire need of replacing. But we needed to repair the hull before we could proceed to Ponta Delgada, and then home to England.'

'Fever is not new,' van Zetten said scornfully. 'I meet it everywhere I go. It is rampant on the coast of Africa and the islands of the Caribbean. Tell me why you did not sail to the main port first.'

'It would have been an embarrassment for a British frigate to sink on the city's wharf,' Mr Parry replied, the serious expression on his face unchanged throughout the exchange. 'However, under the circumstances,' he continued, 'I cannot refuse you entry to the ship but I assure you, sir, you will find nothing of value.'

'I shall be the judge of that.'

'Mr Nightingale,' Simon said, 'kindly advise the cooper we have a visitor coming aboard and to ensure that there are no loose barrels that could roll and injure him.'

Immediately, the lieutenant headed toward the rope-ladder dangling from the hull. But word had already been picked up by the sailors working beneath the ship and conveyed to the crew who were still on board.

'I invite you to inspect our cockpit while you are there, but I warn you, it is filled with dead and dying men suffering from the malignant fever. That is another reason I did not sail into Ponta Delgada. I would have been required to enter the port under the yellow flag of contagion, and I doubt I would have received a cordial welcome.'

Pulling a handkerchief from his pocket, the visitor dabbed it to his nose, its once smooth line interrupted by an old scar cutting across it. The unmistakable musky scent of ambergris wafted on the air as he flicked the piece of dirty white silk before returning it to his coat.

'Perhaps you had not heard of the epidemic that ravaged Cadiz claiming fifty thousand lives only recently.'

It was obvious this information was new to van Zetten.

Mr Parry continued. 'We buried most of our victims at sea, but the recent deaths and those who will die in the coming days, we will commit to the soil of this island. Three bodies were buried his morning over there.' He pointed to the area at the far side of the cove where a group of men had been digging a ditch. While it was human excrement and not bodies lining the bottom of the ditch, it served Simon Parry's purpose.

'But the doctor assures me,' he said, continuing the charade, 'the fever is subsiding. He says that if we remain here for a long enough period then, hopefully, the sickness will end and there will be no need to raise the quarantine jack when we enter the port.'

'If I were to set fire to your ship, you would have no more concerns about the contagion.'

'Ah,' said Mr Parry quickly, 'but once repaired, she is a good fast ship and will exchange for a considerable amount of gold if she was to be sold on the Barbary Coast.'

Van Zetten was not amused.

Simon eyed the man who was a threat to every person on the beach. Was he gullible enough to have believed the story about *Perpetual*'s problems? he wondered. While he was confident of the truths he had uttered, he was less confident of the untruths he had told. They did not come easily to a man of integrity but, at this stage, he had more than himself to consider and could think of no better alternative. He desperately needed the support of Captain Quintrell. He wondered if the guilt churning inside him was showing on his face.

By not sending word to alert the captain to the arrival of a foreign ship, he had failed to follow orders, and the following events had unfolded so quickly he had been caught unprepared. The fact the frigate's company was greatly depleted justified his decision to parley rather than engage in an abortive fight that could have ended disastrously. The bodies of the dead marines and sailors, whose life-blood had already soaked into the sand, furthered his resolve. With the ship, *San Nicola* anchored outside the mouth of the cove, its guns directed at the frigate, and with a company of renegade sailors pointing muskets at his men, he considered the action he had taken had been for the best.

'You have ample food and water aboard the ship, no doubt?'

'No, sir,' Simon Parry said truthfully. 'Believe me when I say we are desperately short of both water and provisions, but before we could make the victualling yard in Ponta Delgada, it was necessary to repair the damage. We were taking on water so fast we would not have made the distance of fifty miles to São Miguel.'

'You disappoint me, Captain,' van Zetten scoffed. 'When I look around, I see many fit men at work. They do not look hungry.'

'It is no lie. We have supplies enough to last us for one week at the most, and until we arrived, we had water but it was limited. I am hoping to find some fresh water nearby during our stay.'

Captain van Zetten was not interested. 'You have many men.'

Simon Parry shook his head. 'Barely enough to man a British frigate. A ship of this size requires over two hundred men. You can see for yourself, at present, I have less than half that number. He chose his words judiciously. 'Many good men died in Gibraltar.'

The pirate's laugh was scathing. 'You have more men than I. My ship was becalmed in the Doldrums for six weeks. There I tossed four dozen overboard, either dead or begging for death. It was the seaman's curse,' he said. 'Scurvy.'

Though van Zetten's teeth were crusted in yellow and brown, they all appeared to be present. It was obvious to the lieutenant that the ship's captain had not suffered from scurvy as his men had.

'So, Captain Parry, you will oblige me with half of your men.'

'I protest,' Simon exclaimed.

The pirate laughed again. 'Who are you to protest to me? In other circumstances I would take your ship, your men and your life without uttering a single word. In this instance, I am being exceedingly generous. I will take forty of your sailors leaving you enough to complete your repairs. I will also take your carpenter and cooper. I will return here in five days and will expect to find your vessel sound and ready to put to sea. Consider this, Captain Parry, and be grateful. My ship will tow your frigate from the sand, but once afloat, I will relieve you of it along with the rest of your crew. Do I make myself clear?'

Mr Parry glanced from the line of bare-chested Perpetuals standing in front of the frigate's hull, to the foreign sailors standing in and alongside the boats in which they arrived, armed with muskets, swords and pistols. Then he considered the frigate lying on the sand. It was as useless as a shark whose dorsal fin has been sliced from its back. Then he caught the evil grin on the face of the man about to take half of the crew who were present.

'You will come with me to ensure your crew do exactly as I command. They will sail my ship, *San Nicola*, into Ponta Delgada, where I will buy supplies. When I return, you will inform your sailors that, if they do not comply with my orders, I will use them as fish bait. Take heed, Captain, I do not make idle threats.'

Without waiting for a reply, he turned to Mr Nightingale. 'I see you are an artist,' van Zetten said, grinding the sketch pad into the sand with the heel of his shoe.

'I am Lieutenant Nightingale of His Britannic Majesty's Navy. I was making a sketch of the beach for my captain.'

Mr Parry's heart sank, in the event, the young officer revealed too much.

'You will remain here, Lieutenant, and make sure these men finish the work they are doing and do not run off into the hills.' Then he pointed to the two midshipmen standing nearby, the only men on the beach in full uniform. 'They will come with me, also,' he said to Simon. 'They will be insurance against me being fired upon when I take my leave. Should that happen, you will see two pretty young men wearing hempen neckties hanging from the main yardarm. Do I make myself clear?'

Mr Parry had no alternative but to accept the conditions, though his feeling of anxiety was increasing with every passing second. Had the sounds from the musket and cannon fire carried to wherever the captain was? Had the men cutting wood and collecting water also been alerted by the noise? If so, would they guess what was happening on the beach or ignore it? There was a possibility at any moment a mob of sailors could descend on the beach only to be cut down in a shower of musket shot. And, on discovering that he had lied about the number of his men, would the ship's guns be aimed at every man on the beach?

'Yes,' Mr Parry said reluctantly, for he was in no position to argue or put up a fight. Had he attempted it, many lives would have been lost. His only hope was that, when Captain Quintrell returned, he would find a solution. One small consolation was that *Perpetual* had not been taken. Contrary to the tale he had told the pirate, the frigate's hull was sound, and already many barnacles had been cleaned from it. There was a slight possibility, that if the tide was in his favour, the captain would be able to refloat the frigate quickly and save it from being taken as a pirate's prize.

Van Zetten was becoming impatient. 'I want your men lined up on the beach this instant. I want your boats hauled down to the water and the sailors put aboard *San Nicola* with all haste. I weigh anchor in half-an-hour.'

With the flash of steel glinting in the sunlight, Simon Parry had run out of arguments and lies, and had no alternative but to comply.

'I beg you to leave some of our boats,' Simon said.'

'Why? What need have you for boats?' van Zetten asked. 'Unless you plan to escape to one of the other islands.'

'No, sir, I assure you we will not do that.' He knew he was perilously close to raising van Zetten's suspicions.

'You would do well to mind your tongue, Captain Parry. I have been known to nail a man's tongue to the cap rail for being greedy.'

'Forgive me.' Simon nodded. 'I will assemble the men and have the boats made ready.'

Captain van Zetten stepped back twisting the greying hairs sprouting from his chin.

'Proceed,' he said. 'But remember, when I return to collect the frigate, do not fire on me or my ship. As a reminder, I will have your sailors lined up along the deck and will slice everyman's throat before pushing him overboard. I do not think you or Lieutenant Nightingale will want that scene playing on your conscience for the rest of your days.'

Simon Parry remained silent. There was no time to lose.

Exchanging glances with Mr Nightingale, the first lieutenant was confident he understood what had to be done. The ship's artist was a sensible man and a good officer. He trusted he would make the right decisions in his absence. Only one thing now worried Simon Parry—as *San Nicola* sailed along the coast, would it meet the captain's cutter returning to the cove? He prayed that would not be the case.

Within minutes, a large group of seamen, including Bungs and Mr Crosby, was marched down the beach in double file.

Looking back to the third lieutenant, the sailing master and the doctor who were standing together on the beach, Mr Parry and the two middies were rowed out in van Zetten's own boat and taken aboard the pirate's ship. The sailors from the frigate followed in the other boats, but before boarding, the men were searched for any weapons hidden in their shirts or tucked under their belt. The knives and chisels that were found were immediately tossed into the sea. As the boats packed with sailors, glided toward the ship, the translucent water was barely disturbed by the dip of the oars. The white sand gleamed reflecting the warmth of the full sun. From the boats' thwarts, the prisoners watched their freedom drifting from them and tried not to focus on the fate awaiting them.

Within less time than it takes for the half-hour glass to empty, *San Nicola*'s anchor had been raised, the sails set and the ship was underway.

On the beach, the remaining Perpetuals, who had buried their tools in the sand, whispered together. Many had ideas and suggestions and it was not long before they were bombarding Mr Nightingale, the doctor and the bosun with their proposals. The sailing master soon put a stop to the upheaval. In his opinion, Captain Quintrell would be returning shortly and he would know what to do. Being the most senior man according to age, Mr Mundy assumed command and called for the doctor to support him. On the sand, the bosun took it upon himself to attend to the men. 'Back to work you dogs or you'll feel the bite of the mate's starter.'

But Mr Nightingale, the most senior naval officer remaining, knew where his responsibility lay. Mr Parry had charged him with informing Captain Quintrell of what had happened, but with no boat available to carry him along the coast, his only alternative was to head over the cliff tops on foot. But, with no idea of the distance he must travel, or the location of the beach, the gallows or village, or the route he must follow to arrive there, he needed help. Only Mr Tully and the two boys knew the way, and Mr Tully was with the captain. His only option was to take Tommy Wainwright and young Charles and trust their memories would serve them when called upon.

Chapter 8

The Plan

'Captain, is that you?' Mr Nightingale called. 'Thank the Lord, I have found you.'

'What brings you here?' Oliver asked. The unexpected appearance of the lieutenant and the two boys on the top of the headland did not bode well.

'I was sent to find you, Captain. I'm afraid all is not well.'

'What has happened? Is the frigate safe?'

'Aye, Captain, but that is about the extent of it.'

'Tell me all. I must know.'

The sailors drew closer muttering together, anxious to learn the news.

'Five of the marines have been shot dead and two sailors.'

'What? How?' Oliver demanded.

'And Mr Parry and two of the middies have been taken prisoner, along with forty of the crew including the carpenter and Bungs.'

The captain was aghast. 'Who did this?'

'A ship came and took them. And it will return in five days. Its captain is demanding the frigate be ready to go back into the water. He's threatened to seize the frigate and take the rest of the men along with it. He's taken all the ship's boats, and we can't defend ourselves because we can't bring the guns to bear.'

'Slow down, slow down,' the captain cried. 'Do you have control of the beach?'

'Yes, sir, there is only the crew on the sand.'

'In the absence of Mr Parry, you are the senior officer, so who is presently in charge?'

'The sailing master and bosun have assumed responsibility while I'm away.'

'And the men, what is the feeling amongst them?'

'They want you back, Captain. They want to get our ship off the sand. They want to put to sea as quickly as possible and rescue their mates who've been taken.'

The tale being related was unbelievable. It was the last thing he expected or wanted to hear. His immediate urge was to head off with all speed to re-join his ship and his men. But with so many unanswered questions and thoughts whirring round in his head, he needed to listen to the full story before making any rash decisions.

'Rest for a moment,' the captain said. 'Catch your breath. Take some water then tell me everything.'

Squatting down on the path, Mr Nightingale and the boys were grateful for the water and drank thirstily. The sailors who had climbed up from the village gathered closer, some sitting on the hard ground, others standing, but all eyes were fixed on the frigate's third lieutenant as he recounted what had happened since they had departed in the cutter.

'Mr Parry had no option but to do as he was bid,' he said defensively. 'This rogue, who had command, believed him to be the captain and kept addressing him by that title. Mr Parry didn't correct him because he was never asked.'

Captain Quintrell was bemused. It was unlike Lieutenant Parry to do anything deceptive. 'This devilish fellow thinks he is holding *Perpetual*'s captain, is that what you are telling me?' Oliver considered the consequences of that situation. 'Hmm, interesting. Do you think the lieutenant will continue with the ruse?'

Mr Nightingale nodded. 'Yes, sir, as long as he can.'

'You called this ship's captain a privateer—what is his name? His nationality? What is the name of his ship? What are his demands?'

'He wants men. He is short of crew to work the ship. His name is Fredrik van Zetten. He speaks English, but sounds Spanish. He sails under a Danish flag but his uniform is neither Danish nor Spanish nor French, nor any other navy I know of.'

'And the ship?'

'A fully-rigged ship by the name *San Nicola*.'

The sailors listened in stunned silence.

'Of what appearance is this captain?' Oliver Quintrell asked.

'Broad in the shoulders, but short. He has a swarthy skin, like the mulattos of the West Indies, and bears an ugly scar across his nose.'

'Apart from wishing to take my ship as a prize and wanting men, what else did he seek?'

'He asked what cargo we were carrying and how well we were supplied with water and victuals. Mr Parry convinced him the hold was empty and that we were still carrying the malignant fever picked up in Gibraltar. That was the reason he didn't climb aboard. But he promised he would be back and said we must have the frigate repaired and ready to go back to the water or he would blow it off the beach or set fire to it. He has the guns and is capable of doing so.'

Oliver's thoughts were still racing, darting from one thing to another. 'What of the two women? Are they safe?'

'Aye, captain, they remained below deck and were never seen.'

Turning his face into the wind and gazing across the sea to the empty horizon, the captain pondered on the information he had been given. He glanced down at the two boys sitting behind the lieutenant, and considered the worried expressions on their faces. He thought of his crew on the beach. What state were they in now?

'What can you do, sir? You have to stop him.' It was the second time in as many hours that this question had been put to him.

'I will stop him,' the captain announced emphatically, 'one way or another. Are the divisions returned from collecting wood and water?'

'Not when I left the beach.'

'That means there are forty members of the ship's company this rogue is unaware of.'

'Indeed. Plus this group of men here with you. Thank the Lord I found you, for I feared I would not. It was a terrible thing that happened, but the doctor said the outcome could have been much worse.'

'The outcome is bad enough,' Oliver replied bluntly, 'but I lay no blame on Mr Parry or anyone else. Perhaps the blame lies with me for leaving the beach.' He quickly shook that idea from his head. He had done what had to be done at the time and he could not have anticipated the events that followed. 'My concern now is for the men who have been taken. I fear the treatment they will receive aboard the *San Nicola* will not be good. I shall find the scoundrel who has taken them and return them safe and sound—every last one of them.'

There was a murmur of approval from the group over an undertone of disbelief.

Having listened patiently to the lieutenant's story, it was Captain Quintrell's turn to relate the events that had transpired in the village. Without interrupting once, Mr Nightingale, Charlie and Young Tom listened wide-eyed to the tale the captain told.

Even as he spoke, his mind was abuzz with a daring scheme he was hatching. By the time he had finished speaking, he was ready to issue his orders to the third lieutenant.

'Return to the ship. Assure Mr Mundy and the crew that all will be well. Tell them to continue working diligently and finish scraping the hull. We are likely to need the additional speed from a clean bottom in the near future. When they return from the hills, have the men continue collecting wood and water as though nothing was amiss, but tell them not to stray far and to be ready for anything.'

'Might I ask what you intend to do, Captain?' Mr Nightingale enquired.

'I intend to take van Zetten's ship and rescue my men.'

The lieutenant was not the only one astounded by the captain's statement. 'Beg pardon, Captain,' he said politely, looking around at the dumb expression of the other faces. 'How will that be possible?'

Oliver considered the sailors' reactions. 'Consider this; there are already Perpetuals aboard *San Nicola*—albeit they were taken aboard as prisoners. Hopefully, they are not all locked in the hold. Hopefully some are working on the decks or on the yards. Captain van Zetten has admitted he is short of men. Isn't that what you told me?'

'Indeed, Captain.'

'But how do you plan to get aboard?' Mr Tully asked.

A quirky grin played on the captain's face. 'I have a plan. I will share the details later, but for the present, there is no time to lose.' Taking off his coat and hat, he handed them to Charlie Pickering. Then he turned to Mr Tully. 'Kindly remove your king's uniform and hand it over. The rest of you will part with your ship's slops at the village. I intend for us to return there and assume the identity of farmers, at least for a short while.'

'But, Captain.'

'Don't worry, Mr Nightingale, I have no intention of losing any more men. However, there is one important thing.' The captain looked directly at Tommy Wainwright. 'I have nineteen men in my group. I need one more to make that number up to twenty. I cannot take you, Mr Nightingale, because van Zetten would recognize your face, and I will not take the boy because he is too young.' He turned to the sixteen year-old lad from the north of England. 'You have proved your courage in the past, young Tom. Are you prepared to fight for your king and country again?'

'Too right, Captain,' Tommy Wainwright said.

'I am sure Ekundayo will give an eye to you.'

The West Indian nodded.

'Then I am satisfied. Go now, and believe me when I say, all will be well.'

Rising to their feet and without so much as a farewell, the artist and the ship's boy set off. Heading over the headland as quickly as they could without stumbling, they made their way back to the beach. Tucked under his arm, each man carried an officer's naval uniform, while grasped tightly in his hand was a bicorn hat.

'With me, men,' the captain called, turning on his heel and leading Mr Tully, Eku and the rest of his group across the top of the windy hilltop and back down to village.

On reaching the sheltered beach the captain stopped and briefly examined the bodies hanging from the length of timber that had once served as a ship's topmast. Leaning down beside one of the corpses, he took off his silver-buckled shoes and rolled down his white silk stockings. Then reaching up, he carefully removed a pair of leather sandals from the feet of the dead man, dropped them onto the sand and slipped his feet into them. 'This man has no more use for them,' he said.

Several sailors followed the captain's example, though the Negro took off his shoes and opted to walk barefoot. The discarded footwear was hidden in the bushes. If all went as planned, they would collect their belongings later. From the beach, the group retraced their steps along the path and headed back to the village.

Before they had even stepped foot on the mosaic patterns surrounding the square, the seamen were greeted with cries of delight from the women who were agog with relief and excitement at seeing them return. Within minutes they were lavished with food and locally made wine for which the hungry sailors were grateful.

Having bowed elegantly when greeting the village matriarch, Captain Quintrell spoke with her, through his translator, as he had done previously. 'You informed me that this foreign captain is returning tomorrow. You said he has demanded your men, and if not, he threatened to hang the women and children. Do you believe he will do that?'

The villagers' heads nodded in agreement.

'He has done it once,' the old woman said. 'He will do it again.'

'Then I will stop him,' Oliver assured her.

'But he is cruel. You cannot fight him and hope to win.'

'I do not intend to fight him, *Senhora*, I intend to join him.'

The captain's plan was met with a frisson of disbelief and amazement, not only from the women gathered around, but also from the men. It was a shocking proposal.

'We are twenty in total, the exact number this fiend has demanded, and you will deliver us to him.'

'But you are English,' the old woman said, a pained expression on her face.

'And you are Portuguese and your people do not understand the Spanish words this man speaks. So, my seamen will pretend they are also Portuguese and that they do not understand him. Believe me; Captain van Zetten is not interested in these men as individuals.'

The women were not convinced and some of the sailors appeared sceptical, also.

'But I will need your help, *Senhora*. My men and I will trouble you for some old clothes. The type of dress your menfolk would wear in the fields.'

A few eyebrows were raised at the request, but no one questioned it.

'I can assure you this charade is necessary and we will return the clothes when the job is done. Can you do that?'

The women agreed.

Dispensing with the black silk ribbon tied in a bow around his queue and giving it to one of the girls, Oliver's hair hung loosely around his face. He quickly powdered it with a handful of dry dirt, hooked the loose strands behind his ears and pressed a straw hat, which was offered to him, onto his head.

'We will leave our weapons here with you. It would be wise to hide them in a place where they cannot be found.'

'You will go unarmed?' the woman enquired in disbelief.

Mr Tully was also confused. 'But if we leave our weapons, what will we fight with?'

'Our best weapon is the ship itself. Trust me, you will see. Once on board, we will not be alone. Your mates will be very pleased to see you and, if the ship is as short of sailors, as this scoundrel claims, it will make for an easy victory.'

Neither Mr Tully nor most of the seamen were convinced.

Oliver turned to the matriarch, who also wore a worried expression. 'I promise we will return safely and collect our clothes and weapons later.'

'May God be with you,' she cried, clasping her hands together. Her sentiment was echoed by the others.

During the evening, the church took on the guise of a schoolroom. With the sailors perched on the benches or sitting cross-legged on the stone floor, Ekundayo instructed them in a few simple words and phrases in Portuguese. Although his efforts were commendable, by the time the lights were doused, the captain resolved it would be better for the men to keep their mouths shut.

Before sleep overtook him, Oliver considered the scheme he had conceived and presented that evening. If all went well and they were taken aboard van Zetten's ship, his plan had to be acted on swiftly. He could not allow the pirate to carry them far out to sea or for many days. He had no idea what the rogue captain intended to do with this new mob of lubbers or where he would be heading. It seemed unlikely he would embark on a long voyage as he was short of provisions. It was more likely, as he had an appetite for sailors, he would offer them to the Dey of Algiers or sail to Cadiz or Toulon and offer the British frigate as a prize vessel to the highest bidder. France or Spain would reward him for the gift of a fighting ship with no questions asked.

Then Oliver considered the response he would receive from the Perpetuals already being held aboard *San Nicola*. That thought raised other questions. Were his men truly aboard the foreign vessel or had they been brutally murdered or tossed overboard? Were his men working the decks or chained in irons in the hold? Was the vessel seaworthy? Was it carrying typhoid fever, plague or some other deadly disease? Were the men held prisoner being fed or starved and, if he succeeded in getting aboard, would they be fit enough to help him? Would the rogue captain keep his word and return to the cove in one week's time? The fact he had treasure hidden aboard had slipped his mind. What other contingencies had he forgotten?

He had so many question and so few answers. But he had one aim in mind—to make sure his men did not end up dangling from a yardarm or hanging from a makeshift gallows on some isolated beach for the hawks to rip to pieces.

The seamen, including their captain and second lieutenant, spent the night on a thin layer of straw hastily spread in the vestibule and along the central aisle of the church. Despite the chill from the stone floor, being packed closely together and being exceedingly weary, the sailors slept surprisingly well.

In the morning, Oliver woke to the winter sun steaming in through the coloured glass of the nave's leaded window. Stepping cautiously over the curled bodies, an old man was struggling to reach the rope that swung from the bell tower above their heads. Mindful of his failing strength and balance, Oliver assisted him. The first resounding clang from the single bell rudely woke all the sleepers and reminded them where they were. It was time to put the plan into action.

With the arrival of several bundles of clothing, delivered by the women, the sailors exchanged their slops and dressed in the local garb.

For Captain Quintrell, a coarse hempen shirt and woven jacket replaced his fine white cotton shirt with frilled collar and cuffs. For his legs, he pulled on a pair of old serge trousers patched at the knees. Around his neck, a hand-knitted scarf replaced the silk neckerchief. On his head, the straw hat he had been given the previous day, and on his feet, the leather sandals courtesy of the dead farmer. Gone was the image of a post captain.

His brace of pistols and sword, which had been hidden in the straw beside him while he slept, were forfeited to the care of the old bellringer. He assured the captain all the weapons would be hidden in a place within the church few men knew of and where no one would find them.

The sailors quickly dressed. Wearing smocks, woven waistcoats, patched trousers and felted hats, they more resembled peasant farmers than members of His Britannic Majesty's Navy. Less than an hour later, after having toileted themselves and partaken of some freshly baked bread liberally spread with butter and honey, the crew nervously awaited the arrival of Captain van Zetten.

He did not disappoint. With the church door slightly ajar, Oliver was able to see the rogue who had murdered the villagers as he approached the square. He came with a greater number of men than Oliver had expected—at least twenty-five ruffians armed with pistols, knives and cutlasses. Some had muskets slung over their shoulders.

The swarthy-skinned, arrogant-looking pirate led his band of rowdy misfits to the trough in the centre of the square. In Oliver's opinion, the dress of the undisciplined crew represented vagrants from the cesspools of Africa, slave-masters from the slave ports of America, deckhands from the whalers of Nantucket and common sailors from any port in Europe. Their muskets, however, all spoke the same language and were, no doubt, primed and ready to fire.

If only he had a 9-pounder and a bag of grapeshot, with one touch of the slow-match, he could blow them all to Kingdom come. But that was not to be. As it was, he was satisfied he had a plan.

Standing with legs apart holding a coiled leather whip in one hand, van Zetten appeared shorter and broader than Oliver had imagined. Turning to the women standing outside their houses, he called out in Spanish. 'I have come for your men? Where are they?'

The huge church door creaked.

Van Zetten turned.

'We are here,' Eku called, using the language of a Spanish slave from the island of San Domingo.

'Hah, that is good. Let me see you,' he demanded, before turning abruptly to face the villager. 'You lied to me, you old witch. Have you more men hiding from me?'

Though the woman did not understand his Spanish, she shook her head.

'Search the houses,' the blackguard ordered. 'Bring me the cowardly dogs hiding under the beds.'

But a quick search uncovered only three old farmers who were dragged from their homes and thrown onto the stones. They swore they had not been hiding. They were crippled and unable to walk. The captain had no time for them.

'Keep the old grandfathers,' van Zetten said, casting his eyes over the motley group that had filed from the church and was standing in front of him.

Pacing up and down, he glanced over them. They were an untidy lot, not unlike the sweepings from the Portsmouth taverns gathered up by a persuasive press gang. A woven scarf, a knitted beret and a felted waistcoat were enough to convince the visitor they were farmers. Stopping in front of the broad-chested Negro, who stood several inches taller, he spoke in Spanish and waved the plaited handle of his coiled whip in front of Eku's face.

'You know the sound this lash makes?'

Eku nodded.

'Turn around,' he ordered.

When Eku obeyed, the shirt was tugged from his belt and lifted. The raised scars criss-crossing his black skin satisfied the pirate. He was not to know that they were not from his days on the plantation, but from his time in the Royal Navy. Mr Tully also carried the scars of service on his back, and though he was not asked to reveal them, the pained expression on his face did not escape unnoticed.

'You with the beady eyes, are you listening to what I am saying?'

Not understanding what van Zetten was saying, Ben Tully did not reply.

'It seems I have your eyes but do I have your ears?'

Standing beside the lieutenant, Eku was nodding his head slightly in an attempt to convey the message to Mr Tully to do likewise. Fortunately van Zetten did not notice. But neither did Ben Tully.

After handing the whip to one of his men, the swish of steel being drawn from his scabbard brought an audible intake of breath from the women. Holding their hands to their mouths, some closed their eyes. They had already witnessed the atrocities this man was capable of.

Van Zetten's voice rose as he repeated his demands. 'You will listen and do as you are bid. You will obey or die.'

Lifting the curved blade, he levelled the tip to within a few inches of the lieutenant's left eye.

'You still do not answer,' he taunted.

Mr Tully shook his head. He didn't understand what was being said, but his lack of response was taken as a sign of insolence.

With a flick of his wrist, van Zetten slid the cold metal down the side of Mr Tully's skull and deliberately sliced through the cartilage of his ear, amputating most of it and leaving only the fleshy earlobe dangling. As it fell onto the paving, Mr Tully groaned and gritted his teeth. He thrust the flat of his palm against the wound, but it did not stop the blood running between his fingers and streaming down his neck.

Screwing the amputated ear onto the tip of his blade, he held it in front of the lieutenant's face. 'Now,' van Zetten yelled in Spanish, 'I have your ear. Perhaps you will give me your attention.'

The pain creased Ben Tully's brow, but he did not cry out.

Showing little fear, one of the younger women ran from her house, stripped off her apron, rolled it into a bundle and thrust it into the hand of the wounded officer. Though his knees quivered and a wave of fear almost toppled him, he stood firm, lifted his bloodied hand from the mutilated wound, smiled weakly at the villager and pressed the coarse cloth to the side of his head.

Van Zetten was amused. Holding the blooded piece of flesh aloft, he flicked it across the square where a flock of gulls immediately dived on it arguing over the tasty morsel. With wings beating furiously, the screaming birds fought over the tough flesh and ripped it to pieces.

The pirate laughed. 'Now you will all lend me your ears. *Allez*! All of you.' Pointing his sword in the direction of the beach he waited for the group to move off. The Negro led the way.

Oliver Quintrell remained silent. He dare not allow his gaze to meet that of his lieutenant or the frightened faces of his men. Remaining where he was in the middle of the pack, he followed Ekundayo from the village, leaving the women clinging to each other for support.

Yet, despite the malicious injury inflicted on Mr Tully, the captain's plan was working. When they reached the beach, he expected to be loaded into boats and rowed out to the *San Nicola*. The next move would depend on the Perpetuals who had been taken prisoner earlier. Their help would be needed, if he was to take van Zetten's ship.

Chapter 9

San Nicola

Climbing aboard the *San Nicola*, Oliver Quintrell was struck by the obnoxious smell. It was not a familiar ship's aroma of Stockholm tar, vinegar, brimstone and bilge water, but the sickening, unhealthy smell of a ship too long at sea—of rotting timbers and rotting men. Apart from the odour, the ship was unkempt and spoke of lax discipline and lack of pride on the part of its captain and his officers. Various objects waiting to be tripped over littered the deck, while loosely lashed barrels rocked to the movement of the waves. Lines, hanging down like lianas from aloft waited to be taken up, while those that had been coiled had been thrust onto the belaying pins in a lubberly fashion. To the observant eye, some ropes, high in the rigging, showed signs of fraying due to constant rubbing against a spar or sail. For the captain, this lack of attendance to basic ship-keeping would eventually result in time-costly accidents and likely loss of life. The final insult was the sight of a meat bone from a previous meal thrown into the scuppers waiting for the next big sea to wash it overboard.

As he and his men appeared slovenly and bedraggled, the captain considered they were in keeping with the tone of the vessel. Scanning the deck tentatively from under his straw hat, he had hoped to see a few familiar faces, but at first saw none. Then he spied a pair of seamen dressed in blue jackets and white duck trousers—regular naval slops' issue, and another three standing beside the windlass. They were under the close gaze of a sailor with a stout rope's end swinging from his wrist. Then he spotted another two, similarly dressed, in the fo'c'sle. They, too, were being guarded, though not closely. Van Zetten's men showed no interest in the new arrivals, which was a relief to Captain Quintrell, but his major concern was that there were very few sailors from the frigate about. His only hope was that when it was time to prepare the ship for sea, the frigate's sailors, who were probably held below, would be summonsed on deck.

The thought had hardly left him when, without drum-beat, pipes or whistles, a raucous voice bellowed a command in Spanish. The foreign words were gobbledegook to most of the newcomers apart from Eku and another sailor who had once served on a Spanish ship in the West Indies. Without understanding the order, the new men were poked, pushed or beaten over the head with a knotted rope to the stations where they were required.

After being shepherded to the capstan, Captain Quintrell and half a dozen of his own men picked up the heavy wooden bars and slotted them into the capstan's head. When the call went out to weigh anchor, they leaned their full weight against them and began walking circles around the drum to raise the anchor from the sea bed.

'Where are the men?' Mr Tully whispered to the captain.

'Hush,' Oliver replied. 'Be patient.'

With the wet cable returned to the tiers and the anchor catted, a stream of commands from van Zetten's first mate was relayed along the deck. This time, sailors spilled up from below where they had been confined. Keeping his face hidden beneath the brim of his hat, the captain recognized the faces of his crew, however, there was no sign of Mr Parry or the two midshipmen.

Like Oliver's group from the village, these seamen were unfamiliar with foreign words, so they too were pushed and prodded to the stations where they were needed. Most were stationed around the fife rails beneath the three masts, or at the pin rails along the sides of the ship. It was here the braces were belayed.

With the work on the capstan finished, the men removed the long levers and placed them neatly on the deck next to the skylight. The hands were then sent elsewhere. There was no time to lose in relaying the captain's plan to the others, but extreme caution had to be taken. If a voice was overheard speaking English, the plan would be foiled.

'Watch yourselves and keep your voices low,' Oliver whispered, as he moved to the starboard rail.

Though the orders screamed at them in Spanish were incomprehensible, for seasoned sailors the sequence required to put a ship to sea mattered little on the vessel's size or nationality. The location of the lines on both larboard and starboard sides followed a logical pattern and was almost identical on every square-rigged sailing ship.

Standing by the mainbrace on the windward side, Oliver was joined by three more members of his crew. On seeing the captain, one of the hands exploded in surprised delight. It took a quick thump in the ribs from behind to quieten him and explain what was about to happen. There were more unwanted shrieks and outbursts as word travelled along the deck, but van Zetten's men, who were overseeing them, took their sounds to be no more than complaints or curses.

If his plan was going to work, Oliver knew it had to be enacted quickly. If his identity became known, all would be lost. Waiting for the ideal moment, he watched the wave of whispering as it spread both forward and aft, whilst on the quarterdeck, Captain van Zetten swayed side-to-side, oblivious to the reason for the undercurrent of murmurings.

'*Silencio!*' he shouted. At the same time, the slap of the bosun's plaited starter on a man's back brought the whispering to a halt. Then a barrage of commands followed. The masts groaned as the yards were braced around them. Crumpled canvas clattered down. Lines were hauled and sails sheeted home, and when the belly of the sail filled, the clew-garnets and bunt-lines were adjusted and made fast. With the helm hard over, the wind caught the jibs turning van Zetten's ship from the coast.

While only a light breeze had ruffled the translucent waters of the cove creating little more than a ripple washing onto the sand, on the open sea outside the shelter of the headlands, *San Nicola* met with a fresh nor'wester on her larboard bow. With the sails taken aback, the jibs luffed, canvas crackled and blocks rattled over the deck as the ship heeled over. For a while it was in danger of being blown onto the lee shore, where the rugged rocks would have ripped open the rotting hull in minutes.

Then another order was given. The helm was put over and the braces hauled, swinging the yards on the fore, main and mizzen masts around in unison. With the rudder adjusted, *San Nicola's* bowsprit pointed north towards the main island of the Azores.

It was time.

Oliver leaned towards the man alongside him. 'Pass word to be ready for the call.'

Sailing close to the wind, the ship's bow sliced the oncoming waves like a hot knife through butter and, while the eyes of van Zetten's crew were fixed on the top hamper, no one payed heed to the messages being passed between the newly recruited lubbers stationed around the deck.

With their eyes focused on Captain Quintrell, the seasoned sailors worked slowly and carefully taking the lines on the belaying pins down to a single turn and placing their hands firmly over them, so they would not slip. The strain on the weather braces was extraordinary.

As the ship pounded through the oncoming swell, the doleful moan of the wind in the rigging was suddenly interrupted. Throwing his straw hat aside, Captain Quintrell leapt into an open space amidships and bellowed so loudly his voice could be heard from bowsprit to mizzen top: 'Let fly all lines! Let the braces run! Hold firm, men and then reach for your weapons!'

Within seconds, the lines sizzled and smoked as they hissed through the sheaves at lightning fast speed. Huge pulley blocks on the stays'l and jib sheets hammered the deck and swung over it like giant pendulums slaying anything in their path. The block on the main topsail halyard swung down wildly knocking one sailor from his feet and slamming him face-first onto the deck. Blood seeped from his skull. On the mainmast, the royal yard dropped onto the topmast cap crushing a sailor's head and sending another cannoning into the sea. The deck heeled violently to starboard, then to port, throwing the officers on the poop deck off their balance and barrelling them into the gunwales.

When the wheel spun free, a spoke caught in the helmsman's jacket and tossed him over the rail like a wad of tobacco spat from a sailor's mouth. Another man grabbed the helm and almost lost his hand as the bow swung around and the rudder took on a will of its own. The spinning wheel pounded his hand ripping his little finger until it was lying flat across the back of his hand.

With the sheets cast free, the great squares of canvas surrendered to the wind, flying out horizontally like giant pennants flapping in a gale. With no one controlling its course, *San Nicola* pitched its bowsprit into the sea, then rose like Neptune's trident pointing skywards. Heeling violently, water rushed in through the scuppers and washed back and forth across the deck, carrying men like pieces of flotsam caught in a maelstrom, dashing them against the bulwarks. For a while, van Zetten's men had lost control of *San Nicola*. The wind and waves had taken command and were pushing the ship towards the deadly coast. As Oliver Quintrell had planned, the ship was their main ally.

Before the renegade crew had gained their feet, the frigate's sailors reached for their weapons—seven-foot long capstan bars and shorter, but equally hefty, wooden handspikes from the windlass, boat-hooks, plus dozens of belaying pins turned from blocks of dense vitae lignum that were now sitting empty on the pin rails. Wielding one in each hand, like cudgels, the Perpetuals descended on the surprised sailors bludgeoning them like wild men.

Van Zetten's officers on the poop deck, struggling to regain their feet, had no time to draw their swords before they were attacked by the prisoners stationed around the mizzen mast.

Enraged, the foreign sailors fought back, throwing punches and kicks and reaching for their pistols, but most were too slow for the newcomers. Quintrell's men lashed out relentlessly cracking skulls, ribs and arms, leaving the deck littered with fallen bodies cradling bleeding heads and broken collar bones,

But the cries of victory were premature as not all van Zetten's men were on deck. On hearing the commotion, those who had remained below rushed up the companionways. They were greeted with a barrage of blows before they could step out on deck and when they fell back from the ladders, their weapons were quickly taken from them.

Van Zetten seethed with rage. His eyes flashed wildly as he screamed orders at his men. Surrounded by a group of his trusted lieutenants, he fired his two pistols indiscriminately blowing the face from one of his own men before throwing the firearms aside and drawing his sword. Lashing out, he showed no regard as to whom he struck. He had no intention of surrendering his ship and fought furiously to keep his command.

Descending the forward hatch, a group of Oliver's men easily overcame the single guard outside the cabin in which Mr Parry and the two midshipmen were confined. Until the door was smashed open, the three prisoners were unaware of what was happening on deck. They had been alarmed by the thuds, the sound of running feet, timbers creaking, pistol shots and screams. They had felt the violent motion as the ship had pitched and rolled, and heard distant calls. But they were unaware Captain Quintrell was aboard and were both amazed and thrilled to hear that he was taking the ship.

'The weapons store,' Mr Parry cried, hurrying forward to locate it, but it was already being rifled. Without the attention of an armourer, many of the blades were blunt and stained with old blood, but they were still lethal if wielded correctly.

While wooden pins whizzed across the ship at head height, some hitting their targets, others ricocheting off spars and spinning along the deck like runaway wheels, blocks continued to strike lethal blows at anyone foolish enough to venture across the bow. The noise was deafening. With the thunderous luff of the sails, the crack of loose lines whipping the air, and the banging of the blocks that bounced off the deck, it was impossible to hear if any shots were fired.

The Perpetuals' were frenzied. Without blades, they vented their anger wildly, gouging eyes, biting noses and head-butting their opponents, but when the cutlasses and dirks were handed up from below, the clang of steel on steel rang out. Men screamed and bodies fell. Initially, Quintrell's men had been in the minority but, with the enemy suffering badly from the surprise attack, the numbers were soon relatively even.

With the sun glinting between the swaying sails, Tommy Wainwright kept low and dived for the feet of a man levelling a musket at his mess-mate. Having knocked the renegade to the ground, Bungs was quick to drive the tapered stem of a belaying pin into the man's bare belly. Tommy cried out as the skin parted and a gush of foul fluid spurted in his face.

'Are you all right?' the cooper called.

'Fine,' Tommy yelled, wrenching the pin from the victim and hammering it into the back of another man's knees.

'Well done,' shouted Bungs, as he stormed aft.

Making his way through the *mêlée* toward the poop deck Oliver Quintrell's sights were set on van Zetten. But when he was almost within arm's length, the giant African, who had carried his master ashore on the beach, sprang in front of him.

Creating a mirror image, Ekundayo did the same for Captain Quintrell, leaping to his captain's defence. With the power of a man who could turn a millwheel single-handed, Eku wielded a capstan bar above his head. Swinging it around in a full circle of three hundred and sixty degrees, he struck the African beneath the jaw. The power of the blow severed the man's head and sent it flying over the hammock netting like a ball from a bat. Blood, dripping from the tentacles of veins, splattered the deck with red spots. The standing carcass crumpled in a heap, while the pool of blood spilling from the neck was quickly sucked up by the thirsty oakum from the dry seams where the pitch had sweated away.

A cutlass from the store was thrust into Captain Quintrell's hand. Though unwhetted and rusty, the weapon with a plain iron hilt was quite capable of killing a man. 'Out of my way,' he called to the men nearby, side-stepping the headless corpse and heading towards his opponent.

Although the foreigner was older than Quintrell and could boast far more practice with a sword, *Perpetual*'s captain was no less capable as a fighter. The gleaming blade van Zetten wielded was slightly curved and razor sharp. It was far more ornate than the old cutlass Oliver presented. But the amount of gold filigree on the hilt provided no advantage.

Oliver knew his own weapon was slower and that his cutlass lacked the length of van Zetten's blade, but fortunately his arm was longer, so they were equally matched for reach.

Dancing back and forth nimbly, avoiding the patches of wet blood on the deck, the pair lunged, cut and parried. Both men seemingly oblivious to anyone near them. Suddenly, a deafening pistol shot exploded at the side of van Zetten's head. For a moment, the shattering sound dazed the scoundrel while the smoke momentarily clouded his vision. Pressing the advantage, Oliver sliced the point of his blade down van Zetten's forearm. The gold-hilted sword fell from the pirate's hand and clattered to the deck. Oliver kicked it out of the way.

'Next time, I'll take *your* ear—and your head with it,' Ben Tully crowed, blowing the smoke from the pistol and tossing it aside.

Disarmed, with the cutlass blade to his neck and blood running down his arm, the pirate was beaten. 'Who are you,' he bellowed, 'to come aboard my ship the way you did?'

'Let me introduce myself,' the captain said, inclining his head slightly. 'I am Oliver Quintrell, captain of His Britannic Majesty's frigate *Perpetual*. I believe you have already met Mr Parry, my first lieutenant, and I am certain the Governor of Ponta Delgada will be eager for an introduction when he learns you have been butchering his innocent citizens. I hope the village you visited was the only one you preyed on.'

Van Zetten spat in the captain's face, but Oliver quickly turned his cheek, and with it changed his tone. 'I am taking your ship. Restrain this rascal, Mr Tully, and take him below.'

'With the greatest of pleasure, Captain.'

'You English fool,' the pirate scoffed, as his hands were tied. 'You will regret this.'

Oliver wiped the stain from his blade. He was disappointed that the exquisite pleasure of finishing the fight had been snatched from him. However, he had achieved what he set out to do—he had gained control of the ship. 'If you were an officer in any country's navy or showed any sign you were a gentleman, I would treat you as such. However, I see nothing in your behaviour to indicate either.'

'Dog. You will pay for this.'

'No,' Oliver replied emphatically, 'This time you will pay. Gag him. Clap him in irons and place him under lock and key in one of the cabins with a double guard outside. If I am not mistaken, you will find a plentiful supply of slaves' shackles in the hold, enough to fit this scoundrel and all his men. Get him off the deck. I do not wish to see his face again.'

The string of blasphemous remarks that issued from the pirate's mouth was unintelligible. But the captain did not ask for a translation.

Fredrik Johannes van Zetten continued to swear, kick and flayed his arms about as Ekundayo and several other sailors dragged him below. He was lucky not to receive a serious beating from the sailors whose hands were still gripping wooden belaying pins.

Breathing a sigh of relief, Oliver Quintrell turned to his crew. 'Take the prisoners below. Throw the bodies over the side. Let us get this ship back in shape. It's a disgrace to the high seas. All hands to the lines! Two men on the helm! Let us right her before she beaches herself. One ship on the sand is enough for the present. Mr Hanson, be so good as to search for a British jack. I'm sure you will find one in a deck locker. Most pirates keep souvenirs of their previous conquests.'

'Aye, aye, captain,' the young man said, as he scampered off eager to impress. Captain Quintrell cynically regarded him as doing something useful for a change.

With the twenty men, including himself, who had come from the village, and more than thirty hands who had been taken from the beach, together with the officers, the carpenter and the cooper, the captain had sufficient crew to man the ship, but before they could make any headway, essential repairs to *San Nicola* were necessary. In its present condition, it was unseaworthy and bobbing on the water like a piece of cork.

The first priority was to attend to the running rigging—to re-reeve, replace or splice the lines that had been cut or damaged during the fight. They needed *Perpetual*'s bosun but he was not on board, there were, however, enough seasoned sailors to complete the work. Not until those jobs were done could the sails be set and the ship returned to the cove where they had left the careened frigate and the rest of the ship's company.

The injured men also had to be attended to, and because the ship's surgeon had also remained ashore, the sailors did the best they could, with improvised bandages and slings, to dress the bleeding wounds of their mates and of the enemy. The dead also required attention. Hammocks were brought up from below and the members of van Zetten's crew, who had paid with their lives, were given a brief, but fitting, Christian burial though, from the murmurs uttered by the men, few of *Perpetual*'s crew thought they deserved it. The bodies of the three of their own who had died were taken below, placed between the guns and covered in shrouds of sailcloth. Oliver ordered they be returned to their own ship and buried later. The name of the topman who had fallen from the yardarm was noted, though his body was not recovered.

Finally, once the blood splatters had been swabbed from the deck and loose items secured or taken below, a ration of food was handed out. One ship's biscuit was allocated to each man, together with a double serve of rum. Not surprisingly, though there was little food, there were ample supplies of liquor in the hold of the pirate's ship.

Several hours later, when *San Nicola*'s bowsprit appeared from around the headland, a call came down from the lookout balanced at an ungainly angle in *Perpetual*'s masthead. On the beach, the crew, including Mr Nightingale, Mr Mundy, the doctor and the men who had returned from the wood and water expeditions, regarded the arrival of the ship anxiously not knowing what had transpired or what to expect. Had the captain managed to get aboard as he had indicated to the lieutenant? Or was van Zetten returning to claim the frigate?

Drifting slowly across the cove's entrance, the men on the beach could see sailors on the yards furling the squares, but as the flag had curled itself around the post, their immediate fear was that the pirate had returned. Then nine small flags were run up on the signal halyard. The flags spelled out the word P-E-R-P-E-T-U-A-L. With a spontaneous cheer, news was quickly relayed to those who could not read the message. It was echoed by a resounding cheer and waves from the frigate's sailors on board the captured ship.

Even before the anchor was let go, the ship's boats and those taken from the frigate, were swung out and lowered to the water. Captain Quintrell was one of the first to descend the steps and take his seat in the stern sheets of a longboat for the short row to the beach.

After greetings and handshakes and their tale being told many times over, the captain made it clear he had no intention of remaining on the beach longer than necessary. It was imperative he deliver his prisoners to the authorities on the main island, and visit the victualling wharf in Ponta Delgada. Before that could occur, the frigate had to be righted and refloated and it would need more than a few feet of rising tide to return it to the sea.

With water pooling around the keel and the clean copper plating gleaming in the late afternoon sun, the topsails were set to back. But it was soon realized that, during the time the frigate had been sitting on the beach, it had settled and was now stuck firmly in a pool of quicksand.

A kedge anchor was dropped in the shallows and a team heaved on the capstan in an attempt to haul the frigate out. At the same time, sailors attempted to dig a channel for the ship to slide along, but their efforts proved fruitless and the incoming waves returned the sand quicker than the men could remove it. This was where the *San Nicola* was needed. It could deliver more power than a dozen boats on the water with sailors pulling on oars.

With a heavy hawser rigged from the stern of the ship and attached to the base of the mizzen on *Perpetual*, the crew waited until the tide was at its highest and water was lapping along the frigate's keel. It was time for the towing to begin. With sails set and the anchor raised, everything was ready. The hawser stretched and squealed, squeezing the water from its hempen fibres, but the frigate still failed to move. The tide had now reached its highest and there was little time left.

As if in answer to everyman's silent prayer, the waves picked up and Providence delivered a heaven-sent breeze off the land. The frigate's sails backed and the canvas on *San Nicola* filled. Only then did the sand relinquish its suction on the keel and *Perpetual* slide back from the beach onto the cerulean waters of the Atlantic Ocean. Even Captain Quintrell joined in the cheers when his ship swam free but before they could depart the island there was much to be attended to.

Stacked on the beach like giant signal beacons waiting to be lit, were huge piles of dry wood. Alongside them were rows of water barrels of various sizes. The men had obviously toiled exceedingly hard. Now all that remained was to ferry both wood and water from the beach to the frigate and load them into the hold.

Knowing that transferring those items aboard and stowing them carefully could take several hours, the captain took the opportunity to return by boat to the other cove he had dubbed Gallows Bay. He owed the villagers a visit and wanted to collect the cutter, and the clothes and weapons they had left behind.

As before, when he arrived in the cove he found it deserted and when he continued up the sand to where the gallows stood, he discovered the victims had been cut down. With no graves nearby, Oliver assumed the bodies had been returned to the village and deposited in a charnel-house, which was the customary practice in that region.

'Pull it down and burn it,' he ordered his boat crew, before continuing up the path with only Mr Tully and Eku accompanying him. The three strode out as quickly as they could.

On entering the village square, the group felt eyes gazing at them but, not until they were almost at the church door did the villagers show themselves.

'Tell them, they are safe. Tell them the pirate will never return.'

Ekundayo conveyed the captain's message to the crowd of women and children.

Their anxious looks quickly gave way to expressions of joy and celebration. Tears glistened on the cheeks as a few came forward to touch the captain's hand or pat the other pair on their backs. The captain had left the village in the garb of a peasant farmer, but now he returned in the dress uniform of a British naval officer with a fine sword hanging from his belt.

The village matriarch, her head bare, approached him. She had a younger woman on her right and the old bellringer on her left.

The captain greeted the woman with a gracious bow. '*Senhora*,' he said, 'I am pleased to inform you that the danger to your village is gone. The fiend, who took the lives of your menfolk, is in chains and will be dealt with in Ponta Delgada. When the authorities learn of the crimes he committed here, he will surely hang. I only wish I had arrived here earlier and prevented this horrible event from happening. However, let me assure you, it will not happen again.'

Ekundayo translated the captain's words, while the women hugged each other and cried.

Two girls, looking rather embarrassed, pushed through the crowd and approached the captain. In their hands they dragged two bulky sacks. Oliver looked to the matriarch.

'Your clothes, Captain. Your swords and pistols. They are all here. We can offer you some fruit and wine,' she said. 'It is very little for all you have done to protect us.'

'My satisfaction is in knowing this sort of dreadful thing will not happen again here or in any other village. But I must bid you farewell.' Oliver did not want to leave so hurriedly, but it was late and he was anxious to get back to boat without delay. Despite wanting no reward, he was presented with several large bags of oranges and bottles of wine, which were loaded onto the back of a donkey-cart and conveyed to the beach.

The women carried their gifts from the cart to the boats ignoring the smouldering remains of the ship's mast and spars that had stood as a gallows. By morning, all that would remain would be a pile of ash on the sand. If the wind did not scatter it, the spring tides would wash away all evidence of the dreadful thing that occurred on this particular beach.

Blessed with a wind, the cutter and the captain's boat were returned safely to the two waiting ships and with the last of the wood and water stowed in the frigate, preparations to depart the island were complete. But by the time the two boats had been put away, it was dark. All that remained was to transfer van Zetten and six of his subordinates to the frigate. It was not an easy job, but the captain insisted on it. He would not rest easy until he had the scoundrel van Zetten, under guard, on his own ship.

It took longer than expected and, when that odious task was completed, the captain ordered both ships to drop an additional anchor. It had been a very long day and he was not the only one who was weary. *Perpetual* and *San Nicola* would proceed to sea in the morning.

Later that evening, having time on his own to reflect, Oliver was relieved the last few days were over. With God's good grace, he had managed to turn the end result in his favour but, if his plans had gone awry, the outcome could have been disastrous. Had he lost his ship yet been spared, he would have been returning to England to face a court martial. And, had his daring plan to take van Zetten's ship faltered in any way, the fate to befall his men would have been unthinkable.

However, he preferred not to dwell on those eventualities. His main concern now was to relieve himself of his prisoners and deliver *San Nicola* to an agent in Ponta Delgada. As soon as that was done, Mr Parry and his sailors, currently lodged aboard van Zetten's ship, could return to the frigate. He would then be in a position to return to his regular duties and follow the Admiralty's orders that he had been distracted from.

Chapter 10

Ponta Delgada

Dawn broke and a puff of smoke accompanied the discharge of a two-pound shot from the swivel gun mounted on the frigate's aft rail. It was the signal for *San Nicola* to follow *Perpetual* to sea. With Mr Parry in command of van Zetten's ship, the prisoners were securely shackled in the hold beneath battened hatches. The complaints and abuse of the previous day had continued throughout the night and, whilst most cries consisted of abusive threats, some voices claimed they had never volunteered to sail with van Zetten but that they had been taken against their will and forced to serve him. While Oliver doubted anything the pirate uttered and, in turn, was suspicious of the voices of anyone sailing with him, it would be the job of the authorities to ascertain who was speaking the truth.

Aboard *Perpetual*, Fredrik van Zetten and six of his closest henchmen were also heavily shackled and under guard. Captain Quintrell was taking no chances.

Being short-handed, the men worked feverishly to weigh anchor and prepare the two vessels to clear Santa Maria's rugged coast. With no regrets, everyone aboard was looking forward to the short daylight passage of a little over fifty miles, heading north-west to the port of Ponta Delgada, located on the main island of São Miguel, the largest and most easterly of the nine islands in the Azores group. If the weather gods looked kindly on them, with easy sailing they would cover the distance in twelve hours. That would see the frigate and *San Nicola* anchored in the outer roadstead before nightfall, where they would remain overnight and enter the harbour the following morning. The prospect of being given leave to go ashore was uppermost in every sailor's mind.

The sighting of a French corvette on the horizon, less than an hour after they had weighed, sent a feeling of uneasy anticipation through everyone aboard. Hull down, heading east, the corvette was sailing well and appeared to be making remarkable speed. The last thing Oliver wanted was contact with an enemy ship. With only an adequate number of hands spread between the two vessels, he was conscious he had insufficient crew to man all the guns. Now was not a good time for a confrontation. Even with his clean hull and harnessing the wind to every stitch of canvas he could fly, the burden he was dragging with him was no longer weed, but the larger, older and slower *San Nicola*. For Captain Quintrell, running from the enemy was not an option and the decision to fight was not his alone to make.

With his telescope trained on the French ship, he was relieved to see it did not alter course or ease its wind, but maintained its heading towards Europe, probably making for Brest on France's north-west coast or Toulon in the Mediterranean Sea. It was possible the lookout on the corvette had reported sighting two ships flying British colours sailing close to the island. In consequence, it was likely the French captain had decided, as he was sailing alone, he was no match for a frigate and a ship-of-war. Whatever the reason, the officers on *Perpetual*'s quarterdeck breathed easier once the Frog disappeared over the horizon.

Throughout the morning and early afternoon, the two ships made reasonable time but, as the day progressed, their speed dropped to two knots. When the sun set, it took with it the final remnants of breeze. Less than ten miles from the coast of São Miguel, the weather gods turned their backs on the British seamen leaving the two vessels floating, almost motionlessly, on a flat sea of obsidian glass.

Taking advantage of the calm, a sailor cast a line from the rail and with the help of his mates hauled in a large grouper. When the initial excitement died, it was cleaned and, with the permission of the officer-of-the-watch, delivered to the galley. Keen to make a similar catch, several sailors baited hooks and tried their luck, but their efforts were unsuccessful.

Dr Whipple was also grateful for the flat water. As the frigate was only half a cable's length from *San Nicola*, it provided him with the opportunity to visit and attend to the wounds of the seriously injured held below deck. The blows from belaying pins, capstan bars, and swinging blocks had cracked a few skulls, while near lethal cuts from cutlass blades, knives and swords still bled or wept and needed dressing. Two of the rogue sailors, who had sustained wounds from pistol shots, were pronounced dead and committed to the deep without ceremony.

Apart from the doctor's boat, the longboat, stacked to the gunwales with sacks and barrels, was rowed across to *San Nicola* to share some of the frigate's remaining rations with the working crew and prisoners.

While the surgeon was absent from the sick berth, Mrs Crosby attended to the injured men in the cockpit with help from Connie Pilkington and Tommy Wainwright. Working with the two women reminded young Tom of his home in the north of England. He remembered his mother, who had farewelled him in tears when he went to sea, yet each time had sent him off with her blessing; and his sister who had died in the coal mine buried beneath tons of falling rock from which he had miraculously survived.

After Captain Quintrell visited *Perpetual*'s sick berth to ensure everything was in order during the doctor's absence, Mr Crosby, the carpenter, approached him for the final time. He politely reminded the captain of the help his wife and her friend had provided in the past few days and begged him to reconsider his decision to remove them from the ship once they reached land. But, once again, his request fell on deaf ears. Oliver was adamant the women would go ashore when they entered the port.

As dawn broke and a light wind blew off the land to the north, the two vessels approached the island sailing to within a mile of the rugged cliffs. The black sand beaches tucked in between the headlands presented a very different picture to that of the bright yellow sandy coves of the smaller island they had left. Changing course and bearing west, *Perpetual* followed the coast heading for Ponta Delgada situated towards the western end of São Miguel. Measuring forty miles long and ten miles wide, like Santa Maria, this island also ran in an east to west direction.

Despite the mists of morning smudging the skyline, the contours of old volcanic mountains worn down over the centuries, were visible. Trees covered the lower slopes and on the outskirts of the town sheep, goats and cattle grazed on the open pasture.

Located in a bay, sheltered from the prevailing north-westerly winds and the rolling Atlantic swells, the port of Ponta Delgada had existed since the 1500s. Having grown in size and significance, it was now the prosperous capital of the Western Islands and, not only home to fishermen, farmers, plantation owners, exporters, bankers and shippers, but also military personnel, civil diplomats, local government officials, and representatives of the Portuguese administration in Lisbon. Plus, there were the clergy of the Catholic Churches, and the nuns and monks of the convents and monasteries.

Only two miles out and a familiar sound rumbled across the water. It was the distant thunder every seaman recognized—the unmistakable thunder of guns being fired in rapid succession, as in a rippling broadside.

'Masthead,' Mr Tully called from the deck. 'What do you see?'

'Nothing, sir.'

'What distance would you estimate those guns?' Oliver asked his sailing master.

'A mile or two, no more.'

'Then the lookout must be blind.'

'But sound carries further at sea,' Mr Mundy explained. 'I'd say it's coming from beyond the next headland.'

Oliver was familiar with the properties of sound over smooth warm waters and was not about to stop and investigate. 'Let us raise Ponta Delgada as quickly as possible. We will learn what is happening once we reach the roadstead. I only pray the French have not brought war to these islands and trust the town is not under attack.'

'Deck ahoy! Two ships astern. A second rate and a frigate.'

Fighting ships! 'What colours?'

'Portuguese.'

No sooner had the officers fixed their lens on the crowd of sails rising in the east, than more calls came down from aloft. Two more ships had been seen. Then, on the sweeping bay around whose shores the main town was nestled, dozens of masts with yards crossed came into view. The stout majestic timbers of a 90-gun man-of-war dominated the impressive array of second, third and fourth rate ships of the line. There were also several frigates of various sizes along with ketches, snows, fishing boats, cutters and lighters.

Reducing sail, *Perpetual*, accompanied by *San Nicola*, entered the roadstead sailing slowly between the fighting ships already anchored in the outer harbour. There were more ships than some of the sailors had seen gathered in Spithead, on the Mother Bank and at St Helens Road at any one time.

'It appears the whole of the Portuguese Navy is in attendance,' Oliver announced to the wide-eyed officers on deck.

Three decks towered from the bulbous hulls of two of the fighting ships. They dwarfed the British frigate as it sailed by.

Mr Mundy conducted a tally of the fleet, listing two 90-gun ships, nine 74s, two 64s, and three 50-gun fighting ships, plus several frigates. 'Thirty-two in all, if I am not mistaken. Old ships, though' he added disparagingly. 'Some are thirty years old or more. See there—' he pointed—'that's *Principe Real*. Her keel was laid down in '71, and *Infante dom Pedro* is even older.'

Oliver was far less critical. 'I agree they are not young, when compared with Bonaparte's fleet, but they are sound and well maintained. See how the brightwork shines. Every metal plate and trim has been polished, and you can smell the fresh paint from here. As for those part-furled sails, I would suggest they are new and recently bent. I am impressed.'

'What would you consider they are doing here, Captain?' Mr Nightingale asked.

'Probably the same thing we are doing, refurbishing their supplies. The wine grown here is particularly good and abundant, as is the supply of wheat, salt, fruit and vegetables. The fleet has, no doubt, sailed from the Tagus River to stretch its new hemp and Lisbon is where it will return to. I expect the firing we heard was from a naval ship exercising its guns.' Oliver felt relaxed. 'Seeing this fleet gives me confidence. This navy is a sound ally. Let us pray Emperor Napoleon is never able to lure the Crown of Portugal into his net.' He turned from the ship and looked to the city.

Having visited Ponta Delgada on several occasions, the sailing master was eager to share his knowledge of the island, its capital and its port facilities but, in his usual vein, Mr Mundy could find nothing positive to say about the Portuguese island, despite the fact Britain was ambitious to embrace it within its empire and benefit from its ideal location. Situated at the cross-roads between Europe and America, between Britain and the Cape, it was an ideal port for ships carrying troops to Cape Town, but it was also desirable territory because of its rich supplies of hemp for cordage and rigging, and its ample production of juicy oranges, flour and fresh beef.

'As to the way it is administered,' Mr Mundy advised, 'you have two choices. On the one hand, there are the nuns and friars of the ecclesiastical orders who have the greatest influence over the inhabitants. On the other hand, the military who are slovenly, insubordinate and undisciplined. The principle fort at the west of the bay has 24 guns, although I heard few are capable of service. A league to the east are two small forts with three guns each. Both of these are useless due to neglect.'

Oliver frowned. 'What of the civil administration and the navy?'

'The government of the Azores comes under the authority of Portugal and is run by a cabinet which stifles the people and shows little interest in them. It supplies them with holy relics in exchange for the island's valuable produce. The people of the Western Isles have no independence and apparently no aspirations. They boast no past to speak of, and look forward to no future. As for the navy, they use this only as a watering hole. Within a few days, all these ships will be gone and they will not return again until their holds are empty.'

Oliver had to excuse himself from hearing more. He preferred to see for himself and form his own judgement. In the meantime, he had a list of priorities to attend to. His first and foremost important duty was to hand over Captain Van Zetten and his crew, and to deliver his written report of the atrocities that occurred on Santa Maria to the governor. The sooner the pirate was removed from his ship and taken for trial the better. Then, he needed to find an agent to discuss the sale of the *San Nicola*.

Most importantly, he needed to take on more water and purchase stores sufficient for a nine month voyage and arrange for their prompt delivery. Apart from that, he had to arrange the departure of the two females from the frigate as early as possible. It was his intention to depart the harbour in no more than five days, during which time he could hardly refuse his men at least a few hours shore leave to make their own purchases before embarking on the forthcoming voyage to the far side of the world. The first challenge, however, was to find a berth in the overcrowded harbour.

'Take us in, Mr Tully, and send a message to Mr Parry to put *San Nicola* as close to the wharf as possible.'

With the wind spilled from the foretops'l, the frigate drifted to a stop and the order was given to drop anchor. The ship, with a hold full of rogue sailors, brought in by Mr Parry, anchored only thirty yards away.

It was past noon by the time both ships were fully secured with their sails furled neatly to meet with the captain's approval. Only then was he confident to leave the vessels and go ashore. For Oliver Quintrell, the first priority was to locate the Port Admiral and appropriate government authorities.

The town itself was a thriving city of single and two-storey houses interspersed with the spires of many churches, some dating back before the time of Columbus's visit to the Azores on his return from his voyage of exploration in 1492. Though it was a busy port, it boasted only one short mole, its length adequate only for fishing vessels and small traders. Vessels of any reasonable size had to anchor in the harbour or further out in the roadstead. Because of this, all victualling supplies, fresh food, livestock, export products, even armaments and powder had to be conveyed by lighters to the various ships. It also meant that personnel had to be ferried on the ships' boats. This would include the transfer of prisoners from *San Nicola* and *Perpetual* to the town.

After wasting almost half a day walking the narrow roads littered with children and untethered domestic animals, navigating markets for fish, meat and fruits, tramping back and forth from one government building to another and being referred by one official to another, until he was exceedingly frustrated, the captain was obliged to heed the advice given to him by his sailing master. He needed to locate Mr Read, the British Consul.

Several years earlier, Mr Mundy had been briefly introduced to him while serving as master's mate on a second rate man-of-war. At that time, he had learned that the long-serving consul had lived on the island for many years. He and wife resided in a fine villa they had built on a farm situated on the hillside overlooking the town. In his spare time, the consul took delight in growing oranges. In the sailing master's opinion, Mr Read was both a diplomat and a man of business. He was a congenial gentleman, born and raised in Bristol, who was very approachable and always willing to assist British visitors to the Islands be they officers, merchants or investors.

An hour later, sitting down over a cup of China tea in the consul's city residence, feeling slightly relaxed, Oliver explained the dilemma that was both confronting and exasperating him.

'Despite the atrocities I have related that took place on the island of Santa Maria, it appears to me no one in this town wants to take responsibility and deal with the situation. The Port Admiral was not available and his subordinates were totally engrossed in dealing with the requirements of the newly arrived Portuguese fleet. One naval officer I spoke to suggested it was a problem for the civil authorities to deal with. The city's administrative representative referred me to the garrison commander, who has no interest in *San Nicola* or its scurrilous captain and crew. Nowhere have I come across such a blatant lack of interest or willingness to accept some responsibility for a heinous crime perpetrated on that country's own soil.'

With no immediate response from the consul, Oliver continued his diatribe. 'The only apparent sympathy I received was from a priest who offered to come aboard and pray for my ship. I argued that he should be praying for the poor villagers who had been murdered, tortured and threatened, and pray for the souls of the treacherous dogs who are traitors to their country, their king and their God, and pray they would be hung within the week. I admit by this time, I had exhausted my patience and he scurried away after apologising that he could not understand my English.'

The captain inhaled deeply. 'You are my final hope, Mr Read. To put it simply, I need someone to receive my prisoners and to accept delivery of the ship *San Nicola*, which is anchored in the harbour.'

Mr Read sat back. Having listened carefully and made an occasional written notation of certain facts, he appeared unmoved and smiled graciously. 'I can sympathise with you, Captain, but must beg the question: Would it be more in your interests to collect the provisions you need and sail to England taking the ship with you?'

Oliver sighed and shook his head. 'That is impossible, sir. Firstly, I have my orders and they do not allow me to return to England. If I were to do so, I would not only be disobeying those Admiralty orders, but also putting my ship and my men into potential danger from attack by our enemy, the French. I can assure you Napoleon's ships would not turn their noses up at the chance of taking both a British frigate and an accompanying ship as valuable prizes. To a fleet of French vessels, we would make an easy target. Secondly, the murderous behaviour perpetrated by this villain Fredrik van Zetten was directed at Azoreans—inhabitants of these islands. God only knows how many islands he visited to purloin young men to serve under him. But he sails under no country's flag and did not attack my ship, therefore, Britain will not declare him a maritime enemy. What he is, however, is a pirate and should be treated according to the laws of the sea which have existed since Roman times!'

The consul rose to his feet. 'Captain Quintrell, be assured you can leave these matters with me. I speak the language of the Islands. I have lived amongst these people for several years—long enough to know how they think and how they perform their duties, which, at times, is not very efficiently. Also, I understand how the administrations, sacred and secular, civil, military and naval operate and in what hierarchical order those operation apply. Do not worry. I will make the necessary arrangements for you.' He paused. 'The first thing we must do is to have your ship resupplied. I shall come with you to the victualling yard forthwith and arrange it. No doubt the British government will be paying.'

Oliver nodded.

'I am concerned that the recently arrived fleet will have priority over visiting vessels, so let us waste no time in placing your orders.'

Early the following morning, the tips of the ripples created by the vast number of small boats ferrying supplies back and forth to the ships at anchor, glistened in the sun. With little wind across the bay, the lateen sails of fishing boats flapped idly from their slanting spars, whilst dozens of oars dipped in the water creating tiny whirlpools with each stroke.

The white-washed buildings of the town gleamed. The city's castellated skyline stretching along the harbour side was dominated by the projecting towers and crosses surmounting its ornate churches. The black chiselled-stone edges contrasted with the brilliant white-painted walls. But the grey mist surmounting some of the distant tops was not cloud or fog—it was steam. The island of St Michael—São Miguel lived and breathed, its sulphurous odour occasionally spilling down the verdant hillsides and floating across the bay to challenge the familiar scent of orange blossom and freshly baked bread.

From the quarterdeck, Oliver watched the boats swarming around the ships like bees round a honeypot. The fleet's visit to this Portuguese outpost, over eight hundred miles from Lisbon, was, without doubt, to fill the holds with provisions. The volcanic soil of São Miguel, like most of the other islands was rich and fertile, the climate supporting both tropical and subtropical fruits, and wheat from which fine flour was milled for the bread baked daily in the ovens built on the side of every house. The green slopes behind the town offered verdant pasture for cattle to graze and supply the ships with ample quantities of fresh beef.

The cargoes stowed on the lighters' single decks, packed in open topped boxes, consisted mainly of fruit—1000 oranges to a box, and lemons, limes and pineapples. Other boats transported barrels of wine, sacks of flour and boxes of vegetables. On the wharf, close by the mole, cattle driven down from the hillside were already penned and voicing their objection to being prodded and crowded into small compounds. Whether they were to be loaded live or butchered on the quay was not certain.

'Beg pardon, Captain,' Midshipman Hanson said, touching his hat. 'Mr Crosby asked to speak with you.'

'Where is he?'

'In the waist, sir. Should I tell him to come up to the quarterdeck?'

'Indeed.' The captain was aware of what the carpenter wanted to speak to him about.

A beckoning gesture from the young middie brought the carpenter to the deck.

'Good morning, Captain,' the carpenter said.

Oliver acknowledged.

'I beg your permission to go ashore, sir.'

'You wish to accompany your wife and her companion into the town.'

'That's right, Captain. I want to see them settled into some reputable accommodation. Then I will visit the shipping office to enquire about a passage for the pair to England.'

'Permission is granted,' the captain said. 'A boat is already in the water and the crew has been instructed to transport the females and their dunnage to the town wharf. I trust they are not expecting the return of the animals they brought aboard.'

'No, Captain. My wife said to thank you for your tolerance, and begs you to accept the livestock as a token of her gratitude for delivering her and Mrs Pilkington from Gibraltar. She said to do with the animals as you see fit.'

'Huh. Is your wife ready?'

'Yes, sir. Waiting below.'

'Then I suggest you get the women ashore immediately. As for yourself, you may take leave for the day to attend to your business,' the captain added curtly, 'I take it that it is your intention to return to the ship.'

'That is correct, sir, you can be sure of that.' He held out his open palms. 'I would not be going ashore empty-handed and leaving my tools in the carpenter's shop, if I was not intending to return.'

'That is well,' Oliver said. 'You will report to me when you come aboard. I will inform the boat crew to return to the wharf promptly at four o'clock to collect you. Do not be late. I have no intention of sending men into town after dark to search for you. Do I make myself clear?'

'Aye, Captain. You have my word. I'll be there on time.'

Having only made the acquaintance with the tradesman briefly since he had come aboard, Oliver was putting faith in his ability to assess the man's character from what he had gleaned from his papers. The carpenter had learned his trade as a shipwright at Deptford before shipping as carpenter's mate aboard a second-rate. Having been given his first warrant on a 74-gun ship of the line, he had served for five years before accepting work at the naval dockyard in Gibraltar. While working in the colony, his wife and sons had taken passage from England and joined him on the Rock, where he had been resident. At first, life had been idyllic and he had valued the time he had been able to spend with his family—something sea life deprived him of. But, as he had explained, when the fever struck, everything changed.

Being a married man and being at least ten years older than himself, Captain Quintrell judged Mr Crosby to be a mature, honest and hardworking fellow. He had also heard that the carpenter had applied himself to the repairs on van Zetten's ship as conscientiously as to those on any British vessel. And though he had not seen him during the fighting, it was obvious he had defended himself adequately against the ruffian crew and survived the fight unscathed.

While any captain relied on the loyalty and efficiency of his senior officers, the next most-valued man aboard any ship at sea was the carpenter. He was responsible for the welfare of the ship itself. Without a watertight hull and a sound vessel, a captain's command was worthless.

Oliver also trusted young William Ethridge who had served on *Elusive* with him on a previous mission. His service on that occasion had been invaluable. But being barely twenty-one years of age and having only recently completed his apprenticeship, he had less experience than Mr Crosby, therefore the captain was obliged to favour the older man for the position of ship's carpenter.

Only a few minutes elapsed before the women emerged from the waist and headed to the entry port. Dr Whipple accompanied them up the steps, but did not linger on deck. Having been grateful for the assistance the women had provided in the cockpit, the doctor was sorry to see them depart, but he did not believe in protracted farewells.

Despite the captain's expectations of tears and tantrums, there was no such performance. Because of the devastating losses they had both suffered, the women carried themselves with a dignity not normally associated with females of their class. Oliver was warmed by their decorum. It was far removed from the outlandish outbursts and lack of propriety he had witnessed demonstrated by ladies of so-called good-breeding who had never suffered any form of deprivation.

The two female companions departed the deck with dignity and little more than a smile to the sailors standing nearby. Only one person gave way to emotion—that was young Charles. Despite being under the keen and critical eyes of the sailors on deck, he allowed the older women to embrace him in a motherly fashion, and when Consuela Pickering reached out her arms to him, he responded to her embrace with heartfelt affection. Stepping back, his lips mouthed, Good-bye, but no sound was made. The wet streaks on his cheeks bore testament to his feelings. The ten-year old was destined to remain alone aboard the ship.

More noise and chatter accompanied the sailors carrying the women's dunnage. It consisted of a bag apiece and a wooden chest between them. The contents of the chests soon became evident when Mr Midshipman Hanson started unpacking and examining them. Having been given instructions from the purser to ensure nothing was stolen from the sick berth, he took it upon himself to remove each item from the chest, remove it from the garment or table linen it had been bound in, then set it down on the deck revealing, for all to see, the women's valued possessions. Most were well-used household goods of little value, though there were a few pieces of fine china, ivory-handled cutlery, a lamp and mirror, plus ornaments and personal mementos that Mrs Crosby had amassed over the years. The process of unwrapping each item amused the men leaning on the cap rail. Mr Crosby stood nearby, but said nothing.

'Mr Hanson!' the captain called. 'Enough of that!'

The young middie stopped and looked up. Only half of the contents had been rummaged through.

'Kindly get that box packed up and over the side. And be quick about it.'

'Aye, aye, sir,' the young midshipman said.

'Mr Tully,' the captain asked quietly, 'what is happening with the boy who came aboard with the women? I believe his name is Charles. I want to know how he has been entered in the muster book.'

'I'll enquire.'

With the crew seated, Mr Crosby climbed down into the boat and assisted his wife to find her footing on the steps. An ample skirt and petticoat did not make the descent easy. When she was seated in the bow, he helped Mrs Pickering to gain a seat and then received the women's dunnage and placed it between the thwarts.

With the call for the mooring line to be released, an oar pushed the boat from *Perpetual*'s hull and, once clear, six oars dipped into the water. From the ship's aft rail, a handful of sailors watched the boat's progress. Apart from a few whispered conversations, there were no calls or cries. It was a solemn farewell.

Standing on the quarterdeck away from the rail, Oliver was also watching the water, but his interest was on a line of lighters heading directly towards *Perpetual*.

'Mr Tully, have all hands ready to hoist the supplies. Get Bungs to attend to the barrels. I want to see them stowed as quickly as possible.'

'Bungs is not well, Captain.'

Oliver was not impressed. 'Then speak to the bosun.'

'Yes, sir.

As the morning wore on and the sun rose higher, a breeze blew across the bay allowing small squares and triangles of sails to replace the rise and fall of oars on the small boats servicing various ships with stores.

At one point, a black-hulled schooner swam smoothly around the warships and edged its way towards the wharf and dropped anchor close to *Perpetual*. It was flying the red and white striped flag of a British East Indiaman, the small union jack in the corner was hardly visible.

'A nice line,' Mr Nightingale commented, when he came on deck. 'I imagine she could make ten or twelve knots in the right conditions. Returning home, or heading south, would you say, sir?'

'From the colour of the men's skin, I would suggest she is heading north, and from the fine condition of her canvas and cordage, it would appear she has been blessed with a smooth passage.'

'Perhaps with a cargo of silks and porcelain from China,' the lieutenant said. 'I'd wager the crew are happy to be breaking their voyage here before heading home.'

With lots of activity on the water, replenishing *Perpetual's* empty hold continued all day. The supplies from each lighter were loaded into netting before being hoisted up, swung inboard and lowered into the waist. From there, depending on the nature of the goods, they were conveyed to the hold, pantry or bread room as indicated by the purser. As each supply-boat was emptied, it returned to the victualling wharf to collect another consignment.

Satisfied the work was proceeding well, Oliver returned to his cabin.

'You asked about the boy who came aboard in Gibraltar,' Mr Tully said, before he left the deck.

'What of him?'

'He's been entered as a ship's boy and allocated to Mr Hanson's division.'

'Thank you, Mr Tully.'

Promptly at half-past three in the afternoon, the captain's boat crew pushed off and headed to the town. Standing at his stern window, with the telescope to his eye, Oliver could see Mr Crosby waiting on the wharf as instructed.

He was alone.

Chapter 11

Foreboding

On the third day in Ponta Delgada, four boats headed towards the frigate. They were rowed by Portuguese oarsmen and carried uniformed marines and armed soldiers. Mr Read, the British consular representative with whom Oliver had spoken, was seated in the leading craft. The coxswain hailed the frigate as they approached.

After being given a dignified welcome aboard *Perpetual*, Mr Read introduced the officer in charge of the military guard. 'This is Captain Ferreira. I am afraid he is lacking in English. He is here to take charge of the ship you escorted in and the prisoners you have confined below deck in both vessels.'

The consul anticipated some of the many questions that were foremost in Oliver's mind. 'I can guarantee you nothing with regard to the fate of these foreign sailors. They are not enemies according to Portuguese naval definitions, therefore, they cannot be held as prisoners of war. It is likely, however, they will be questioned and, once you have departed the port, they will be freed and be at liberty to sign on any other ship.'

'But they are riff-raff—nothing but rogues and cut-throats.'

'I don't doubt what you say, Captain, but let me explain. You admitted yourself that many of them are possibly common seamen, who will claim they were forced to follow the orders of Captain van Zetten. It would be impossible to prove differently. Being captain of a naval frigate, I do not need to remind you that seamen who sail under your command are obliged to obey your orders to the letter, and argument and dissent are dealt with harshly in the British Navy.'

The captain could not disagree.

'Furthermore, this town does not have an adequate jail to house all these men pending the arrival of a judge from Lisbon to hear their pleas. However, Captain Ferreira will ensure these sailors remain confined for the present on board the ship *San Nicola*. It will serve as a temporary floating prison similar to the hulks you have on the Thames and at Portsmouth.'

'I had hoped to have the ship vacated in order that it could be sold to a prize agent.'

The consul smiled sympathetically. 'I am sure you will agree technically the vessel you have brought in is not a prize of war. The Royal Navy is not at war with whatever nation this captain professes to sail under and from what you told me, he denies any allegiance to either France or Spain. I fear our judges in Ponta Delgada will also argue that point of law. But as this pirate attacked residents of Santa Maria and committed heinous crimes against them, I feel the authorities will thank you for bringing him to justice and, as a consequence, the Portuguese Navy will commandeer his vessel.'

'But what of Captain van Zetten?'

'You advised me you are holding him and his lieutenants aboard this ship. Is that so?

'Indeed.'

'Good. I have here a letter from the military commander of the port who is acting for the governor. It gives me the authority to take these men and deliver them to the jail where they will be held for trial for crimes committed against the citizens of the Western Isles.'

Some consolation, Oliver thought. It appeared the consul had taken control of the matters and there was little more he could do. His immediate concern was to get the worst of the prisoners off the frigate with the assurance they would stand trial and receive their due desserts. When that was achieved, he could wash his hands of them. The question of *San Nicola* being sold was of little importance to him personally but his men would be sorely disappointed to learn they would not benefit from their part in the action that could have cost them their lives.

'If you are in agreement,' Mr Read continued, 'I require your signature on this document. Once that formality has been taken care of, I will receive van Zetten and his six officers from you. Kindly have them ready to leave. From here, Captain Ferreira will take charge of them and convey them in two boats to the quay where extra guards are waiting to escort them to the jailhouse. The soldiers and marines in the other two boats will head to *San Nicola*, relieve your men and take responsibility for the ship and its prisoners for the present.'

Oliver thanked the consul, though not without some second thoughts. The prospect of dispensing himself of the responsibility of the prisoners relieved him but he was unconvinced the fate deserved by the pirate and his cohorts was assured. He regretted not having meted out a seagoing sentence to van Zetten when he had the chance. Hanging was his due, as it was for any man who perpetrated such evil on land or water. For Oliver Quintrell, the only consolation was a degree of satisfaction at having done his duty. The problem was now in the hands of the authorities to administer their own judgment against the men who had committed atrocities against their people. *So be it.*

'I have the seven ringleaders confined below, including the ship's captain. I believe they are all equally guilty.'

Mr Read offered his reassurance. 'Captain Ferreira promises me they will be tried for their crimes as soon as the governor returns from Lisbon.'

Oliver acknowledged the commitment, though his faith in the Portuguese system of administration was not unwavering.

'Have the prisoners brought on deck,' the captain called. 'Transfer them to the boats. Make sure they are all manacled.' He turned to Mr Read. 'I suggest you warn Captain Ferreira to be very wary of these rogues. They are more slippery than eels.'

From the quarterdeck, Oliver Quintrell watched as the pirate, who declared himself a ship's captain, was brought up from the hold. Of all of the prisoners, he was most obstreperous, complaining about the dire treatment he had received and claiming he had Letters of Marque from both Spain and Denmark. He claimed he had lost many of his men to scurvy and had visited the island of Santa Maria in desperation because he lacked enough men to sail his vessel to Ponta Delgada. He swore he had offered to reward any volunteers who sailed with him and had promised to return them to their own island within the month. From what Captain Quintrell had experienced of the man, every word he uttered, apart from the reference to scurvy, was a lie.

Whether van Zetten was Dutch, Danish, South African or Spanish, Oliver had not discovered but his nationality made no difference. As he was paraded along the frigate's gun deck before climbing the companion to the quarterdeck, he directed a barrage of threats and foul-mouthed curses at anyone who put a hand near him.

Shuffling along with his hands and feet dragging iron chains, he was unable to physically retaliate other than spit obscenities at the crew. Once on deck, his final curse was directed at Captain Quintrell.

'English pig. You thought you could beat me with your pantomime. But hear this. I swear you have not seen the last of Fredrik van Zetten. I will find you and, when I do, I will haul you up by the neck till your tongue swells and when it pokes from your mouth I will slice off the end and watch the blood spurt from it like water from a gargoyle's mouth. Let me see how ingenious you are then.'

'Gag him!' Oliver ordered. 'Tightly! Let him drown in his own spittle.'

But before the gag could be fastened across his mouth, Fredrik van Zetten let out an evil laugh that sent a cold shiver down the spines of everyone on deck.

'Get that scum off my deck,' the captain yelled, turning his back on the prisoners as they were herded to the waiting boats.

Waiting patiently in the boats, the soldiers sent to guard the prisoners appeared to be little more than boys of sixteen or seventeen years of age. The muskets held between their knees were dirty. The bayonets rusted.

How long will this military guard hold this monster? Oliver wondered.

'Once Mr Parry and the rest of the crew are returned aboard, and I am satisfied the ship is fully provisioned, we make preparations to sail. Is all in readiness?'

The sailing master confirmed the purser's and quartermaster's reports. *Perpetual* was well supplied.

'There is just one matter to be—'

A musket shot rang out across the waters of the bay. Then another. All eyes on deck turned to the water and the two boats heading towards the mole. Aboard both boats, the prisoners were standing upright and rocking the boats from side to side. The oarsmen planted their blades on the water in an attempt to stop the boats from going over but despite the threats from the soldiers and wild shots flying over the oarsmen's heads, the prisoners took no heed. Their aim was to capsize both boats and tip everyone into the water.

'All hands!' the captain boomed. 'Away the boats. Quick as you can! Marines with me. I will not have the fiend escape.'

Another shot rang out and a man fell or dived into the water from the second boat. It lurched violently throwing another shackled prisoner into the water. When it rolled back, water poured over the gunwale and within seconds the boat filled and sank. The soldiers seated on the thwarts were stunned into immobility.

'Shall I order the marines to fire?' the lieutenant asked.

'No. At this distance. It would be impossible to hit the right target.'

Splashing frantically for a few moments, the soldiers were weighed down by their heavy uniforms, muskets, belts and powder and ammunition pouches and quickly disappeared under the water. Three prisoners with iron shackles also slipped silently below the surface and did not return. Two of the oarsmen swam in circles and were able to grab onto an oar which acted as a life preserver. Swimming in a strange dog-like fashion, one prisoner turned from the boat and, despite his irons, made for the nearby shore. No effort was made to shoot him or catch him.

It was the passenger in the first boat Oliver did not take his eyes off. Seated in the bow, he appeared completely at ease, and though the gag covered his mouth, the deep curling creases around his eyes made it evident he was enjoying every moment of the commotion. No doubt van Zetten had engineered the plan over the past few days and was now relishing the success of his scheme. The cheers and jeers from sailors lining the rails of the nearby Portuguese war ships encouraged him.

Oliver Quintrell was sickened by the fiasco and impatient for his boat to be on the water.

After what seemed like an age, the launch was pushed off from the frigate's hull but, despite the best efforts of the boat crew, by the time they reached the mole, the two local boats were swaying off an iron ring in the stone sea wall. On the quayside, four prisoners, under heavy guard, were being marched under the great arches of the old town to the jail. Fredrik van Zetten was one of them.

'I pray that is an end to it,' Oliver said, more to himself than to any other ears. Glancing across the water to the Indian-built *San Nicola*, he considered its motley crew confined in the hold and wondered how long it would be before they engineered some plan of escape.

'Return to the ship,' he called to his coxswain.

'Aye, aye, Captain.'

The sailors who had been granted a few hours leave to go ashore gave not a thought to the events of the past few days. Like most sailors, their one desire was for the swarthy-skinned women selling pineapples, seafood and sexual liberties. Others preferred to titillate their palates with the locally grown grapes, crushed and bottled and flowing cheaply in liquid form in the taverns. For a few of the older hands, sitting on the quay under a warm sun, tempered by the fragrant breezes, invigorated them. Others preferred to take a stroll along the lanes lined with flowers and enjoy the sound of the land birds flitting about above their heads. Despite the way each man chose to spend his leisure time, it passed all too quickly and after four hours they were obliged to return to the boats waiting for them at the wharf.

An unexpected visit from a navy boat that pulled alongside *Perpetual*'s hull delivered an invitation for Captain Quintrell to meet with Captain Ruiz on board one of the Portuguese ships. Oliver was delighted to accept, and two hours later, accompanied by Mr Parry, he climbed aboard *Principe de Brazil*, a 74-gun third-rate built in 1802—a little over two years old.

Wearing full dress uniform, with elegant swords hanging from their belts, the captain and his lieutenant were afforded a formal welcome on deck, where they were greeted by the Portuguese captain before being conducted to the great cabin. It was a very fine large and airy room, elegantly furnished with galley windows stretching the full width of the ship's stern and wrapping around on both sides. The cabin smelled of cigars and beeswax.

After an offer to partake of some refreshments, the Portuguese captain apologised profusely that the admiral was unable to acknowledge the British frigate. He had not sailed with the fleet due to an indisposition which, on the advice of his surgeon, had necessitated him remaining in Lisbon.

With the formalities quickly observed, Captain Ruiz wasted no time in embarking on the matter that was of interest to him. His English was excellent. 'I hear that you successfully delivered Fredrik van Zetten into custody?'

'Indeed I did.'

'That name is not unknown to me. That rogue is well known on the coast of Brazil.'

'A truly unsavoury character,' Oliver said, then anxiously added, 'I trust he has not escaped.'

'No, Captain Quintrell, you need have no concerns on that score, although it would have been more fitting that you delivered him into the hands of the naval and not the civil authorities here. I can assure you, with the evidence you have provided, our justice would have been delivered more expediently.'

'I regret, that was not the case,' said Oliver, concealing his frustration. 'Unfortunately, I had difficulty involving the local authorities, despite my written report detailing the crimes he committed against the villagers on Santa Maria.'

The Portuguese captain's expression was grim. 'You may not be aware, but this man at times flaunts our flag and was previously engaged in the slave trade. As both merchant and master of his own vessel, he has purchased and transported slaves from West Africa and delivered them to Peru. I believe they were destined for the Potosi silver mines.'

Captain Quintrell did not take his eyes from the speaker. He was anxious to hear more.

'It was a particularly lucrative business for him as he was accused of barely feeding his charges once he had them chained in the hold. Two years ago, reports reached Lisbon that he had been lost in a storm around Cape Horn. It was thought that was the last anyone would hear of him. But it appears he escaped that watery grave.'

Memories flooded into Oliver's mind. 'Do you know the name of his ship?'

Captain Ruiz' brow furrowed. 'I fear I cannot remember.'

'Could it be *Adelina*?'

'Yes, *Adelina*. Does it mean something to you?'

Oliver shook his head in disbelief. 'It foundered in the Strait of Magellan.'

'On the outward or homeward voyage?' Captain Ruiz enquired.

'As the hold was packed with African slaves, I would assume it was the outward passage.'

'All souls went down with the ship, I believe.'

'Indeed. They all perished. A terrible loss.'

'Not for the ship's master,' the Portuguese officer replied. 'The insurance would have paid handsomely, both on the loss on the ship and on such a valuable cargo.'

Simon Parry was also shocked by the revelation. 'Captain Ruiz, are you saying the master of that slave ship was van Zetten?'

'It is quite likely.'

The pirate's evil laugh came into Oliver Quintrell's head. He thought of the old men from the village, strung from the gallows on the beach. Then his thoughts shifted to the scene that confronted him when he boarded *Adelina* in the Strait of Magellan.

He cursed himself. And cursed, once more. He had had the scoundrel at the end of his sword but, being a man of honour, he had not run his blade through him. Now he wished he had severed every vein, muscle and sinew in the scoundrel's throat and cut through to his yellow backbone. The best he could now hope for was that this pirate and his band of cut-throats would be given a brief hearing and would be delivered in chains to the gallows where a short drop on an old rope would guarantee him a slow death.

The meeting left a foul taste in Captain Quintrell's mouth, though he could not blame the Portuguese captain for the information he had shared. 'If you will excuse me,' he said. 'There are several matters I must attend to.'

'I understand,' Captain Ruiz said. He stood and bowed politely. 'However, there was one question I wished to put to you. Are you able to advise me of the intentions of the British fleets?'

Oliver was instantly aware this very leading question was probably the main reason he had been invited aboard the Portuguese ship.'

'Sir, if I was privy to such information, I would not be at liberty to share it with you. I am sure you understand.'

'Of course.' Captain Ruiz smiled diplomatically. 'I raised the question because I was surprised to see a British frigate in Portuguese waters so far from home. We had heard that all the British fighting ships, apart from those engaged on blockade duty, had been urgently recalled by your Admiralty.'

'And why would that be?' Oliver asked bluntly.

'How long have you been on the water, Captain?'

Oliver's brow furrowed. 'I sailed from Gibraltar in mid-December and, for your information, I am heading across the Atlantic and have no intention of returning to England at this time.'

'Then you are not aware that Spain succumbed to Napoleon's overtures. Having signed an allegiance with France, that country is now at war with Britain.'

'What? When did this happen?'

'In December. This sort of news travels fast in Europe. It was conveyed across France by semaphore immediately after an alliance was reached. Days later the Spanish fleet sailed out of Ferrol and headed south to Cadiz. I understand it presented an impressive sight off the Portuguese coast. Imagine what a formidable force the combined fleets will present when they join up with Napoleon's ships.'

In Oliver's mind, it would be an invincible force that would stop at nothing to give the British Navy a thrashing it would not forget in a hurry. He also wondered if the treasure taken illegally from the Spanish treasure fleet at Cape Saint Mary had been the spark that had ignited the allegiance. The King of Spain was dependent on his treasure ships to pay the dues demanded by Napoleon. Without that silver, the Spanish Royal House was penniless and had no alternative but to comply with Napoleon's demands. If Spain had failed to capitulate, Napoleon would have marched over the border and taken the country.

Though the likelihood of a Spanish/Franco alliance had been spoken of for several years, confirmation of the pact hit Oliver like a bolt from the blue. His mind churned. From now on, no matter what direction he headed, every sail that poked up from the horizon would be regarded as a potential enemy.

If what Captain Ruiz had told him was correct, perhaps he should return to a British port and report for fresh orders. But Gibraltar was the closest British garrison and he had no intention of sailing back into Algeciras Bay and the arms of the waiting Spanish gunboats. Alternatively, he could head north and report to the Commander of the Channel Fleet or sail home to Portsmouth. However, in his cabin, he had his orders from the Admiralty and until he received instructions to the contrary, he must follow them.

'Begging your pardon, Captain Ruiz,' Oliver said. 'May I venture to ask what the views of your country are on this catastrophe?'

The officer needed no time to contemplate his answer. 'Both our military and naval forces are committed to defend Portugal's borders by land and sea. Like Great Britain, it is our intention to withstand any invasion force should Napoleon choose to follow that path. Unlike England, however, we do not have a convenient channel of water separating us from our neighbour.' He stood up and wandered to the stern window and gazed at the fleet of ships at anchor.

'It is apparent that Napoleon intends to bring Europe under his command and place his relatives on the thrones of those countries he conquers. As you will have observed, the Portuguese Navy is prepared for action. Our fighting ships are well equipped and well maintained. Though I admit our sailors lack the discipline of the British tars, I am confident their performance will improve. Our fleet, though not huge, is capable of defending the Portuguese coast from our naval base in Lisbon, but providing sufficient trained soldiers to guard our inland border with Spain is not such an easy proposition.'

With that, Captain Ruiz moved towards the door. Oliver Quintrell and Lieutenant Parry followed him. The interview was over.

As the officers emerged onto the deck, sunlight glistened on the glassy waters of the bay. The fleet of fighting ships, taking up much of the harbour and roadstead, was impressive—90-gun ships of the line, 74s, 64s, frigates and numerous others. Amongst them were *Perpetual* and a black-hulled Indiaman, several schooners that traded between the Azores and the mainland, plus the now infamous three-masted *San Nicola*, hanging off her anchor only a cable's length away. Before Captain Quintrell was piped over the side, the officer had a final question for him. 'When do you intend to sail from here?'

'If all is ready—two days from now. In the morning.'

'We sail then, also. Therefore, I bid you farewell and God speed.'

'And to you, sir. I pray this war will soon be over.'

Not waiting for an answer, Oliver Quintrell followed his first officer down the steps to the waiting boat. A faint smell of sulphur wafted across the bay reminding him of the shivering island in the southern ocean that he had visited two years earlier.

'Let us hope the smoke and steam rising from the craters in yonder mountains will not erupt into the fires of war on these islands.'

Chapter 12

Ill Fortune

'Captain.' The voice came in a whisper rousing him instantly from his fitful sleep.

'What time is it?'

'Half an hour after midnight,' Casson whispered.

'Is there a problem?'

'Mr Parry says he's sorry to disturb you, but requests you join him on deck.'

'Tell Mr Parry, I will join him directly.'

'Aye, aye,' the steward replied.

Being in a neutral port, surrounded by a neutral fleet, with a deck beneath his feet as still as the bedroom floor at his house on the Isle of Wight, and with not a single creak or groan from the frigate or a sound from the men who were sleeping soundly in their hammocks, he was puzzled as to the reason for the call.

Having had no undue concerns the previous evening, he had taken to his bed and allowed himself the liberty of undressing and donning his night shirt. It was a luxury he seldom afforded himself when at sea. The light from the lantern was dim, though his eyes quickly adjusted to it. The glim revealed his clothes draped over the back of the chair where he had left them.

The possibility of the frigate casting its anchor and drifting close to one of the other ships came to mind, or the possibility of a fire on board, or a sailor falling from the yard, or of being boarded, or water rising rapidly in the well. But, in any of those instances, he would have heard the shrill of the pipes and the rumble of feet, and his steward would surely have informed him.

Dressing as quickly as he could and slipping bare feet into his shoes, he left the cabin with his neckerchief in his hand. Climbing the companionway and emerging from the waist to the quarterdeck, he noticed a few sailors leaning over the cap rail on the larboard side near the entry port. But there was no sense of urgency or alarm.

He joined his first officer. 'You wanted me, Simon?'

Mr Parry looked weary. 'I have a dilemma on which only you can pass judgement.' He moved to the rail and glanced down to the water. 'If you would care to take a look.'

The captain joined him.

It was a black night with stars dotting the sky with a half-moon shining, but the larboard side of the hull was shrouded in darkness. The nearest lantern was at the wheel but it threw only a dim puddle of light on the deck. Looking down to the water, the captain could make out the shape of a small boat pulled up alongside. It carried no light. Two figures were seated side by side on the central thwart while another figure sat with an arm resting on the rudder. Whether the occupants were male or female was impossible to tell. Behind the rowers, in the bow, was the boat's cargo. Was it a bundle of skins, or a crumpled sail? Or bags of oranges covered with tarpaulin. Oliver concentrated his gaze.

'I'm afraid it is Mrs Crosby and her friend returned from the town. From what I can understand from these local fishermen, both women have been sorely beaten. Apart from that, I do not know their condition. I have not been aboard.'

'For goodness sake, man, call the surgeon.'

'I have done so already,' Mr Parry murmured.

'And muster enough hands to help get the women aboard. You will need rig a sling to lift them.'

The orders were conveyed quickly and quietly. Hands were soon standing by.

Leaning over the side, the captain could detect no movement in the boat. 'We need more light,' he demanded, as two sailors climbed down into the boat. 'As soon as you have the women aboard, have them taken to the sick berth. I will speak with Mr Whipple later.'

Mr Parry nodded. 'Thank you.'

Oliver looked quizzically at his first lieutenant. 'As I have said before, I am not entirely without feeling. I merely endeavour to follow the strict regulations that every man in the service is obliged to follow.' Then his defensive tone changed and he lowered his voice. 'I suggest you do not rouse Mr Crosby until his wife is settled in the cockpit. Seeing her in this condition may cause undue distress. And,' he added after a pause, 'I appreciate your diplomacy in dealing with this matter. Any commotion would have raised unnecessary questions from the crew, and tittle-tattle is best kept to a minimum. Hopefully the answers to those questions will be forthcoming in the morning.'

Mr Parry could not resist the question burning within him. 'Will the women be permitted to stay with the ship?'

The captain avoided a direct answer. 'I will know more in the morning. For the present, attend to the women. Thank the local boatman and, if payment is required, pay him off, then see the boat away from the side as quickly as possible.' Turning away and heading to the waist, Oliver shook his head and spoke aloud to himself. 'What is so damned special about these islands? I have found nothing *fortunate* about them.'

On his knees, beside the fixed bunk his wife had been placed into, Mr Crosby dabbed a dampened cloth to the cut on her lip. 'I should not have left you,' he said.

Her voice was faint, her mouth appeared twisted from the swelling and her left eye was closed. 'You cannot blame yourself,' she whispered. 'It was my fault. I should have known better.'

'Hush,' he said. 'Don't talk.'

'But I must explain. I want you to know the truth.'

The carpenter tried to quieten her, but her mind was made up.

'One minute it was twilight. The next it was dark. Night fell so quickly. Connie and I were hungry and had stepped out onto the street to buy some supper.'

'And you were set upon and robbed.'

'That would have been a kindness,' she said, reaching her right hand down to her pocket and fingering the bundle of coins still safely tied in her handkerchief. 'We had only walked a few yards when a group of men surrounded us grinning and making lewd gestures. They were young—little more than lads and it was Connie they were interested in. I told her to keep her head down and not look their way, but they began taunting her, reaching out and touching her in a disgusting manner. I linked my arm in hers and we hurried to get away from them, but they followed us. It was obvious what they wanted.'

'Did they touch you?'

'They had no interest in an old lady like me. Their eyes were set on Consuela. When they grabbed her, I tried to stop them, but I couldn't.' She sobbed. 'Her arm was pulled from my grip, and in an instant, she was pressed against the wall and her dress almost ripped from her. Oh John!' she cried, 'I called out and begged them to stop, but they jested and jeered and jostled each other. When I tried to pull one of them away, he turned on me and sent me reeling to the cobbles. The next I remember was waking to the sound of heavy footsteps, like clogs on paving stones. It was a group of soldiers. They, too, were young and when they surrounded us, I feared they would take up where the others had left off. I tried to crawl over to Connie to help her. She was lying in a heap beside the wall. I feared she was dead. I begged the soldiers to help us and they asked questions of me, but we did not speak the same language. I answered the only way I could. I said we were *English* off a *ship* and I remember pointing to the harbour.

'With my mind in a fog, I felt myself being lifted up and carried along, but I had no idea where I was being taken or if Connie was with me. I admit, in my weakness, I allowed myself to succumb to sleep. The next recollection I have was being bundled into the bottom of a boat. I could feel the rocking motion and hear the splash of the oars. I opened my eyes and could see the heavens above and, I thanked the Lord, I could feel Consuela beside me. Best of all, I could hear her breathing. Then, it was like my prayers were answered. I awoke up in this bed and heard Dr Whipple speaking softly as he attended to her. Poor Connie, I hear she is in a terrible state. I can only imagine what horrors she endured.'

Mr Crosby was distraught. 'I should have left the ship with you. I should never have signed on this voyage. I should be heading home with you to England.'

'Hush, husband. It is over. We are safe now.'

'But,' he said anxiously, 'the captain will not allow you to stay on board. You will be returned to the shore as soon as you are recovered.'

Captain Quintrell stepped out from the shadow of the doorway. 'A word in your ear, if you please, Mr Crosby.'

The carpenter stood upright. 'Beg pardon, Captain. I did not mean to speak out of turn.'

Oliver drew him aside. 'I suggest you do not tax your wife any further. The doctor tells me she needs rest if she is to recover quickly. But let me say that I understand your concern. However, you must give a little thought to the unfortunate position I find myself in. I have strict orders to adhere to, but I am human and will not tolerate the mistreatment of women such as your wife and her companion have been subjected to. Under less traumatic circumstances, I would order them ashore. Furthermore, I would permit you to rescind your warrant without penalty and to leave the ship in order to accompany your wife back to England.'

The carpenter listened closely as the captain continued.

'The facts are, the women are far from fit and, under no circumstances, would I return them to such an inhospitable place as this. As to your situation here, my decision is not founded in the goodness of my heart. My reasons are purely selfish. I need you aboard my ship. We are embarking on a long voyage and it will be over a year before we return to England. As ship's carpenter, your services are essential. Therefore, I will permit your wife to accompany you on this voyage and allow Mrs Pilkington to travel as her companion. I charge you with ensuring they continue to behave in the manner they have so far demonstrated. Do I make myself clear?'

Tears welled in the carpenter's eyes. 'God bless you, Captain. God bless you.'

'I have already spoken with Mr Tully. At first light, only an hour from now, you will go ashore. I have suggested to the lieutenant that you visit the boarding house where the women were lodging. Hopefully you can recover some of their possessions. Failing that, I would encourage you, with whatever money you have between you, to purchase some women's attire suitable to clothe them for a long sea voyage. Mr Tully and two of the marines will go ashore with you.'

The carpenter was unable to express his gratitude.

'I will speak with you later in the day. In the meantime, let us pray both women survive this ordeal. I would not wish this sort of violent unprovoked attack on any of my men, let alone a pair of defenceless females. But, let me assure you, Mr Crosby, they are in very good hands. Mr Whipple is an excellent doctor and will do all he can.'

Oliver glanced across the sick berth to the young woman lying in the swinging cot. The sight of her long black hair on the pillows, her warm olive skin, her slender neck and the bloodied saliva running from the side of her mouth brought back memories of Susanna. As he turned away, he could feel tears filling his eyes. Brushing them with away on the back of his hand, he headed to his cabin.

After three days in port, although most of the stores had been loaded aboard *Perpetual*, van Zetten's crew was still being held in the hold of the captured ship. At times, their cries, curses and complaints could be heard half-way across the harbour. Despite having fought to the death on *San Nicola*'s deck, they argued they were not pirates but common sailors who had no particular allegiance to the captain. They also claimed they despised the man and would rather throw themselves overboard than serve on another voyage under him. They complained about being held in irons and being given little to eat.

As a result of the disturbance and the adverse reports from the soldiers who were guarding them, the ship received a visit from the colonel of the garrison's guard. The outcome was received with mixed feelings. While all shackles were removed, the prisoners had to remain confined and under the supervision of the local military. The colonel guaranteed they would be adequately fed and a decision as to what to do with them would be made very soon.

Captain Quintrell regarded the whole affair as unsavoury and unsatisfactory. He conceded that the picture both Mr Mundy and Mr Read had painted regarding the state of affairs on the Islands was not far from the truth. He did not intend to remain in port to bear witness against van Zetten at his trial, but trusted that the statement he had dictated and left in the hands of the British Consul provided sufficient evidence to damn the pirate and see him hanged for his crimes.

'I should have run him through and sent his body to the bottom,' Oliver vowed in frustration. There was nothing more he could do or say. It was important he serviced his own vessel and was off the roadstead and heading for Brazil as soon as possible.

When one of the ship's boats returned with members of the ship's company who had spent several hours on shore, Captain Quintrell was surprised to receive Mr Read, who had taken the liberty, and the only spare seat in the boat, to travel with them.

'Welcome aboard,' the captain said. 'For what do I deserve this pleasure?'

'I have come to beg a favour of you,' the consul said.

'Anything,' Oliver replied.

'I am asking on behalf of six men who are seeking passage on a ship heading west.'

'Local men?'

'No, sir, British from Liverpool.'

'Sailors?'

'I think not, but good workers and sober men besides. They have been working on my farm. They desire to sail to America, but there have been no suitable ships willing or able to take them. It is their wish to stay together. If you can assist them, this will be the only favour I ask of you.'

At this stage of his mission, Captain Quintrell had no desire to embark anyone on his vessel who did not have papers, or a trade, or was known to him or his men. However, Mr Read had been an invaluable help over the last few days and, without his assistance and guidance, it was likely van Zetten would still be his responsibility. With this debt to repay, and with no specific reason why the men could not be signed, he was obliged to accept.

'I will speak with my first lieutenant. I am sure he will find something useful for them to do. I trust they are aware we are not heading to America. My next port of call is Rio de Janeiro.'

'I made that clear to them,' Mr Read replied.

Having agreed to accept them without first seeing them left Oliver doubting his decision. A stream of questions ran through the captain's head. Why were these men at liberty on the Azores? Had they been stranded, shipwrecked or merely arrived at Ponta Delgada from a ship heading south with the intention of taking passage on another ship? Did they have money? How old were they?

He was putting his trust in Mr Read's recommendation and he had faith in the consul. He would not go back on his offer. Any question that arose would be for Mr Parry to pursue but, for the present, he had more important matters to deal with.

'Are you aware I am sailing tomorrow?'

'I am,' the consul replied.

'Where are these men presently?'

'They are waiting on the wharf for word from me.'

'Do they have their dunnage with them?'

'They have very little baggage and are ready to come aboard immediately.'

Oliver considered it odd that six men had few possessions but presumed there was good reason for it. 'Return to the wharf and inform the men they can come aboard. Tell them to report to Mr Parry when they do so.'

Bidding his visitor farewell, Oliver remained by the rail until the boat had pushed off. He then headed for'ard to speak with his first lieutenant.

He could well do without further encumbrances at this time. Much had transpired in the last few days and dealing with the various problems had occupied more time than he would have wished. Because of this, the captain had given little thought to the voyage ahead. It was imperative he speak with the sailing master about plans to depart the port the following morning.

He was not sorry to be leaving the Azores and looked forward to heading out into the Atlantic. As to the fate of Fredrik van Zetten, although he had wiped his hands of him, he was finding it hard to convince himself that this was the last he had seen of the blackguard.

The following morning, as the sun rose over the mist-shrouded peaks to the north, the crew waited the order to weigh. Since daybreak, they had watched the activities and listened to the buzz of foreign voices on the nearby Portuguese warships. Like ants, hundreds of sailors had followed each other up the ratlines and swarmed out along the yards. Gaskets had been unfastened and some of the sails unfurled in preparation to sail.

Though there was little wind, the outflowing tide meant there was sufficient current to float the ships out of the bay. With permission granted to depart before the fleet, Oliver Quintrell had no intention of waiting and becoming entangled with a mob of more than thirty vessels heading east. His course was west-south-west to the coast of Brazil.

With the first kiss of breeze from the north-west, which favoured the fleet more so than the frigate, Oliver gave the order to make sail. Fifteen minute later, *Perpetual* was sliding across the bay leaving the Portuguese fighting ships in its wake.

Looking back to the island, Oliver breathed a sigh of relief. He was not sorry to be leaving the Azores—The Western Islands the French had once named *Les Îsles Fortunées*. A more apt name in his mind was *The Unfortunate Isles*.

Three days later, at his villa in the hills, Mr Read relaxed in his armchair. Although he had been home two days, he was still a little stiff in the joints after deciding to ride to his farm in the country rather than being driven.

His wife had been delighted at his unannounced arrival. She complained that he worked too hard, was at everyone's beck and call and that she did not see enough of him. Mrs Read was very fond of her husband and pampered him whenever she had the opportunity.

Sitting on the tiled veranda, which surrounded his home, the British Consul inhaled the fragrances from his orchard and listened to the music of the birds. Perched on the hillside, the villa offered a commanding view of the city and its spires, the harbour and its fishing boats, the roadstead and its ships, and inland to the cultivated fields, farms and villages. The rich soil that produced fruits, flowers and vegetables at every season of the year masked the layers of marble-hard lava hidden just beneath the surface.

Having soaked in the surroundings, the consul asked for his bag to be brought to him. His wife immediately obliged. A well-worn leather case contained a bundle of letters recently arrived in the port from England on a ship heading to Cape Town. Apart from Bills of Lading and invoices, there were assorted papers including local correspondence, invitations and appointments that needed his attention.

His wife was delighted when he announced he would accept the invitation to dine with the governor upon his return. She relished the rare opportunities to partake in the social events of the town. Also included in the case was a newssheet that he had folded carefully and put aside to read later. It had been delivered to him personally, fresh off the press the morning he left Ponta Delgada. Being British Consul, he always received a copy. The same newssheet, containing lists of local events and shipping movements, was distributed to all government offices and businesses in the town. Spare copies were displayed in shop windows or nailed to lampposts for the townsfolk to read.

Having opened and read his letters and put aside those that demanded a reply, by the time he turned to the newssheet, his eyes were drooping. It was printed in Portuguese and, because his eyes were tired, he begged his wife to sit with him and read out the items she thought would be of interest to him.

Mrs Read was only too pleased to oblige him and began: 'A fire destroyed part of the slaughter yard and spread to three adjoining cottages. Six cows were burned alive and the owner of one of the cottages also perished.'

'That is not good,' he said.

'Oh, dear,' she continued. 'The collapse of five houses and damage to the walls of several government buildings was blamed on ground movement caused by activity from the volcano on the island. Because of the fear of collapse, the prisoners currently held in the jail were removed to the watch-house at the garrison.'

Movements in the earth were not uncommon. 'Pray continue,' he said. 'I am more interested in the shipping news.'

'The East India Company's schooner, *Silver Cloud*, made an unannounced departure from the harbour overnight, leaving its cargo of pottery sitting on the wharf. And,' she read, 'the ship, *San Nicola*, slipped its mooring overnight. Its destination is not known.'

'One problem less for the authorities to concern themselves with,' he commented. 'Is there anything about the price of oranges? I heard they were selling for two dollars and a half a case.'

Chapter 13

Bungs

The cooper's gaze was intense, as he leaned from his perch on the sea chest and studied the caulking between the timbers on the floor of mess. After tracing the pitch-stained lines down the length of the deck, his eyes returned to where he had started and began again. He was mesmerized.

Tommy looked at Eku, broke a piece of hard tack in his teeth and threw it at the cooper hitting him on the chest. It fell onto the mess table and rolled to the deck, but Bungs was oblivious to it.

Tommy laughed.

William Ethridge, sitting opposite the lad, shrugged his shoulders. 'Eh! Bungs,' he said, tapping the cooper on the elbow. 'We've hardly heard a peep out of you since yesterday.'

He got no reply, so tried again. 'Ain't you got no yarns to tell us or complaints to make? What's got up your nose recently?'

Bungs sat up straight and looked at the empty seat at the end of the table. 'Where's Muffin?' he said.

Tommy Wainwright laughed again but Eku elbowed him in the side.

'That's a daft thing to say,' Tommy said.

'He's late again,' Bungs continued.

'He's no longer with us,' Eku said slowly.

'What do you mean? Didn't he sign for this cruise?'

Tommy was about to answer, but his West Indian shipmate elbowed him again. Harder this time.

'Watch it!' Tommy cried, rubbing his ribs.

With no answer to his question, the cooper got up from his seat and headed for the companionway mumbling to himself, 'I know where he'll be lurking. I'll find him.'

Tommy was open-mouthed. 'What's wrong with him?' he said innocently. 'He sat with Muffin every day in the cockpit. He nursed him right up to the day he died. I should know, I was there too.'

Ekundayo shook his head. 'I've seen it before. Sometimes the mind blots out things best forgotten.'

'That's not like Bungs,' Will said. 'From the stories I heard him tell in the past, he's seen men cut to pieces and he'll tell you all the grizzly details. He knows the whys and wherefores and whereabouts of everyman on the ship, better than Mr Parry does. And, besides that, he's a damned good worker and a fine craftsman. I've heard it said he can turn out a barrel quicker than any other man in a shipyard, and a sounder one at that.'

'Never mind that,' Eku said, grabbing Will's arm. 'You come with me. We best go look out for him before he gets himself into any strife.'

But, by the time the pair had left the table and climbed the forward companion ladder to the deck, it was already too late. When they found Bungs, he was standing over a seaman who was rolling about on the deck, his hand over his nose with blood oozing between his fingers.

'Belay!' Mr Hanson yelled, running along the deck. 'Belay, Bungs. What did you hit him for?'

The cooper rubbed his knuckles and turned to go.

'Don't you walk away from me, sailor. Marines!' he called. 'Restrain this man. You there,' he said to one of the ship's boys, 'go fetch Mr Tully.' But, before the lieutenant arrived, Eku and Will had rested their mate against the windlass and were supporting him, one on either side.

'What's going on here?' Mr Tully asked.

'Just a misunderstanding, I think,' Eku said.

'Well, it is pretty clear to me. It looks like Bungs clobbered Prescott and, for that, Mr Hanson has put him on a charge. And rightly so. There will be no fighting on this ship. Take that man below. The captain will decide his punishment.'

The following morning, the peeps of the Bosun's pipes called all hands to witness punishment. Escorted by a pair of marines, Bungs was brought up from below. Standing in the centre of the ship's company gathered on deck was Prescott, the left side of his face swollen and his eye half-closed.

Swinging a hammer for his lifetime's toil meant the cooper could deliver a fair blow whenever he needed to. Only this was the first time, apart from in a serious fight aboard an enemy ship, that he had ever let fly at another sailor—though he had threatened to do so many times. Those who knew Bungs well swore his bark was worse than his bite.

'Did you witness this fight, Mr Tully?' the captain asked.

'No, sir. Mr Hanson brought the charge.'

'You saw it, Mr Hanson?'

'Not exactly, sir. I arrived a moment after and found Prescott down on the deck.'

The captain frowned. 'Step forward, Prescott.'

Despite a swollen lip, the smug expression on his face was undeniable.

'This is not the first time you have been brought before me for fighting. Did you provoke the cooper to strike you?'

'Not likely, Capt'n. He's bigger than me. I didn't say nowt to him. I was just minding my own business and he came up and walloped me.'

With no alternative but to address the charge that had been laid, the captain turned to the cooper. 'You are charged with fighting on deck. What do you have to say for yourself?'

Bungs remained silent. It was as though he had either not heard the words or could not understand them.

'I asked you a question, Bungs. You will give me your answer or I will add dumb insolence to your offence.'

'He's not well,' Eku shouted.

'Who said that?' Mr Tully called.

Eku stepped forward. 'I did, sir.'

'And what would you know? Are you his keeper?'

'No, sir. I'm his mate.'

'Then keep your nose out of the captain's business or you'll find your name in the book also.'

Still seemingly oblivious to the undercurrent of talk concerning him, Bungs neither struggled nor blinked. Even when the sentence was delivered and he was led across the deck and his wrists seized to the grating, he did not speak. Only when the first stroke of the cat clawed his smooth back, did he struggle against the cords holding him, but the gag across his mouth prevented him from calling out. With the repeated strokes of knotted leather slicing his back, the cooper tensed and groaned and tears welled in his eyes. More than forty years in the service and, remarkably, this was the first time he had suffered the cat's sting. The whisperings from amongst the crew received glares from the midshipman who had brought the charge. Questioning glances were exchanged between Bungs' mates.

When the punishment was over, Mr Whipple examined the man's injuries and, as was the usual procedure, recommended he be taken to the sick berth for his wounds to be attended to. The captain agreed with the request. After dismissing the gathering and watching the men disperse, he turned to Mr Parry. There was something about the atmosphere that troubled him.

'See the men have some worthwhile occupations to keep them busy,' Oliver said. 'Bungs is popular and I fear this sort of thing leaves a nasty taste.'

The events of the following day did nothing to improve the men's spirits. John Fairclough, one of the men who had been injured in the fight aboard *San Nicola*, died as a result of his wounds. A musket ball had shattered his collar bone and, though the ship's surgeon had managed to remove both the shot and the loose fragments of bone, he could do nothing to prevent the blood poisoning spreading throughout the sailor's body.

With all hands gathered on deck for the burial service, Captain Quintrell glanced up from his open Bible and considered the crew's faces. Usually a few men demonstrated some degree of genuine grief but, on this day, all the expressions were blank and emotionless. Even after the body had splashed into the Atlantic, there were no sighs, no inappropriate jokes and false laughter, no tears, and not a single word was spoken. With several weeks sailing ahead before they raised the coast of Brazil, Oliver was concerned for his men.

The celebrations the crew had all enjoyed after taking van Zetten's ship was the type of euphoria shared after a successful sea battle, but it never lasted. As days went by, the feeling of elation quickly drained from them. The sullen mood, the expressionless faces, even the lethargic way the men climbed the rigging or swabbed the decks appeared infectious and no one was immune.

Boredom was almost as demoralising for the men as defeat. His only hope was that, when they crossed the Equator the mood would change. He prayed the Doldrums would not drift north into their path and that nothing else would interrupt their passage. Very soon they would be entering the tropics and the thermometer would show an increase in temperature, but with the oppressive heat came lethargy and listlessness.

Crossing the line was an excuse for an extra ration of grog and half-day of leisure, providing the captain permitted it. While the form of sadistic pleasure it often entailed was not something Oliver usually condoned, on this occasion he decided to encourage the ritual with a view to raising the men's spirits.

Standing on the quarterdeck observing a group of men leaning on a gun in the waist, Oliver questioned his first lieutenant.

'I want to know about the six men you signed in Ponta Delgada. Mr Read told me very little. I have since discovered they are all Irish.'

'Indeed they are,' Simon Parry said. 'They are landsmen not sailors. They claim they were shipwrecked on a passage to America. This is the reason they had very little dunnage.'

'I trust they are not spies hoping to be taken aboard a French ship,' Oliver responded flippantly. 'Continue.'

'One claimed he was a baker, so I allocated him to the bread room. Another professes to be a clerk. The other four have no trades, or admitted to none. I put two of them in the fo'c'sle, one in the hold and one volunteered to help with the animals. When on deck, they follow whatever orders they are given and appear to comply without complaint, but I thought it best to separate them.'

'Very wise.'

'Allocate one of the men to the cooper,' the captain suggested.

'I don't think Bungs will take kindly to having an assistant.'

'Bungs will do as he is told. Better he is kept busy at his horse and vents his anger on barrels and not on members of the crew.'

The lieutenant nodded. 'The man who called himself a clerk said he worked as a writer in the office of the East India Company in Liverpool. He had noticed your bandaged hand and asked if he could be useful in assisting you.'

'He did, did he? What is his name?'

'Michael O'Connor.'

'I will speak with him in due course. In the meantime, the division captains should treat these new arrivals as if they are pressed men. Don't expect too much at first but don't be lenient either, and report anything about them that seems unusual or troubling.'

'Yes, sir,' Mr Parry said.

'I have spoken briefly with the doctor about them. Being of Celtic forebears, Mr Whipple tends to be a little wary. He is all too familiar with the antics of the United Irishmen and their bitter hatred of British rule. "Once a rebel always a rebel" was the phrase he coined.'

'But the Irish Rebellion was in 1798—six years ago. If I am not wrong, most of the ringleaders ended up on the gallows or died in jail, while others were transported overseas. As for the poor farmers, it is said that many lost everything—their land, their houses, and their families. And the atrocities perpetrated by both sides were horrific.'

Oliver agreed. 'The doctor reminded me that in certain parts of Ireland, many still bear a grudge. Yet he has spoken briefly with these men and finds no spite or malice in their attitudes.'

The lieutenant continued. 'Perhaps we should not forget the large number of Irishmen who already serve in the British Navy. As for the other Irish seamen aboard *Perpetual*, they are loyal and good seamen.'

'Thank you, Simon. Let us hope that is the case with these fellows.'

After a long tiring night, that saw a storm drench the deck, Oliver returned to his cabin just before sunrise, removed his boat cloak and flopped down into his armchair. He intended to remove his shoes and urged himself to climb into his bunk but, before either could be achieved, he was asleep.

'Captain,' Casson called.

He woke immediately. For Oliver Quintrell, like any other man of naval or military discipline who had courted danger for many years of his life, the speed with which his mind, body and senses could transition from near unconsciousness to complete alertness was remarkable.

With the call from his steward came the sound of distant cries. Was it an argument? Were the voices raised in anger or alarm? At least there were no peeps or drums or echoes of distant guns, and with the roll of the sea having eased, the ship was sailing smoothly.

'You're wanted below. In the hold. Mr Parry asked me to fetch you.'

'What is the commotion about?' Oliver asked, thinking his steward was close behind him. But Casson had returned to the cabin to collect the captain's pistols.

Around the ladder, leading down into the bowels of the ship, several sailors had congregated and were muttering together.

'Out of my way!' the captain called.

The men stepped back.

At the bottom of the ladder, a seaman was holding a lantern. 'They are down yon far end, sir,' he said, swinging the lantern in a forward direction. But the beam of light merely threw shadows around the frigate's hull, pitching the spaces between the barrels into blackness.

'Bring more light,' the captain ordered, as he stepped down onto the gravel ballast.

Despite the faint glimmer from up ahead, he was guided by the sound of men shouting. Seeing the silhouette of a seaman standing with his legs apart gripping an adze in his hands alarmed him, especially as he was without a weapon. Then, as he moved closer, he saw a group of men struggling on the deck. The sight of Mr Parry and Mr Tully behind the mob was reassuring.

'What is going on here, Mr Parry?' he called.

Before the first officer had chance to reply, one of the seamen answered for him. 'Bungs has gone raving mad! He's been smashing the barrels.'

Oliver looked down at the struggle going on at his feet. The five sailors were not fighting each other. Four of them were attempting to restrain a single man—the ship's cooper. Having wrestled him to the ground, two were holding his wrists, another holding his legs while Ekundayo, the Negro, was straddling his chest. All four were urging him to be still, but Bungs was cursing them and ignoring their demands.

Mr Parry spoke up. 'It appears Bungs took to the barrels with his adze.'

'Been mixing turps with his grog? Looking for hidden treasure?' Smithers added.

'Who said that?' the captain demanded, shocked at the mention of treasure. Was that word used in jest or did the sailor know something?

'Enough, Smithers!' Mr Parry yelled. 'On deck, this instant! If you utter one more word, I guarantee I will have you in irons.'

'Only telling it as it is, Mr Parry, sir.'

'Enough. Back on deck anyone who is not lending a hand.' Oliver turned to the marine who was standing by with his musket lowered. 'Put that away before you kill somebody. Go fetch some rope and shackles.'

He was puzzled and shook his head at the troubling sight. Bungs had sailed with him on several cruises and was known and respected by most of the crew. Although he was a cantankerous and bombastic old coot who did not contend well with criticism, interference or new crew, he was an excellent craftsman, a useful member of his gun crew and an honest and loyal seaman. If that had not been the case, he would never have charged him with the task of hiding the valuable chests of coins in the hold.

Looking around, it was not hard to calculate the damage that had been done. The top hoops of three water barrels had been removed, the liquid having spilled onto the gravel and seeped through to the bilge. The sides of two other barrels, one of pork and one of potatoes had been smashed and their contents wasted. But what was odd was that the area where the commotions had taken place was some distance from where the chests of Spanish treasure were hidden.

'This makes no sense,' Oliver said, taking his lieutenant aside. 'Why would the cooper do this?'

Mr Parry already knew the answer. 'He wasn't looking for treasure. He was looking for Chips.'

The captain shook his head. 'What? Chips is on deck. I passed him on the companionway only a moment ago.'

'No, not Mr Crosby—the new Chippie, he said he was looking for Percy Sparrow.'

Oliver's heart sank.

'He was bellowing out for help saying Percy was stuck in one of these barrels and he had to find him and get him out.'

Oliver turned to Mr Tully. 'Ask the surgeon to come down here immediately.' Then he leaned down to the man spread-eagled on the ground. 'Settle down, Bungs. You must come to your senses.'

The cooper relaxed to the sound of the captain's voice, but his eyes were unable to focus as he looked up with an expression of child-like innocence on his face. 'You don't understand, Captain,' he said, tears filling his eyes. 'Percy didn't go ashore in Rio like you thought. He's down here somewhere.'

The accusation came as a painful reminder. Oliver leaned closer to the man's ear and spoke quietly. 'We haven't reached Rio yet, and the last time we did was two years ago. Percy Sparrow died two years ago.'

Bungs turned his head away and fought to free his arms, but Ekundayo was sitting across his chest and had his knees firmly planted on the cooper's upper arms.

'That's not true,' Bungs yelled. 'I was talking to him on deck just a while ago.'

While he was still struggling, Dr Whipple and one of the marines, carrying a set of leg shackles, arrived at the same time.

'Get your black carcass off me,' Bungs bellowed, but Eku was not to be budged. Only when the cooper's legs had been secured did the Negro slowly release his hold and slide off. With his wrists tied behind his back, the cooper was permitted to sit up.

'Bastards, all of you,' he swore. 'You'll have Percy's death on your conscience for the rest of your days.'

For Oliver Quintrell, there was a painful truth in that final statement.

'Don't put him on a charge, Captain,' Eku pleaded. 'He meant no harm. He just ain't been himself lately.'

The doctor had already arrived at a similar conclusion. 'If this man is seeing ghosts of sailors long dead, he is hallucinating. If not demented, he is certainly very confused. I need to examine him in the cockpit.'

'Is that wise? He could become violet again.'

'Don't worry, Captain. I will make sure he is restrained and a good dose of laudanum will soothe his outbursts.'

Oliver accepted the doctor's opinion.

'You there, Ekundayo, you are one of the cooper's mess-mates, are you not? Is this the first time you have witnessed such an outburst.'

Eku looked over to William Ethridge, who had also been assisting.

'Speak!' the captain ordered. 'The doctor and I cannot read your thoughts.'

'Nothing like this, Capt'n, but me and Will and Young Tommy have noticed how strange he's been these last few days.'

'In what way?'

'Like he didn't answer the bells when he should have, and sometimes he burst out laughing for no reason as if he was listening to a joke, only no one was telling it. And if you spoke to him on deck, he'd ignored you like he didn't see you.'

'We all know what Bungs is like,' Mr Parry argued. 'A canny beggar at times.'

'Aye,' Mr Tully agreed, 'but he's far from stupid. He's usually sharp as a tack and has an answer for everything with a joke or a serve of lip to go with it. Besides, he never misses anything that is going on in the ship. You could always trust Bungs to get the first whiff of any whispers passing around.'

William Ethridge added his support. 'It's not like Bungs at all. It's like he's a different man. And after the lashing he took the other day, I asked him what made him do it.'

'Rightful punishment for his crime,' Mr Tully pointed out.

'What did he answer?' the captain asked.

'"What lashing?" Bungs said. "In all my days in the service, I ain't never had one." It's got me beat,' Will said. 'This ain't the Bungs we know and he don't seem to know us.'

The doctor was listening and scratched his head. 'Apart from his recent punishment, I don't recall him visiting the cockpit or presenting himself at sick call for any ailment lately. Do you know if he has suffered any injuries lately?'

Will glanced at his new mess-mate. 'Aye, he took a bad knock on the side of his head on the deck of the *San Nicola* during the fighting. He told me he was on the foredeck when the ship almost went over and said one of the blocks swung loose and gave him a fair whack on the temple. He swore the force would have knocked any other man clean over the rail. I saw him on deck soon after, wiping away the blood that had run into his ear.'

Eku took up the story. 'He complained about the pain in his head for the next three days and said he couldn't see straight.'

'So why didn't he report to me?' the doctor asked.

'We told him he should, but, you know Bungs, he'd never admit to nothing, especially a bit of pain. Stubborner than any old mule. After that, we let him be and he moped around like he was in a day-dream.'

'And this fellow Percy Sparrow, who he calls Chips, did he really believe this man was hiding in the hold. Were they friends?' Mr Whipple asked.

Will explained. 'Bungs and Percy were old mates. They'd served together on the Calcutta Station long ago before they joined Captain Quintrell in *Elusive*—a frigate just like this one. That was in 1802 during the Peace. There were some mighty strange happenings on that cruise, not least poor Mr Sparrow being murdered and his body being stuffed in a barrel.'

'Do you think Bungs was guilty of the crime and the fact is still playing on his conscience?'

'That's not so,' Will argued adamantly. 'They caught the ones who did it. The problem with Bungs is that he's just confused.'

'Thank you, men, you have been very helpful. Now, kindly assist the cooper to the sick berth. This man needs my attention.'

With the morning sun streaming in from the stern windows and the men at breakfast, Oliver left his cabin and went below to visit the cockpit to speak with the doctor.

'It's brain fever,' Mr Whipple said quietly. 'I have put him in a cot with feather-filled cushions around his head. He did not appreciate having his hands restrained but, the laudanum has taken effect and he is calm compared with his behaviour in the hold.'

'What can you do for him?' Oliver asked.

The doctor pondered before replying, 'Very little, I am afraid. He must remain very still and quiet and be watched day and night. Presently, he is burning with fever, which does not surprise me. Brain fever is a dangerous malady and, of the cases I have seen in the Borough Hospitals, few victims survive.'

The captain had little recollection of the weeks he had spent in the Seamen's Hospital at Greenwich when he suffered from brain fever. Only when he was recovering did he recognize the people who were visiting him and become aware of the smell of old, dead and dying men around him. Against the odds, he had survived. He would pray for Bungs to recover also.

'Is the fever infectious?' he asked tentatively.

The doctor shook his head. 'It is possible the blow he received fractured his skull and caused his brain to bleed.'

'But you said you didn't treat him when we returned to the beach.'

'That is correct. I did not treat him as there was no necessity to do so. I do, however, remember speaking with him briefly, along with all the other men when they returned to shore. But, as a surgeon, one tends to remember the most horrific injuries and forget the minor scratches. I now recollect he told me he had received a blow to the side of the head and pointed to a slight cut on his temple, but when I examined it, the bleeding had stopped. I was certain the injury was only superficial and would heal quickly, but obviously I was wrong. The bruising is deep and, in my opinion, there is now fluid collecting around his brain. This has resulted in a new swelling. My fear, because of his confusion, is that this has led to blood poisoning.'

'Is there anything you can do for him, doctor?' Oliver asked.

'I can bleed him, but mostly he needs rest and quiet. And someone to attend to him and keep his body cool.'

'Will he survive this?'

'I cannot answer that question.'

'Who is watching him now?' the captain enquired.

'Mrs Crosby is with him. She is remarkably patient and caring. And young Tommy Wainwright is on hand to call me if I am needed urgently. His other mess-mates, the Negro and William Ethridge, have volunteered to sit beside him when they are not on watch.'

'Is there anything I can do?' Oliver asked.

'Pray for smooth seas and fair winds. Beyond that, the life of the cooper is in God's hands.'

Chapter 14

The Irishman

Having spoken Michael O'Connor, the Irishman who claimed he had written letters and made copies of documents in the offices of The Honourable East India Company in Liverpool, the captain sat the man at the table in his cabin. After supplying him with paper, ink and pen, he dictated several lines from the first book that came to hand from his bookcase. The Irishman quickly proved he had a fine flowing hand and his writing was legible. As a result, the captain was prepared to engage him, when necessary, to undertake a small number of secretarial tasks.

He did not, however, permit O'Connor access to his cabin in which to do his copying. That would not occur until Oliver had full trust in him. In the meantime, with Dr Whipple's approval, he was allocated a small table in one corner of the sick berth with a lantern hanging above it. He and the two women were given strict orders not to disturb each other, and he was not allowed to invite his Irish mates to visit him.

There were only certain documents the captain allowed the scribe access to, such as inventories, weekly accounts from the purser and carpenter, warrant officer's reports and the ship's daily log. Though Oliver's hand was much improved from the scratch he had suffered in his fight with van Zetten, he was happy to pass over some of the mundane but necessary tasks he was required to attend to.

These special duties, however, did not prevent the new seaman from participating in gun practice and daily shipboard chores. Being rated as an idler meant he worked daylight hours, unless all hands were called to action stations at any time of the day or night.

Michael O'Connor was unmistakably Irish in appearance, with bright orange hair and green eyes. He spoke with a strong accent that had a poetic lilt about it but, because he spoke so quickly, Oliver found it hard at times to understand what he was saying. However, that was something the captain would soon get used to. At only a little over five feet in height and with a soft fair-skinned but freckled complexion, he looked more like a boy than a man, but he assured Captain Quintrell he was all of three-and-thirty years.

Oliver pondered over the man's background, but did not question him at length. He wondered if he had left Ireland before the uprising or had escaped to Liverpool after it was over. He had assured the captain he had only met the Irish fellows, with whom he had boarded, in a public house in Liverpool, and though they had their heritage in common, they had not known each other before setting sail on a merchant ship bound for America.

Like all Irishmen, they believed America was the land of opportunity and, with no families to support, they had outlaid the last of their savings on a passage to New York. What they did not know when they embarked at the Liverpool docks was that the ship was old and wormy and, before they reached the Western Isles, they found themselves working the pumps to help keep it afloat. After everything that could be jettisoned was thrown overboard, the group of Irishmen, along with the other passengers and their families, could do nothing more than pray for a miracle.

Before that arrived, the ship succumbed to the sea north of the island of São Miguel. Fortunately for most of the passengers, the hull floated for two days but sadly some of the women and children were unable to hang on in the cold and were washed into the sea.

But the prayers of the remaining souls were answered when a whale-ship was sighted. The captain of the whaler had little choice but to take the survivors aboard, but being in pursuit of a pod of right whales, he had no intention of losing his quarry. This meant that the destitute passengers and crew of the shipwreck were obliged to remain within the whaler's stinking hull until this was achieved. Confined in the narrow spaces between the barrels, they hardly had space to turn around while the air they breathed was a stinking fug from the pots of blubber boiled on the deck above them. The smell invaded every inch of the ship.

Though they were adequately fed, they were obliged to endure the discomfort for four full weeks. Only when the captain was satisfied with the number of barrels of oil he had filled, did he agree to deliver the unfortunate survivors to the wharf at Ponta Delgado. It was on the wharf that the six Irishmen, along with the other passengers, were greeted by Mr Read, the British Consul, who offered the men work on his farm for a few weeks.

Having survived with little but the clothes they stood up in, the Irishmen were grateful for the chance to work and, though their wages were paltry, they were fed and housed and looked after. The warm sun and mild climate quickly healed their memories. Even though they were rough and unkempt in appearance, Mrs Read particularly appreciated their company. They entertained her with descriptions and stories of the parts of Ireland they had originally come from and, though it wasn't England, she always enjoyed hearing news from Britain.

Despite their rescue, the group of Irishmen still aimed to reach America and settle there. But, over the past two months, the only American ships entering the port had been heading east and not west. When they learned that a British frigate was about to set sail across the Atlantic, bound for Brazil, they jumped at the chance of a passage. Whatever port the ship stopped at on the continent of South America, they didn't care. They intended to work and save and eventually make passage north. Word was spreading, however, of opportunities to buy cheap farm land in Chile, and three of them, including O'Connor, considered heading around the Horn and trying their luck in a country that had no objection where a man came from, providing he was prepared to work hard for a living.

As far as Oliver Quintrell was concerned, the future of the six men was their concern and the least said about it the better. His own concern was to bring *Perpetual* safely into Rio de Janeiro.

The wardroom aboard His Majesty's frigate *Perpetual* buzzed with the sounds of young midshipmen eager to advance themselves, wanting to learn and anxious to impress—especially when invited to share a meal with the ship's senior officers. They were all endowed with an ample dose of high spirits and bravado on the outside, but for the youngest ones, not long torn from hearth, home and a doting mother, the idea of escaping on an adventure, of fighting for one's country, of proudly wearing the uniform of the British Navy and rising rapidly up the ranks and returning home to a hero's welcome was merely the illusion they brought with them when they stepped aboard. But, within weeks of sailing, that illusion was packed away beneath a pile of neatly ironed shirts and handkerchiefs in the bottom of their sea chests. The few occasions when they donned their best stockings and clean shirts, were the times the illusion was allowed to re-surface. For some, it served to remind them that a successful naval career was generally a glorified dream of their fathers whereas for the young men themselves it was often a nightmare.

Within the safe and enviable environment of the wardroom, a sanctum just one step away from the captain's cabin, the proud young middies thrived on the thought of advancement and, for the moment, were in their element. While invited to share their anecdotes and quips with the lieutenants, their lack of worldliness failed to warn them that they were often being goaded and held to ridicule. The longer-serving midshipmen were more cognizant of the fact and often joined in the play at the expense of the tender-aged newcomers. That evening's ribald tales, teasing and titillating taunts ceased abruptly when Captain Quintrell joined the gathering. Chairs screeched on the deck as the officers attempted to stand upright, though for the taller ones, the height of the overhead beams made that impossible.

'Be seated, gentlemen,' the captain said, after being invited to take a seat at the head of the table. A servant was quick to fill a glass for the captain and refill those of the officers that were empty.

'Thank you for joining us, Captain,' Mr Parry said, his words echoed by a murmur of applause from the company. With space for only a dozen chairs placed closely together around the table, several of the middies sat on the sea chests that ran down the sides of the oblong room.

'I appreciate the invitation to dine with you,' the captain said to the row of young faces eager with expectation. 'It has been some weeks since we sailed from Gibraltar and during that time we have been obliged to overcome one thing or another that has threatened to engulf our wooden world. At times it has not been easy for any of us. At times you have felt fear. But let me remind you, fear can be an insidious disease. Yet, during battle, when you are faced with a broadside, you have no time to give way to fear. Your attention must be totally consumed by the action—the speed and agility of your gun crews, the correct elevation of the gun, the welfare of the men in your division. Whether you are dowsing a fire on a burning deck or dragging a man's legs from beneath the wheels of a gun carriage, you must forget all fear. You must do what has to be done and only by those means will you succeed. I give you a toast, gentlemen. To success.'

The toast was received with the clatter of hands beating on the table, and the atmosphere relaxed.

The captain continued. 'You can tell the men in your divisions that the work carried out on the island has proved worthwhile.' He turned to the sailing master. 'Mr Mundy informs me that for the past three hours we have been making eight knots. That is most satisfactory. Let us hope we can continue across the Atlantic at this speed.'

There was a general feeling of approval with heads nodding and glasses being emptied.

'On a more serious note, gentlemen, although we suffered only four deaths when we took the *San Nicola*, the doctor is still concerned about half a dozen men who have not yet fully recovered from the injuries they sustained in the fight. That includes four from Mr Tully's division, one from Mr Nightingale's, and also the cooper. I ask you to include the recovery of these men in your prayers as the good doctor needs all the help he can muster in such cases.'

'You did not include yourself in the list of injured,' the surgeon ventured to add.

Glancing down to his right hand bound in bandages, the captain made light of it. 'There was little of the hand remaining to injure,' he said flippantly, 'However, without realizing it at the time, I managed to acquire a scratch from van Zetten's sword. The doctor tells me I was fortunate the blade was well whetted and cut cleanly. Had it been a rusted cutlass, he would have been less confidant of it healing so quickly.'

He continued. 'Let me not hold up the meal, gentlemen. I don't doubt the cook has been preparing this for hours. I'm sure the smells issuing from the galley oven have heightened everyone's appetite including the crew's. I trust the beef, freshly butchered on the island, will satisfy the mess. I am pleased to announce that we now have ample supplies to carry us to Rio de Janeiro. Let us acknowledge our safe delivery from the Western Isles and drink to an uneventful passage across the Atlantic.'

The second toast was echoed around the table as the first dishes of the meal were delivered to the table.

Two hours later, when the last of the empty platters were removed and fresh candles lit, the young midshipmen were prompted to take their leave. As was customary, each in turn, politely expressed his thanks to the senior officer of the wardroom then made his obedience to the captain. In a few cases, the apparent lack of balance could not be entirely blamed on the movement of the ship. Once the last of the middies had gone, the remaining company relaxed.

'Gentlemen,' the captain said, looking across the table at the gathered company, 'as you are aware, our destination is the coast of Brazil. I know the men have not been idle over the past two weeks, far from it, but their attention has been taken from their regular duties. Therefore, during the coming week, if we lose the wind, and I can almost guarantee that we will, we shall practice the guns. I intend to heave to and take advantage of the open ocean. Let us see the divisions put in their very best efforts. A little competition between the gun crews will not be a bad thing. Besides that, now is a good time to attend to other items that have been neglected.'

The men waited for further orders.

'The sun, while pleasant, dries out the deck and rots the hammock netting. I have observed much of the netting, running the length of the ship, is encrusted in salt and fraying in parts, not to mention shot holes from previous action. If any man aboard was a fisherman, he will know how to knot a net. Hammock netting, while thicker and bulkier, is little different. It is not a difficult task. I know it for a fact, because I learned that skill from my grandfather and I am sure the sail maker or bosun will be happy to provide instruction. But, let me remind you not to discard any good lengths of hard, dry rope. I want those kept for hanging the next band of pirates we encounter.'

Chapter 15

Unwelcome News

'Sail, astern!'

'How does she bear?' Mr Nightingale demanded.

With only a smudge of canvas visible on horizon, it took the lookout a few moments to consider the direction.

'Heading south-westerly, sir.'

Mr Parry, who was also on the quarterdeck, passed a message to the midshipman. 'Mr Hanson, please advise the captain that a sail has been sighted. He asked to be informed.'

'Aye, aye, Mr Parry.'

Standing at the taff rail with telescopes to their eyes, the officers offered their opinions as to what the vessel was.

'Evening, Simon,' Oliver said, when he stepped on deck. 'What do we have?'

'Sail astern. The lookout did well spotting it.'

The captain took the glass offered to him and ran it along the eastern horizon. From the setting sun, the scrap of square canvas was rose tinted, but with the eastern sky already growing dark, it would soon be swallowed up by the night.

'I wonder what its business is,' Oliver said, more to himself than to his lieutenant. 'What are we making?'

'Three knots on the last heave of the log, but we are losing whatever breeze there is. Unless the wind picks up, it's unlikely that ship will gain on us in the next few hours and then we'll likely lose him in the night.'

'Unless it is following us for some reason,' Oliver said, holding the glass steady on its target. 'I suggest you double the lookouts and, at first light, advise me of its position.'

He snapped the telescope shut. 'The Atlantic is a broad stretch of ocean. I have crossed it a number of times and found that invariably I can sail four thousand miles and never see another ship. At other times, however, if I see one then I see several.'

Simon Parry did not comment.

'When did we see the American barque?'

'Four days ago. But that was heading east.'

'And nothing else sighted until now?'

'That is correct.'

'Maintain your course, Mr Parry, but have the men keep a keen lookout. I shall go below.'

As the sun rose the following morning, the golden orb fanned the eastern sky and the lookout reported on the sail in their wake.

Mr Tully was on deck when the captain stepped up. 'There are two of them, Captain,' he announced. 'Frigates, I believe.'

'What colours are they flying?'

'The lookout can't say.'

Oliver acknowledged with a nod.

'They've gained a little on us. Not a great deal. They are maintaining the same course we're on.'

The captain and his first officer watched Mr Tully scamper up the rigging like a regular foremast Jack. He always appeared more at ease in the crosstrees than in the wardroom.

After joining the lookout, he talked briefly with the lookout, searched the horizon with his telescope and pointed to what, from the deck was but a pair of grey smudges on the rim of the sea. After nodding in apparent agreement, the lieutenant slid down one of the stays to deliver his findings.

'Two Portuguese Frigates from Ponta Delgada, probably heading for the coast of Brazil and Rio de Janeiro.'

'How can you know they are not Spanish or French?'

'I recognized the foretops'l of the leading ship. It was flying the same sail when it arrived in the roadstead at Ponta Delgada.'

'Are you certain?'

'Absolutely, Capt'n. It's been patched recently. The whole centre panel is new hempen canvas still thick with gum. It's almost brown and stands out against the white sun-bleached panels of the rest of the sail. If you ask the sail maker, he'll tell you I'm not wrong. He commented on it when we were entering the harbour. That sail belongs to one of the frigates of the Portuguese fleet.'

Oliver was impressed. 'Thank you, Mr Tully. A useful observation.' He turned to Mr Parry and the sailing master who had joined them on the quarterdeck, 'it appears we may have company.'

'Do we beat to quarters?' the lieutenant asked.

'Not necessary,' the captain said. 'It is unlikely Portugal has transferred its allegiance to Emperor Napoleon during the short time we have been at sea. We must welcome our ally. However, it will do no harm to have all hands at the ready.'

With the change of watch, sailors from the starboard watch streamed up from below and the deck hummed with the sound of feet and muffled voices as word of the two frigates passed quickly from one man to another. With an estimated time of many hours for the two ships to come within speaking distance, the captain ordered sail to be reduced. He was eager to receive any news they would be carrying,

Two hours later, the two Portuguese frigates swam alongside and all three ships hove to within half a cable's length of each other. While preparations to lower a boat to the water from one of the frigates were observed, *Perpetual*'s officers and crew prepared a welcoming party to greet the visiting captain.

Captain Espada was a man of about forty years. He was accompanied by a lieutenant who appeared to be slightly younger. After a formal greeting on deck, the pair was conducted to the captain's cabin where refreshments awaited them.

'I understand you are heading to Brazil, Captain Quintrell.' The officer's English was remarkably good.

'That is so. And you, Captain?'

'We are heading to South America, also. Our government is concerned about any recent activity by the Spanish on the *Rio de la Plata* since the signing of the alliance with France.'

'Do you think Napoleon will try to extend his empire to South America?'

'It is a long way from France, but who can tell?'

Oliver invited the visitors to join him at his table. 'Perhaps you would care to sample some of the fine cheese from your Western Islands? I admit I could easily become partial to this particular variety.'

'Thank you, Captain Quintrell, but this is not a social visit.'

Oliver studied the face of the officer across the table from him.

'You were in Ponta Delgada a little over a week ago, I understand.'

'Indeed. After a lengthy stay in Gibraltar, we left the colony in mid-December and sailed to the Azores to pick up food and water.'

'I was surprised to learn that you were not heading back to England.'

'I follow Admiralty orders,' Oliver said.

'As do I.'

For a moment there was silence.

'I must be honest when I say I was disappointed when I sighted your frigate last evening.'

'Why is that, Captain?' Oliver asked.

'I was hoping to see a ship and perhaps a schooner sailing with it.'

Oliver shook his head. 'The only ship we have seen is an American barque heading east.'

'We saw her also and spoke her briefly.'

'Do you have a message you wish passed to these ships should we encounter them?'

'No message,' the Portuguese captain said. 'My orders are to find these ships and escort them back to Ponta Delgada. They departed the harbour unexpectedly one day after the majority of the fleet sailed.'

'I pray the ship you are referring is not the *San Nicola*?' The sickening feeling of utter disbelief coursing through Oliver's veins was reflected on the face of his first lieutenant.

'Indeed I am. The very ship you escorted into the harbour, I am told.'

'My goodness,' Oliver exclaimed, refraining from delivering the stream of the less dignified expletives on the tip of his tongue. 'How could that possibly be? That ship had prisoners confined in the hold awaiting judgement. Were those men released?'

'I cannot answer that,' the Portuguese captain said. 'I do not know. It was a time of confusion with the fire and disturbance and all the upheaval that was going on in the town.'

'What?' Oliver was dumbfounded. 'Pray tell. I know nothing of these events.'

Captain Espada explained. 'On the afternoon following the departure of most of the vessels in our fleet, smoke was seen rising from the inner city. It appears it came from two separate fires, one at the slaughterhouse and another at the jail that abuts the courthouse. Both fires quickly spread to adjacent houses.'

'What caused the fires? Were they deliberately lit?'

'I understand they were caused by the movement in the earth. It is blamed on the volcanoes from which these islands originally arose. Such activity is not unusual in the Azores. It may be that lighted candles were knocked to the floor igniting straw used for bedding. Who knows? Of course, the jail had to be evacuated and the prisoners relocated to the watch-house at the garrison. It was during the chaos and panic at the fear of the fires spreading that *San Nicola* hauled its anchor and departed the harbour.'

Oliver took a deep breath. 'I presume you are aware, I captured that ship and its piratical crew and brought them into the port. When I sailed, I understood those prisoners would remain aboard awaiting the arrival of a judge from Lisbon. Are you telling me that these prisoners overpowered the guards and took the ship?'

Captain Espada shrugged. 'Again, I do not know what happened, but I am instructed to watch out for her and, if I find her, to escort her to into Guanabara Bay and hand the ship and crew to the Portuguese authorities in Rio de Janeiro.'

'And the prisoners from the jail? Were they all secured elsewhere?'

'Unfortunately, a handful escaped. A thorough search of the town was made but the escapees were not found.'

'What!' Oliver could not absorb what he was hearing. His worst nightmare was unfolding before him. 'Do you have the identities of the men who are still roaming the streets?'

'No, Captain, I do not have that information. I sailed before the problem was resolved. If you want to learn more, you will have to return to Ponta Delgada and speak with the civil authorities there.'

Oliver felt the blood draining from his cheeks and clenched his teeth.

Understanding his captain's state of utter disbelief, Mr Parry politely continued the conversation. 'That is not good news, Captain. However, we appreciate the information, but what makes you think this ship would be heading this way? After all, it had just completed a long voyage from the South Atlantic. I hardly think it would be retracing its course, especially as it was in dire need of provisions and water at the time we departed.'

'I asked myself the same question, Lieutenant Parry, but it was sighted south of Pico, one of the other islands of the Azores. The American barque, we encountered two days ago, confirmed he had seen two ships heading west.'

'Two?' Oliver queried. 'The ship I delivered was sailing alone.'

Captain Espada inclined his head. 'It appears it is now in the company of a schooner. You may have seen it in the harbour—the *Silver Cloud*, a 400 ton three-masted schooner with a black hull. A Company vessel. It berthed at the wharf in Ponta Delgada two or three days before the fire. It was returning from the East Indies and broke its voyage intending to fill the remaining space in its hold with fruit and pottery. Its destination was London. On the night of the fire, the schooner sailed without advising the port authority and, the following morning, boxes of oranges were found sitting on the quay along with some of its cargo of pottery. There was no sign of the ship. When I was preparing to weigh, the schooner's master was on the wharf at his wit's end. He had spent the night ashore at the invitation of an East India Company shareholder. Can you imagine the shock he would have experienced on returning to his ship, only to discover it had gone?'

Oliver shook his head in utter disbelief. 'In a harbour filled with ships, you are saying that no one witnessed these events?'

'Believe me, sir, I do not jest.'

'Captain, I spoke with Captain Ruiz of your navy and warned him of the man who captained the *San Nicola*. His name is Fredrik van Zetten. He is a murderous cut-throat and a pirate to boot.'

'Strong words, Captain.'

Oliver continued. 'Is it too much to hope that this man is not at liberty and has not taken command of one or both of these vessels?'

'If that is the case and you happen to see either of these ships, it would be wise to steer clear of them and advise the Portuguese authorities of their whereabouts when you reach Rio. If this Captain van Zetten is indeed in command and I find him, I will deal with him myself.'

'Captain Espada, I wish you luck, but advise you now if I encounter this villain before you, he will not reach Rio de Janeiro—or any other port for that matter. It will give me the greatest of pleasure to blow him and his crew clean out of the water.'

The Portuguese captain did not respond to Oliver's threat.

'However,' Oliver said, 'as we are on the same course heading for Rio, perhaps we can *rendezvous* off Fernando de Noronha. Do you know the islands?'

'Naturally. They are only two hundred miles off the coast of Brazil.'

'And a good source of wood and water that van Zetten will be in dire need of.'

The captain agreed. 'We will meet at the islands. In the meantime, we will scour the seas to the south from here, if you will scan the waters to the north.'

The meeting with the Portuguese frigate captain had begun cordially, but the disquieting news left a bitter taste. Though Captain Espada was in no way responsible for the events that had occurred in Ponta Delgada, and was merely conveying a message, the impression his words delivered was that it was regarded as unfortunate the ships had disappeared, but that the authorities were not unduly concerned. The fact Captain Espada's ship and the other frigate happened to be on the lookout for them was merely a fortunate coincidence because, by chance, they were heading in the same direction.

With no time to waste on further trivial conversation, Captain Quintrell thanked his visitor and ended the meeting abruptly. On deck, the guests were given a hasty, but dignified farewell, and the captain immediately returned below to consider the devastating news with his first officer.

'One thing puzzles me,' Oliver said. 'Why would van Zetten head back across the Atlantic? From what we saw, his men were half-starved, his ship was ill-supplied and, if he wanted prizes, the African coast or the Mediterranean Sea would have offered far richer pickings.'

Simon Parry's answer confirmed an idea Oliver had fostered in his mind. 'As you said, this man is the epitome of evil. He cares for no one but himself. Only one thing will now satisfy him and it isn't a hold of filled barrels, or a contented crew, or even prize money or cases of silver coins. This man takes what he wants whenever he wants it and, so far, no one has been brave enough to stand up to him. What Captain van Zetten demands is to wreak revenge on the one person who blocked his path and almost cost him his life. And that is you, Oliver. I believe his sights are set on finding you and killing you.'

Chapter 16

The Mermaid

The lookout scanned the horizon searching for any sign of Fernando de Noronha, the small group of twenty-one isolated islands lying three degrees south of the Equator and only two hundred miles off the coast of Brazil.

Word, that the frigate was nearing land was reason for excitement. It quickly spread through the ship. To sailors, land meant one of two possibilities—shore leave, taverns, tobacco and women; or working parties, either to satisfy the on-going appetite of the galley fire, or to wet the parched throats of thirsty crew.

Like the Azores, the small archipelago had risen from the seabed aeons ago. The active volcanoes had once formed a high mountain range but, over the millennia, the sea had slowly drowned them and now only the cores of the dead peaks remained.

As a general rule, there were few geographical locations around the world the seasoned hands had not visited, and even if their ship had not anchored to allow them to sample the ports and all they offered, at least someone knew something of the place—the bars, the beauties, the bounties and the things to be avoided. With Fernando de Noronha, however, though questions were asked in the mess, not a single man aboard had ever heard of the location, let alone ever stepped ashore on the beaches. Someone claimed that Bungs would have known, but the cooper was still confined to his cot in the sick berth. The fact he had not died from the brain fever was encouraging.

Under a cornflower blue sky with the sea a slightly darker shade, the glassy surface was broken only occasionally by the head of a turtle popping up, open-mouthed, to suck in air, or a pod of dolphins showing off their aquatic skills. With the equatorial air blowing warm on the sailors' bare chests, the frigate was making a respectable five knots ahead of a following wind.

A gull landed on the bowsprit and was content to rest for a while. Even the occasional slap from the flying jib did not disturb it. Being a land bird, the seagull never strayed too far from home, so the arrival of several more of its kind meant land was not far away.

Despite the buzz of anticipation, decks still had to be holystoned, hammocks aired and brightwork polished, but once the morning's chores had been completed and breakfast finished, the duty watch was able to relax on deck and wait for the next call.

It was mid-morning when the first peak of the island group was sighted.

'Land!' the lookout called down. 'It's a towering sugar loaf.'

'We have raised Fernando de Noronha,' Oliver said, when he heard. 'That is well. We shall circumnavigate the main island and, hopefully, meet with the two Portuguese frigates as arranged. '

Heading south-west, skirting the broad bays and inlets of the main island, *Perpetual* glided across a translucent sea. The colours of the water reflected the changing depth—turquoise to emerald, aquamarine to peacock blue, and lapis lazuli to sapphire. Edged by narrow bands of golden beaches, the coast was breathtakingly beautiful even to the eyes of seasoned sailors. Littering the bays were tiny islets and giant rocks rising vertically from the seabed. Their sharply-chiselled, coal-black faces reared up in stark contrast to the gleaming sand.

The verdant forest that covered the hills and ran down to the shores appeared too thick to be penetrated. It provided an ideal sanctuary for the many birds nesting there. Apart from the birdsong and lilt of the lapping waves on the shores, there were no other sounds. There were few places on earth that offered such an idyllic setting.

Suddenly, a dull thud vibrated from the forward strakes and jolted everyone's senses.

'What was that?' the captain called, haring up the companion from the gun deck. It was like the sound of a solid four-pound shot hitting the hull, but there had been no calls and he had heard no cannon fire.

'We must have struck something,' Mr Parry replied. 'It came from the bow.'

Hurrying forward, the pair scanned the water expecting to see another ship or submerged rock, but there were neither. The six fathoms of water beneath the keel were crystal clear, revealing a clean sandy bottom free of seaweed. Bare feet padded along the deck as sailors ran around the ship peering from the rails on both sides, but nothing could be seen.

'Masthead, ahoy. Do you see any ships or boats?'

The lookout turned a full three hundred and sixty degrees. 'No, Capt'n.'

'On your feet, Smithers,' Mr Tully bellowed, after almost tripping over the legs of the sailor sitting on the deck. 'Out of the way!'

'You there!' Mr Parry called to another sailor who had leapt off the head in such a hurry his trousers were still wrinkled around his ankles. 'For goodness sake, man, attend to your dress. The captain is talking to you.'

The captain continued. 'From where you were perched, you must have seen something.'

Prescott hitched up his trousers, but didn't answer. His face was drained and his hands were shaking.

'What is wrong with this man?' Oliver asked his lieutenant.

Smithers was smart with an answer. 'Stupid dawcock said he saw a mermaid. I told him he was as barmy as Bungs. Then he changed his mind and said it wasn't a mermaid, it was an angel.'

'Mind your tongue!' Mr Parry reminded.

The captain raised his eyebrows and exchanged a puzzled look with his first lieutenant.

But Smithers hadn't finished. 'The oaf said he heard it knocking like it wanted to come aboard, and when he leaned over to see what it was, it rose up from the water and tried to bite him. If you ask me, I think it was trying to kiss him.'

The men standing nearby sniggered, but Prescott's expression did not change.

'Thank you, Smithers,' Mr Tully said sarcastically. 'We don't need any of your stupid remarks.'

The captain turned back to the sailor. 'Enough of this cock-and-bull rubbish, Prescott, what exactly was it you saw?'

'It's just what Smithers told you, Capt'n. And it scared the livin' daylights out of me.'

'Just as well he was sitting on the head!' the sailor quipped, with a toothless grin.

'Smithers! Go below this instant!'

Mumbling and dragging his feet, the old topman left the deck.

The captain continued. 'And what did this *mermaid* do after it popped up from the water?'

'It sank back down and I didn't wait around to see if it would come up again.'

Oliver turned to the other members of the fo'c'sle division who were standing within earshot. 'Did anyone else see this apparition?'

Murmurs about mermaids and sea monsters ran round the foredeck, but no one had seen anything, although several admitted to hearing the sound of knocking.

'Sounded like the carpenter in the hold tapping the hull with a wooden mallet,' one said.

'It was no bloody apparition,' Prescott claimed adamantly. 'I tell you it was real and I don't ever want to see it again.'

'Watch your language,' Mr Tully warned.

'Masthead!' the captain called. 'Keep a keen look-out.'

'Aye, aye,' the reply came down. But there was not a soul on the island's beaches and the rim of the sea carried nothing on it.

'It's over there!' Midshipman Hanson called from amidships, causing all heads to turn and sailors to rush to the starboard side.

'What do you see?'

'Can't rightly say, sir. It could be the back of a whale, an upturned canoe or a mighty big turtle. It's swimming just below the surface.'

'Bring us about, Mr Tully,' the captain ordered. 'Back to your stations, men.'

Mr Hanson, keep an eye on its position. Don't let it out of your sight for one instant. I want to know what hit us. And get the carpenter to sound the ship and check the hull for damage.'

'Aye, aye, sir.'

The calls went out. The sailors scattered. The yards creaked and the staysails rattled as they were hauled across to the other tack.

'It's still there, sir. It must be a log to float like that.'

'Tell the helmsman not to get too close. Have the deck hands ready to fend off if it gets too close.'

It took some time to wear the frigate around and bring it back to where the midshipman claimed the submerged object was lurking just below the surface.

'It's over there!' one of the topmen shouted from the main yard, causing a rush of bodies across the deck. It was now on the opposite side of the vessel and more than twice the ship's length away. Either Prescott's mermaid had dived and swum with the speed of a porpoise or Mr Hanson had lost sight of it when the frigate turned.

With the wind spilled from her sails, the helmsman steered to where the topman was pointing and brought the frigate to within a few feet of it. When *Perpetual* drifted slowly alongside, the waves combined with the ship's wake caused the large piece of flotsam to roll over. The realization of its source was greeted with an explosion of shrieks and jeers from the company gathered on deck.

Lifting her head from the water was Prescott's mermaid. Yellow wavy hair trailed over her lily-white shoulders. A loosely fitted blue cowl framed the angelic face. With her arms reaching out in front of her, the delicate hands cradled a white dove, its wings extended as if attempting to fly. For a few moments, her blue eyes gazed directly at the frigate's crew and her voluptuous curves were shown to best advantage. Then, as if embarrassed by all the attention, she turned over again and buried her face in the sea. Only then was the extent of the injury to her back evident. The timbers running down from the centre of her spine to the short platform on which her feet rested had been badly damaged. Though once securely fastened to the bowsprit of a ship, the splintered timber revealed where the proud effigy had been hacked away or shot clean off.

'Your mermaid,' Captain Quintrell announced.

It was a great joke to almost everyone, but a joke Prescott would not live down in a hurry.

'Do you want the men to fish it out?' Mr Parry asked.

The captain shook his head. 'It's of little use to us. However, enter it on the board with the time and position. I will report it when we raise Rio de Janeiro. I can only deduce that it belonged to a ship that has gone down in the Atlantic and the current has floated to this spot.'

'How long would you estimate it has been in the water?' Lieutenant Parry asked.

'Not long, I'd wager. It is perfectly clean.'

'Do you think the ship sank close to these waters?'

Oliver had already drawn his own conclusion, but he was more concerned about the ship that had fired the lethal shot than the item floating in the water.

Having just returned to the deck with his sketch pad and pencil, Mr Nightingale was eager to make a drawing of the mermaid he had just heard about. But, like most modest women, the carved lady appeared embarrassed by the artist's attention and insisted on turning her face from him.

'Too shy to stay long enough for the men to get a good eyeful,' Mr Tully said, with a cheeky grin.

'I've seen it before,' Mr Nightingale announced to expressions of surprise. 'In the harbour at Ponta Delgada and again only a week ago.'

He had the captain's full attention. 'Of course,' Oliver said, as his memory was pricked. 'It's the figurehead from one of those Portuguese frigates.'

'Begging your pardon, Captain,' Eku interrupted. 'That ship's name was *Pomba Branca*. In Portuguese it means—white dove. That's the bird the lady's holding in her hand.'

'Thank you, Eku.' The information was interesting, but the fact the figurehead had been blown off the bowsprit of one of the naval vessels confirmed his worst fears. Having arranged to *rendezvous* with the two Portuguese frigates at this group of islands, he expected to find them in these waters at this time.

Had the pair had been ambushed and sunk by van Zetten and the other ship? he wondered. *God forbid.* But they had heard no sounds of gunfire. He thought of the two days he had spent hove to in the Atlantic practising the guns. *Damnation.* He should have arrived here earlier. Then he wondered if the frigates had sailed together or had separated and entered the waters alone. Surely it wasn't possible that both would be lost.

'Mr Parry, all hands on deck, if you please.'

'Deck there!' the call came from the masthead.

'What is it? What do you see? Is it a sail?' the midshipman called back.

'Something the captain would want to know about,' the lookout replied.

'If you have something to report, you will report it to me.'

'I can't exactly say. I need Mr Tully or Mr Parry to take a gander first.'

On the quarterdeck, the third lieutenant's ears were alert to any messages flowing down from the lookout. Noting the concerned tone of the sailor's voice, he strode briskly along the gangway to where the midshipman was standing gazing up into the maintop. 'Is there a problem, Mr Hanson?'

The young middie was obviously not happy, firstly, for not being given the information from the lookout he had demanded and, secondly, and more aggravatingly so, because the lieutenant had witnessed the brief exchange. He was conscious of his shortcomings, especially his inability to handle situations like this in an authoritative manner. Now he was unsure of himself also. Perhaps he should have conveyed the message to the captain without question. Annoyed, and unable to hide his feelings, he pointed aloft. 'The lookout said he saw something, but he is incapable of forming an opinion as to what it is.'

'I'll speak with him,' Mr Tully said, but rather than wasting words with the middie, he leapt up onto to the weather rail, grabbed the shroud and swung himself into the ratlines. It was another opportunity to climb into the tops and, for him, the more swell there was on the ocean, the more he enjoyed the challenge.

'I'm glad it's you, Mr Tully,' the lookout said, when the officer climbed onto the platform.

'I warn you, Brown, you'd best watch yourself with young Mr Hanson. If he thinks you are being obstreperous, he's likely to pin a charge of insolence on you.'

The lookout shrugged. 'Better that happen than him going off half-cocked to the captain, if I happened to be wrong.'

Mr Tully was not interested in the lookout's problems. His concern was with the reason for his call to the deck. Hooking his arm around the main's topmast, he scanned the sea and shoreline, but there was nothing in particular to attract his attention. 'Where should I be looking?' he asked.

'You must wait a moment until that great rock slides away and you can see into the next bay. Then you'll spy it. I just caught a glimpse, but I'd bet a week's ration of grog that it's a submerged wreck.'

'A ship? A boat? What was it?'

'A ship, but what she was is hard to tell. She'd not smashed on the rocks. Looks like she's filled and gone down. I'd say she's sitting on the sand with water over her rails.

'What is she? How many masts?'

'Three stumps,' the sailor said bluntly.

'You mean the masts are broken? Is she dragging canvas in the water?'

The sailor shrugged.

Mr Tully frowned at the description he'd been given but, while they were speaking, *Perpetual* rounded the large rock to reveal a small semi-circular bay with a narrow beach of golden sand. The water lapping the beach was aquamarine and as translucent as any tropical lagoon. Sitting half a cable's length from the shore was a submerged hull. Stripped of all its tophamper—topmasts, yards and rigging, and displaying a clear deck, it resembled the hull of a recently launched ship built at a private shipyard when it was ready to be floated to the Portsmouth Naval Dockyard to have its masts stepped and be fully-rigged and fitted out.

'That's mighty odd,' Mr Tully said, 'the remains of the masts appear to have been sawn off a few feet above the deck, and there's no sign of spars or sails or an inch of line anywhere.'

'That's what I thought. Strange, isn't it? I didn't want to shout it down in case I was wrong. I'd have sounded like a regular idiot.'

Mr Tully nodded. 'You did right. I'll inform the captain. He'll want to see this for himself before we get too close. And, he'll want to get some canvas off if we are going to investigate. Keep watch,' he reminded, as he swung himself down from the platform. 'Don't worry about the wreck, that ain't going nowhere. Just keep a keen eye out for other ships.'

Grabbing one of the stays, the lieutenant, wound his left foot behind it and locked the right in front and slid down the rigging to where the midshipman was waiting.

'So what did he see?' Mr Hanson asked rather defiantly. But Mr Tully was not about to reveal his findings to the middie and headed straight down to the waist. He needed to pass on the information to the captain.

Within minutes the captain and his second lieutenant were heading back along the deck. As they passed the binnacle, Mr Tully grabbed a glass from the quartermaster.

'All hands on deck, Mr Parry,' the captain called. 'Prepare to heave to.'

'Aye, aye, sir.'

The order was given and men streamed up from below peering about to see what the reason was for the call.

After quickly removing his coat, the captain handed it to the midshipman who was peeved at being ignored. Following Mr Tully, he climbed the rigging with dozens of eyes watching his every step.

'Brown?'

The topmast man knuckled his forehead. 'That's me, sir.'

'What do you see?'

The sailor pointed, 'It's a hulk, sir. Little more than the top of the cap rails above water.'

'By God, if I'm not mistaken, it's one of the Portuguese frigates.'

The sailor looked hard. 'How do you know that, sir?'

'The size of it. The shape of the stern and the position of those masts—or what is left of them.' He examined the wreck through his glass. 'How strange, they have been sawn off, as you suggested. I don't understand. Who would take masts yet not bother to un-step them?'

'I don't know, sir,' the lookout answered, but it had been a rhetorical question that Captain Quintrell had already formed an answer to.

'I'll tell you who would,' Oliver said. 'A piratical blackguard who would give his right arm for spare spares, sails and rigging, yet does not have enough men to do the job properly.'

'Deck there,' Oliver shouted down, leaning away from the mast. 'Mr Parry, all hands to quarters and bear away from the coast.'

With nothing more to be gained from the position in the maintop, the captain climbed down to the deck by the ratlines. Below the familiar sounds of the ship being cleared for action were evident. Mr Parry and the other officers waited anxiously on the quarterdeck for further orders.

'That pirate, van Zetten, is lurking in these waters. I am sure of it,' Oliver said.

'What could you see, Captain? What happened here?' Mr Parry asked.

'I believe one of the Portuguese frigate captains encountered this madman when he least expected it. The smaller frigate was well armed and carried 22 guns, but I believe he was probably taken by surprise and attacked by two ships, not one.'

'Does he need our assistance?'

'No. We have arrived too late. She has gone down.'

'Are there any boats on the water? Surely the crew would not have given up their ship without a fight.'

'I agree. There are many unanswered questions. As to survivors, there was no sign.'

'What about flotsam or bodies?'

'From this distance, I could see nothing, only some seals hauled up on the sand. What worries me, however, is that there is not a single gun on the weather deck.' Oliver Quintrell had already formed an opinion as to where they would be, and it was unlikely they had been pushed overboard.

'What are your orders, Captain?'

'We stand off the coast and watch and wait. It may be a trap. I put nothing past the evil cunning of Fredrik van Zetten. The men will remain at their stations throughout the night. In the morning, when I am certain we are not being lured by this predator, I will take two boats and go ashore. I want to examine the wreck and search for survivors. It's possible some of the crew have escaped inland to hide, but it is equally possible they are strung up on a quickly constructed gallows made from the mainyard, or drowned beneath hatches in the hold, or slaughtered like beasts, or perhaps they have been taken prisoner to serve on one of his ships, as seems to be his usual practice.'

The expressions around him were as grave as his own.

'Because the spars have been deliberately removed, I would expect the holds have been ransacked. The powder and shot has no doubt been stolen along with cordage and spare sails, even tools from the tradesmen's workshops.'

'But why?'

'Think about it, Simon. The *San Nicola* had been at sea for months. We know the hold was empty and the men were limited to meagre rations. We know van Zetten was short of men—hence, the reason he kidnapped the villagers from Santa Maria. And, because of this man's history, neither he nor his ship would be welcome in any British port. If his ship needed repair, he would not have access to any reputable naval yard. Therefore, he would have to repair at sea and careen his ship as we did. The only small consolation is that the lives of any shipwright or carpenter he captured would be safe for as long as their services were required. At this stage, I would suggest, Captain van Zetten needs all the wrights he can get.'

Standing at the cabin door, the red-headed Irishman looked uncomfortable. 'Beg pardon, Captain,' Michael O'Connor said.

'What is it? Are you having problems with your work?'

'No, sir, no problems, it's just—'

'It's what? Spit it out, man. I have enough problems to attend to.'

'Might I come in, sir?'

Oliver frowned. It was a bold request. 'Step inside and close the door.'

173

The Irishman lowered his voice. 'Being disloyal to your fellow countrymen is about the worst sin you can commit in Ireland. You can make enemies real fast and get a knife in your heart even faster.'

'Has someone been threatening you?' the captain asked.

'No, sir, nothing of that nature.'

'So, what is the problem?'

'Well, it's like this, you see,' O'Connor said. 'My mates have been whispering about jumping ship at the first sight of land.'

'Indeed.'

'And here we are already. Yet from what I've heard about the sort of company you've come up against recently, I think it might not be a wise thing for them to do. I've told them so.'

'Telling tales to the ship's captain might not be very wise, either. It will certainly not win you any friends. I warn you, O'Connor, be careful with whom you speak. As for your countrymen, I can do nothing based on tittle-tattle. However, if these men decide to run and are caught, they will be brought back and punished accordingly. I presume you know what that means?'

The Irishman looked sullen and nodded.

'Approximately two weeks from today, we will drop anchor at Rio de Janeiro. Those men will then have the option to stay with the ship or be paid off, though with a deduction for the slops they collected when they came aboard and the short period of time they have served, there will be very little money due to them.' Oliver turned back to the chart he was studying. 'Now go about your business and stop bothering me with such trivia. And the next time you have a problem, speak with one of the officers on deck. Now get back to your station.'

'Aye, Captain.'

Chapter 17

Pomba Branca

At first light, with no sign of sails in any direction and no activity seen on the beach, *Perpetual* worked slowly around and hove to a mile off-shore. Although it was a long pull for the crews, the captain was not prepared to take the frigate in any closer.

In accordance with his orders, two boats were lowered. Apart from the crews, six marines and a dozen sailors armed with cutlasses and pistols accompanied the captain and Mr Tully. Although the state of the sunken vessel was a troubling sight, not a word was spoken as the boats swam past the submerged hull.

As the boats drew nearer to the beach, the captain was confronted with an appalling sight. The objects he had observed on the sand, but paid little attention to, were not seals that had hauled themselves from the water to bask in the sun, but naked grey and purple bloated carcasses. Lying face-down on the beach they little resembled the scrawny olive-skinned sailors who, until recently, had served on one of the Portuguese naval frigates.

'Don't touch them,' Oliver said, as he climbed from the boat. 'We shall bury them later.'

'Do you think these men were washed up from the wreck?'

Glancing back to the remains of the hull, Oliver cast his eyes around the bay and shook his head. Prising the toe of his shoe under one of the victim's heads, he lifted it from the ground. A tiny crab instinctively retracted its feeding claws and sidled back into the gaping hole that stretched from one side of the man's throat to the other. There was no blood. What the sand hadn't swallowed, the sun had baked into a hard black lump the size and shape of a large ship's biscuit. It was under the victim's head.

'It is obvious these men have been murdered,' he said. 'Be cautious. Corporal, guard the boats. You men come with me.'

The beach was firm under foot, as the group of ten headed along the sand. Having found nothing unusual after a brief search, the party split into two groups to check the rocks at each end of the bay. Again their search uncovered nothing, not even the men's clothing. Any footprints that had been tramped in the sand the previous day had been washed away with the previous high tide.

Overhead the equatorial sun burned down from a clear sky dotted only with circling birds. While the forest would have offered some shade from the sun, Oliver was unwilling to venture into the steep-sided woods that appeared so thick they were almost impenetrable. Frustrated, the captain returned to the waiting boats.

Unable to offer the deceased a formal burial service, the captain decided the bodies should be buried on the beach where they lay. Trying to drag them from the sand would have been impossible. He remembered the fate of the sailor who had been cooked in the boiling waters of the volcanic island in the Southern Ocean. The dead man's arm had slid from his shoulder like a bone from a well-cooked piece of salt pork. In Oliver's estimation, the condition of the dead men on the beach would be similar. The combined heat from the hot sun and burning sand would have cooked the carcasses within the casing of stretched skin.

'Corporal, remain here with your men, I shall return to the ship and send a party to bury the dead. I have a group of Irish men who are eager to step ashore.'

The crew were anxious to return to the ship, but when the boats were being pushed back into the water, a faint call was heard from the woods. Though the words were incomprehensible, the tone was disturbing. A moment later, a young man emerged from the trees. After waving his arms over his head, he stumbled to his knees. The marines grabbed their muskets, cocked them and aimed.

'Hold your fire,' Oliver called.

Regaining his feet, the man tried to run to the boats but his legs would not carry him. After falling face-first in the soft sand, he crawled on all fours. His strength was sapped and when his arms collapsed, the desire to stay alive started ebbing from him. He was only twenty yards from the water.

Oliver Quintrell and several of the sailors jumped from the boats and hurried to the man's aid. With the sand dusted from his eyes and a flask of water pressed to his lips, he responded. The expression on his face showed his relief at being found.

'Are there others?' the captain asked. 'Were you alone?' But the man's eyes rolled back in his head and his eyelids closed.

'Mr Tully, get this man aboard as quickly as possible and have the surgeon attend to him. I need to question him. I need to find out what occurred here. He is our only hope to learn the true facts.'

Several hours later, with the five Irishmen relieved to return on board from the distasteful job of burying the corpses, and with the boats secured on deck, *Perpetual* bore away from the coast.

In the cockpit, under the care of the ship's surgeon, José, a Portuguese sailor was resting peacefully. He was young, little more than sixteen years of age but, though his thirst and hunger had been replenished, his face and hands washed and a clean shirt put on him, fear still creased his face during his waking moments. That was not something which could be easily washed away.

The captain spoke slowly and, once again, his every word was translated by Ekundayo. 'Where are the men you served with? Where is the other Portuguese frigate?'

'I do not know,' the young man replied. 'I don't know where anyone is.' A tear trickled down his cheek and sank into the cot's pillow.

'Tell me what happened,' Oliver asked. 'From the beginning.'

After a rush of words and an outflow of sobs, Eku related his story as best he could. 'He said the two frigates had sailed together to Fernando de Noronha. The crew had heard the captain was to *rendezvous* with a British ship. He said that some of the men argued he was looking for two ships, others said he was meeting three. He explained that, below deck, the stories often get confused. He said they had already sailed around the islands once and didn't meet any, so while the other Portuguese ship intended to continue searching, the captain hove to and ordered two boats off to collect wood.'

'Did you go with one of the boats?' the captain asked.

The seaman's eyes glazed and his head rolled to one side. 'I went with the woodcutters.'

The doctor gently eased José's head back on to the teased-oakum pillow and dabbed his forehead with a damp cloth. 'Is this really necessary at this very moment, Captain?'

'It is,' Oliver replied, and continued with his enquiries. 'Was your ship attacked?'

'Not then. My ship *Pomba Branca* sailed off to continue searching and left a party of us on the beach. We were told the captain would return to collect us later.'

'Were you not worried?'

'Why should I be?' he said, through the interpreter. 'I was with my friends. We were happy. There was no senior officer with us, only a carpenter's mate. We felt free, even though we had a job to do. After dragging the boats up on the beach, we climbed the steep hill and went into the woods. We had our orders and knew we would be in trouble with the lieutenant if we didn't get the work done quickly.'

'How long were you away from the beach?'

'Three hours or more,' he replied. 'When we returned down the hillside, the men were loaded with wood. They carried it in their arms and had their axe handles stuffed through their belts. Some had tied twine around the bundles of kindling and balanced them on their shoulders. I had charge of the two saws. They were the length of pit saws and, as I walked, they swayed like waves on the sea. Because they were cutting into my shoulder, I stopped to find some leaves or soft bark to make a cushion to rest them on.' He pulled back his shirt and showed where the saws' teeth had chewed into his skin.

'I was last to arrive on the beach and when I came from the trees, I saw the boats were still there but Captain Espada and *Pomba Branca* had not returned. But there were two ships flying British flags hove to only a few hundred yards from the sand. One was a ship and the other a nice looking tops'l schooner. I had seen it in the harbour in Ponta Delgada. The sailors from those ships landed two boats on the beach. I thought they must be the ships the captain was meant to *rendezvous* with. The sailors from the boats seemed friendly and held out their hands to assist the wood cutters with their loads. But no sooner had they arrived near the boats and put down their axes, than these scoundrels leapt on them, throwing them on their backs and cutting their throats in the manner you would a sheep's.' The Negro translated José's faltering words. 'I could see the blood spurting from their throats and, from where I was standing, I could hear the gurgling sounds of my friends dying.'

The doctor looked anxious, but the captain persisted.

'What did you do?'

'I turned and ran like the Devil himself was after me. I knew if they caught me, I was a dead man.'

'Were you followed?'

'Yes, but they didn't catch me. I raced up the track we had cut through the woods and climbed as high as I could. I went so far I was over the top of the hill and looking down on the next bay. When I stopped, I remember my heart was thumping so loudly I was sure it would be heard on the ship. I don't know how long I was there.'

The captain and his interpreter waited for the boy to continue.

'I never saw *Pomba Branca* return but the noise I heard was like all Hell had broken loose. Even though I was scared for my life, I had to see what was happening. I climbed higher till I found a clearing where I could look down on the beach and see everything.'

'Tell me,' Oliver begged.

'*Pomba Branca* had returned, but Captain Espada could not have expected the sudden bombardment he received from the two ships waiting for him. Canister, chain and bar shot sliced across the frigate's deck, ripping the sails from the yards, the yards from the masts and tearing the men on deck to pieces. The captain was not in a position to fight though he managed to get some shots away.'

'Dear God, didn't I warn them?' Oliver cursed. 'Why did they take no heed of what I said?'

With no response from the small group gathered around the cot, Eku took José's hand and held it until the captain had composed himself and returned to his questions.

'You saw this as it happened?'

The young sailor nodded. 'I watched the tattered remains of our colours being hauled down and heard the firing stop.'

'Was *Pomba Branca* boarded?'

José nodded again. 'Four boats went alongside. I saw bodies being thrown into the sea. Those who had survived climbed down into the boats and were rowed away under guard. Then the schooner moved alongside and barrels were hoisted from *Pomba Branca* and transferred into it.'

'Just as I expected. Provisions and powder,' Oliver said.

'And cannon,' José added.

'God in heaven, imagine how many guns van Zetten now has at his disposal!'

After a sip of water, José continued. 'It took several hours to clear the ship. I was hungry and thirsty, but I dare not move. It was almost dark when the remaining stays were cut and the mizzen crashed to the deck smashing the wheel as it fell. The hull was listing badly but it was still afloat. The boats returned to collect the yards, and then the remains of the masts were sawn off and towed away. When they had taken everything, the hull was abandoned and left to drift. I hid in the forest all night and in the morning climbed to the top of the hill again. This time, the only sound I heard was the birds. Below, there were no ships apart from the wreck of *Pomba Branca* floating in the bay. The hull was sitting low in the water and the tide was washing her closer to the beach. As the day wore on, she went down and settled on the sand. Not knowing what to do or where to go, I stayed in the woods for another day and night. I was too afraid to return to the beach. And then you arrived and I recognized the red coats of the British soldiers and I knew my life was saved.'

Oliver leaned back from the swinging cot where the boy was resting. It was just as he had expected. This disastrous event confirmed his worst fear that Fredrik van Zetten now had two ships under his command. Not only was he well-supplied with ample provisions and powder, but had sufficient men to work both ships and guns, albeit the Portuguese sailors would probably be working with a cutlass blade held to their throats.

The sailing master scratched his head. 'It beats me how an undisciplined horde of pirates aboard a merchant ship managed to take a well-armed 22-gun frigate. And how could an experienced Portuguese naval captain be so easily deceived? Such a catastrophe could never happen to a British naval vessel.'

Captain Quintrell raised his eyebrows and scowled at the sailing master. 'Did it not almost happen only a few weeks ago? The only difference being that *Perpetual* was careened on a beach and could not be taken to sea. And were the frigate's officers not also fooled into complacency?'

Having been on the beach when van Zetten first came ashore, the sailing master recoiled from any further comment.

The captain continued. 'I put nothing past the cunning of this individual.' Then he turned back to Ekundayo. 'Please thank this seaman. Tell him he need have no fear now he is aboard my ship. And inform him that I intend to find this cut-throat and rescue his captain and the rest of the crew.'

The sailing master, Lieutenant Parry and the ship's surgeon regarded him quizzically.

'You heard what I said. I intend to catch this man and, when I do, I will make sure he swings from the royal yard and remains there until every ounce of flesh has rotted from his foul-smelling carcass.'

The sailing master shook his head. 'With respect, sir, he has more cunning than a starving alley cat. This atrocity happened two days ago. For all we know, he could be half-way to the Caribbean by now or on the coast of Brazil skulking in one of its slave ports.'

'I wish that were the case, but I think not. I sense Fredrik van Zetten is lurking not far from here. I cut him to the quick when I took his ship and turned him over to the authorities in the Western Isles. Little good that did.' He laughed coldly. 'In my opinion, this mongrel will not be satisfied until he has taken his revenge. It is me he wants, not my ship or my men. Me. And I don't doubt he has given a considerable amount of thought and evil imagination to the way he intends to see me die.'

'Shouldn't we make for Rio immediately and alert the authorities there?' Mr Mundy suggested. He was aware other members of the crew were of a similar mind.

Oliver Quintrell was adamant. 'Prepare to make sail. Follow the coastline.'

The expression on the sailing master's face was blank.

'That is an order, Mr Mundy. Follow the northern coast until you raise the last stone or pebble belonging to this island group, then tack and head back along the southern coast. I intend to circumnavigate the archipelago. The other Portuguese frigate is somewhere in these waters and I must locate it. As for that felon, van Zetten, I will not leave here until I have found him.'

Chapter 18

The Storm

Gazing blankly through the stern window, Oliver Quintrell clenched his teeth. 'Damn his eyes! I cannot believe he is at large again.'

Simon Parry tried to appease him. 'It's no fault of yours, Oliver. You did all you could. You delivered him into the hands of the authorities and passed the responsibility of dispensing justice to the Governor of the Azores.'

'Hah!'

'Your conduct goes without question.'

'You think so?' the captain replied sharply, not seeking or waiting for an answer. 'I had the point of my blade to his throat. I should have run him though and thrown his carcass to the sharks. Why on earth didn't I?'

'A code of honour, perhaps?'

'Honour!' he scoffed. 'Huff! Would you spare a rat if you found it in the bread room?'

There was nothing more the lieutenant could say to mollify his captain's black mood. Nor was there anything that could be done to alter the situation that now existed.

Oliver stared at the empty horizon. 'I promise you this, I will not rest until I find him.'

Simon placed his hands on the edge of the table and took a deep breath before speaking. 'The men are not happy that we continue to circle the islands.'

'Damn the men. Damn the mission. Damn my orders. This is my command!'

The lieutenant continued unperturbed. 'They know you are searching for van Zetten. It's all they talk about.'

'What of it? I shall continue to search for him as long as I deem fit. I don't understand what the problem is.'

'There is an underlying current of discontent. I'm not sure what has caused it. Perhaps it is fear. Perhaps it was sparked by the atrocities the men witnessed on the beach or by the treatment received by those who were held captive on the *San Nicola*. But whatever tales are circulating about this pirate, they are growing out of all proportion. Besides which, the crew are aware this scoundrel now has two ships and probably more guns in total than we carry.'

'Tittle-tattle, Simon. I am surprised you listen to it.'

'With respect, sir, if you walked the deck, you would recognize that morale is low. While the crew that has served with you for several years has always held you in high esteem, questions are being asked. The men are anxious to sail from here and reach Rio de Janeiro but, I fear, if this state of tension continues, when we make port many will depart the ship and sign on any available ship heading north.'

'Anything else?' Oliver demanded.

Given the opportunity to speak, he continued. 'The men argue that sailing into the Southern Ocean offers little chance of rich prizes, or any prizes for that matter. At the present, they are confronted with the possibility of being blown to pieces, or being captured and subjected to torture and death.'

Controlling his temper, Oliver said nothing, walked to the cabin door and opened it. 'Casson!' he called.

There was a muffled reply from without.

'A bottle of brandy and two glasses.' After closing the door, he returned to the table and sat down.

Simon Parry's revelations came as no surprise. He was aware of his own shortcomings but was loath to admit them to anyone, not least himself. The depressed mood he had suffered in Gibraltar had never fully left him. He had blamed himself for Susanna's death and now those gnawing pangs of anger and guilt had been reignited by the frustration of not dealing with the pirate effectively.

The tension between the two officers was not eased when Casson entered balancing two Waterford crystal glasses and a bottle on a tray. 'A fine drop of French Brandy courtesy of Monshure Napoleon,' the steward said with a smile.

'Thank, you,' Simon Parry replied politely.

Oliver poured the brandy and pushed one of the glasses towards his first officer. After swilling the liquid around the glass, he inhaled its bouquet, filled his mouth and swallowed. Leaning back in his chair, he spent several minutes musing over the words his lieutenant had delivered so directly.

Simon Parry was correct. It was no fault of his that Fredrik van Zetten was back at sea and, for this, he had no reason to feel any guilt or recriminations. Certainly, he was justified in feeling angry, especially after the effort it had taken to bring the man to justice, plus the fact he had put every man under his command at risk. But his abhorrence of the pirate was all-consuming, as was his present preoccupation with recapturing him and his ship. He realized the desire to do so had become an obsession.

Glancing over his shoulder to his writing desk, he thought of the Admiralty's orders enclosed in an envelope in the top drawer. They clearly indicated that he should proceed on his mission with all haste. Thus far he had not complied with those instructions. Sailing north via the Azores, then chasing a foreign ship, not even an enemy ship, in endless circles around the Fernando de Noronha islands was not part of them. The fact the pirate had followed him across the Atlantic was no fault of his either, therefore, he was not responsible for the situation he found himself in. Yet, knowing all this, the fate of the Portuguese frigate, *Pomba Branca*, and its crew lay heavily on his shoulders.

'Simon,' he said. 'I admit, you are right in all you say. We must prepare to sail for Rio. As for van Zetten, if he is determined to find me, let him do so. It will save me the time and trouble of searching for him.'

Less than an hour later there was another knock at the captain's door.

'Come in,' the captain called.

The two men who entered looked rather sheepish. Both were artisans, first and foremost, and sailors second.

'Begging your pardon, sir, but Mr Parry suggested that what we had to say was best for your ears.' The carpenter turned to the young man beside him. 'I think you know William Ethridge.'

Oliver acknowledged him with a nod and a feeling of guilt for not taking time to speak with the shipwright who had saved his previous command in the freezing waters of the Southern Ocean. 'Good to have you aboard.' Then, as if to excuse his omission, 'My time had been occupied. What is it, Mr Crosby?'

'It's about that privateer, sir.'

'Mr Crosby, let me remind you, a privateer is an armed ship under the command of a private individual who holds a government licence authorizing the attack and capture of enemy vessels during times of war. Captured ships, under such authority, are brought before an admiralty prize court for sale. The prize money is then split between the state that issued the Letter of Marque and the privateer who captured it. Furthermore, privateers agree to the humane treatment of prisoners. Tell me Mr Crosby, do you believe Captain van Zetten complies with these requirements?'

'No, Captain,' the carpenter admitted.

'Indeed. That is why I prefer to call him a pirate.'

'Yes, sir.'

'What is it you wanted to speak with me about?'

'Well, as you know, young Will 'ere and I was sent aboard to fix up the leaks in his ship so we know what condition it's in. Now, we hear he's taken on spars and guns from the frigate he sank in the cove.'

'I am listening,' the captain said.

'When we were aboard the *San Nicola*, we were told we had repairs to make—and plenty of work there was, too. We learnt the captain had lost his carpenters weeks earlier from scurvy, so when anything went wrong, nothing was done about it. He kept us busy twenty-two hours out of every twenty-four and hardly fed us.'

'I'm sorry to hear that.'

'I ain't complaining,' Mr Crosby said. 'I've known worse and I don't mind hard work. The fact is, when we went aboard, the well had over two feet of water in it and some of the empty barrels were just floating about in the hold. You couldn't walk over parts of the ballast. It was like quicksand even though the pumps were being operated all day. But me and Will had a job to do and we set about fixing the worse of the leaks as best we could.'

The expression on the carpenter's face grew serious, 'She's a tired ship, Captain, and she's very wormy. She's never been coppered and she's spent years in tropical waters. Will and I agree most of the hull is riddled with holes. Both sides of the hull seep constantly, like tears running down an infant's cheeks.'

Will Ethridge took up the story. 'But apart from being given the job of fixing the leaks, which was near impossible, the captain wanted ports cutting into the hull on the lower deck. He wanted to create another gun deck and make the ship into something like a man-of-war.'

'And did you do that?'

'No, there wasn't enough time. We had marked out where the guns could be located along both port and starboard sides, but we never laid so much as a chisel or a drill on the planks before you arrived and took the ship.'

'So what are you telling me?'

Will explained. 'If Captain van Zetten took some of the nine and twelve-pounders from the Portuguese frigate and hoisted them onto his own ship, he had no carpenters or shipwrights to prepare the lower deck to accommodate them. That means the guns would have to remain on the weather deck, if he intended to fire them. So, Mr Crosby and I reckon the ship is not only unseaworthy, but it's top-heavy.'

'That's just our opinion for what it's worth,' the ship's carpenter added. 'But I, for one, wouldn't want to be aboard a top-heavy ship in a rough sea.'

'Thank you, Mr Crosby. I will certainly take your advice into consideration if we should encounter the *San Nicola* again. However, my searches have proved unsuccessful and I can only presume she had headed west and is probably anchored at one of the slave ports on the Brazilian coast right now.'

The men knuckled their foreheads and turned to go.

'Your wife and her companion—how are they faring?' Oliver asked.

'As well as can be expected, Captain. Like everyone aboard, they are looking forward to making landfall before too long.'

'Indeed, I think we all are.'

Oliver was still not convinced van Zetten had left the location, however, he knew he could waste no more time chasing shadows. Despite the assurance from his officers the danger was long gone, he insisted the crew remain at their stations until the volcanic peaks of Fernando de Noronha had turned from purple to mauve, before eventually sinking beneath the horizon.

The port of Rio de Janeiro was fifteen hundred miles away and it was imperative the sinking of the naval frigate was reported to the Portuguese authorities there. Oliver's hope was that, when they arrived, they would find the other frigate safely anchored in Guanabara Bay.

With the wind failing and the ship reduced to only two knots, Captain Quintrell took to his cot and slept well for the first time in days.

It was February and, in the tropical latitudes, the air was oppressive and clouds seen as infrequently as land gulls. Though the wind was in danger of dying completely, a strong swell was rolling beneath the keel. Driven by the South Equatorial Current, the troughs were broad and deep, the undulations visible on the horizon. *Perpetual* was heading south-south-west running parallel with the coast of Brazil, but staying well clear of it. According to the sailing master's calculation, they were now nine hundred miles from Rio de Janeiro.

Overnight the wind dropped even more, with only the occasional light zephyr to tease the sails. The swell, however was relentless slowly pushing them toward the coast. Making little headway, the frigate pitched and rolled uncomfortably sliding side-on into the troughs of non-breaking waves while being twisted and lifted to the top of the next ridge of sea.

Having resolved to take time to catch up on his journal entries, Oliver was frustrated by the ship's movement. With every roll or pitch, the inkpot was in danger of emptying its contents over the page he was writing or sliding off his desk and staining the deck. Closing the lid, he returned the writing materials to his desk drawer.

'Begging pardon, Capt'n. Mr Parry requests your attendance on deck. He said to tell you it was fairly urgent.'

'Thank you, Casson. I will come immediately.' Having no need for a coat, he proceeded to the waist and climbed the companionway steps to the quarterdeck.

'Two sails, dead astern, Captain. The lookout says they have been a smudge on the horizon for a while but now he's sure they are ships and most likely the ones you were expecting. He says they are following on the same course we are heading. What are you orders, Captain?'

'We can do nothing, Simon, until we find some wind. In the meantime, have their progress monitored and report any change to me. I want a good man on the log.'

'I doubt we are barely making a knot or two at the most,' the sailing master advised.

Taking his glass, Oliver looked dead astern and ran his glass along the horizon. It was not easy to see the specks of canvas the lookout had identified as ships, but the height of the masthead above the deck gave the sailor an advantage. Even so, at this distance it would be easy to confuse two grey dots with flecks of cloud and ignore them.

'The man has good eyes. Is he convinced it's van Zetten's ship and the schooner?'

'Without a doubt, sir,' Mr Parry said. 'Trust him.'

Two hours later, there was barely a breath of wind over their stretch of ocean, yet according to the lookout, the two following ships had gained on the frigate, albeit only slightly, and the hulls were now visible.

'What does the lead read?'

'No bottom, sir,' Mr Tully replied.

'No chance of kedging her,' the captain murmured. He turned to the officer-of-the-watch. 'I want four boats in the water. We tow.'

Mr Tully responded with a burst of enthusiasm in his tone. 'Aye, aye, Captain,' he said. Striding from the quarterdeck, he called for the boat crews and for hands to sway out the boats. Though the men were quick to respond, they were less enthusiastic in their performance. The task of towing a fully crewed and laden frigate with four boats was near impossible, particularly with the rising and falling ocean swell. But, at least, putting the boats in the water was a break from the monotony on deck.

Oliver observed the creases furrowing Mr Parry's brow, but the lieutenant did not speak. 'I presume you are wondering why I do not heave to and wait for those two ships in order to stand and fight.'

'Captain, I don't question your orders but you had expressed a desire to meet this predator head on.'

'That is so,' Oliver said. 'I intend to stand and fight when we have the advantage. However, whatever little wind there is at present is not favouring us. For as long as those ships have the weather gage, I will not turn and fight. For the time being, I desire to stay ahead of them until the wind changes. However, when that happens, you are at liberty to put the same question to me and you will receive the answer you were hoping to hear.'

With the boats in the water hauling on four heavy hawsers, the attempt to make any headway was proving to be a futile and exhausting exercise. To exacerbate the situation, at times a mischievous wind whirled across the water, luffing the sails and halting the frigate, at times pushing it back in the direction from which it had come. The addition of the lower studding sails made no difference, as there was no air to fill them. Fortunately, for the present, the two following ships appeared anchored to the horizon and unable to make any headway from there, either.

Oliver studied the sky. Ominous dark clouds were gathering far off in the west emanating over the vast areas of tropical jungles that covered much of the country. The officers on the quarterdeck argued about the possibility of any wind or rain reaching them, but it was speculation and only time would tell if that was going to eventuate.

'Return the boats, Mr Tully.'

'Aye, aye, Capt'n.'

It took half an hour for the crews to return to the ship and the boats to be swung aboard and stowed. Then the order was given for all hands to their stations. From the quarterdeck, the officers were watching the men in the waist when a loose barrel rumbled across the deck and crashed into one of the gun carriages. As the staves separated from each other, the top iron ring rolled along the deck like a boy's hoop being hit by a stick down an alley. Fortunately, the barrel had only been used to hold brooms and mops and did not hit anyone. But a rogue barrel could easily break a man's leg if he got in its way. It was a reminder to have everything lashed down securely.

Having maintained the same heading throughout the day, Oliver ordered a change.

'West, helmsman. Let us see if our visitors follow our lead.'

While making little headway, the stern swung across and the prow pointed to the west. The change in direction was mirrored by the following ships.

As the afternoon progressed, the ominous clouds grew and darkened, the curtains of a gathering storm closed across the sky.

'There is a squall coming,' Mr Mundy observed. 'If we stay on this heading, it will hit us head on. Shouldn't we spill some wind from the sail?'

'Take the studding sails in. Stow the royals and t'gan'sls, and the fores'l and mains'l.'

'Aye, Capt'n.'

'Mr Parry, I need you to watch the storm as it approaches. When it is almost on us, give the order to come about. I want the weather to engulf us so the manoeuver will not be seen.'

'But if the squall slams into us, it could lay us on our beam ends,' the sailing master said.

'Not if we make the turn before the wind hits. The timing will be crucial.'

'Once we are around, we will have the weather gage in our favour. Then we head directly for the two ships.'

'That will be uncomfortable.'

The captain paid no heed to the sailing master's remark. It was something he already anticipated. In fact, the motion of the sea was one thing he hoped to harness to his advantage. 'If the squall is as strong as I expect, it will bring heavy rain, and possibly hail and we will be completely lost to view until it has blown over.'

'What if the wind drops or changes direction?' Mr Mundy asked.

'And what if St Elmo's fire dances along the yards and strikes down our main mast?' Oliver replied cynically. 'You have your instructions.'

Chapter 19

The Noose

The roiling mass of black and charcoal clouds was tinged with swirling bursts of orange and pink while, beneath it, skirts of dark rain moved silently back and forth over the sea. Lightning flashed from within the twisting mass like a distant beacon, but the storm was too far away for the sound of thunder to carry. At times, rays of sunlight broke through like spokes on a wheel slicing the storm into wedge-shaped portions and delivering pools of shining white light onto the dark ocean.

With all hands on deck ready to bring the frigate about, the men knew they would have to work quickly. To be caught in irons would spell disaster.

'Once we come around, head for the following ships and, hopefully, surprise them. Helmsman, your job is to put *Perpetual* between them.' Oliver's bold plan, when he reached them, was to fire from guns on both port and starboard sides. The gun crews had been instructed to aim for the masts and rigging.

'Do not sink the *San Nicola*,' he ordered. 'She has probably got half the Portuguese Navy in her hold.' He also warned them not to open the gunports until they had completed the turn.

'But what if the rain is not heavy enough to provide cover?'

'Mr Mundy, if the conditions change, I will issue new orders. I have no time for your negativity. Repair to your station.'

The captain's tone was sufficient to disperse the midshipmen who had been hovering around.

Oliver Quintrell's brow furrowed. Though he sounded confident, he was far from it. It was a daring plan riddled with danger, improbabilities and unanswered questions. The points Mr Mundy had raised were all valid, though he did not appreciate being reminded of what could go wrong. It was not possible to be sure when or where the squall would hit or what direction the wind would blow from. The gathering curtains of rain were moving, coalescing and then dividing again and there was no guarantee they would envelop the ship when most needed. Furthermore, if *Perpetual* did not come about in time, being hit head on by a gale of wind with too much canvas flying could easily bring down a mast or rip the sails to shreds. As the sailing master had pointed out, if the wind slammed into the ship before the turn was complete, it could lay the frigate over and, if any of the ports were open, the sea would flood in and take her to the bottom.

Then there was the question of the two following ships. Would they hold their course and stand and fight, or turn from the storm as he was doing? Another thing the captain did not know was how many guns the two ships had between them. And how determined was van Zetten to catch him? He considered he already knew the answer to that question. Apart from that, if the hull of *San Nicola* was as riddled with holes as the carpenters has indicated, would a single shot below the waterline sink her?

Before the squall hit, the schooner and fully-rigged ship were gaining a little. Both could be seen as they were lifted to the top of the swell before sliding down into the next trough. The motion was that of a rocked cradle, the masts arcing dramatically from one side to the other.

Observing the *San Nicola* through his telescope, the sailing master saw a section of the cap rail suddenly blow out, as if it had been hit by a shot fired from within the ship. It soon became apparent that, as the ship heeled, a gun on the weather deck had broken its lines and crashed through the rail. With its rear carriage wheels firmly lodged in the splintered gunwale, the cannon balanced precariously. When the hull slid beam-end towards the bottom of the trough, the barrel dropped into the sea trailing its tackle behind it, leaving the carriage dangling over the side of the ship held only by its breeching lines. If there were any other guns on the deck that had not been securely fastened, they, too, could cause havoc and cost lives. Never were a ship's gun crews in such mortal danger.

Having watched the drama unfold and provided his own commentary, the sailing master closed his telescope. 'She's top-heavy,' he announced.

'Thank you, Mr Mundy. I have been aware of that for some time and have been expecting such an event to occur.' Turning his back on the sailing master, Captain Quintrell made his way to the binnacle and waited for the storm to arrive.

The fierce squall was violent, and the speed with which it descended on the frigate was amazing. A cross-wind rattled the luffs. It preceded a brief and ominous calm before a solid front of rain charged across the sea churning up the surface like a huge pod of porpoises bearing down on them. The rain bounced back off the surface as if hitting solid rock. The sea heaved in response. Then the sky closed in completely, enveloping the frigate in a pocket of weird aqua light through which they could see no further than a few yards in any direction. When the full force of the wind struck, it ripped foretopsail, carried away the outer jib and pitched the bowsprit deep into a wall of water that wanted to hang onto it. The foremast creaked and swayed but held. As the head came around, the frigate heeled over, listing far further than when she had been careened.

Perpetual's crew completed the manoeuvre successfully, though with no time to spare. Had the crew not worked quickly, the vessel would not have survived. Now the wind was behind her driving her towards the point where the two ships had last been seen.

When the cloud suddenly lifted and the rain cleared, only *San Nicola* could be seen ahead of them. The schooner had parted company and was heading south making good time. Was it possible the original crew of the East Indiaman had managed to retake the schooner during the confusion? Oliver wondered. He hoped that was the case. Or perhaps van Zetten's men who were in command of that vessel were tired of being at the beck and call of a murderous dog and had decided it was time to part company.

'Should we go after it?' Mr Parry asked.

'No, let it go. I will deal with that one later. It's van Zetten I want.'

But, like himself, the pirate had anticipated when the squall would strike and had worn his ship around. He was now completing his turn, tacking and coming back on his previous course and the distance separating the British frigate and *San Nicola* was less than a mile.

Suddenly a ball whizzed through the air and splashed into the water dropping a hundred yards short of *Perpetual's* bow.

'Forward guns. Prepare to fire.'

The captain's plans had been dashed. But at least he had the weather gage in his favour and he intended to take the pirate before he had the chance to escape. While the frigate had 32 guns, it was possible van Zetten had more, but he doubted his opponent had sufficient trained gun crews to fire them, and, with a top-heavy ship, anything could happen.

He repeated his previous instructions to his lieutenants. 'Have your crews fire for the masts and rigging. I want that ship brought to its knees.'

The challenge for the gun captains was to choose the exact moment. To fire on the up-roll was to discharge the shot into thin air, and to fire on the down roll would lodge the ball in the ocean. There was little point in ordering the marines into the tops, as they needed two hands to climb and were more likely to drop their weapons than get off a successful shot.

With the gap shortened *Perpetual* sailed to within firing distance. A shot splashed into the water after failing to reach the deck. On deck, the men ducked when grape and canister sailed overhead poking holes in the canvas.

On the call from the division captains, the frigate's guns jumped into life, deafening those on the gun deck and rattling the frigate's fibres from bow to stern. As the frigate was manoeuvred parallel to the ship, the muzzles were raised to fire at the rigging, the guns loaded and rolled out and fired. Choking on the acrid smoke, the gun crews could barely see as they swabbed out the barrels, reloaded and rolled out the guns again.

In response, the numerous small swivel guns on *San Nicola*'s deck peppered the frigate's deck, putting more holes in the topsails and topgallants. Smoke belched from the 9-pounders on the pirate's deck but the crew's aim was poor.

San Nicola's forestay twanged and whipped wildly when a shot from one of Perpetual's guns severed it. A loud crack followed. The foretopmast toppled but it failed to reach the deck. Threatening to drop at any minute, it hung suspended by its lines draping a huge curtain of sail across the width of the foredeck.

'From here, I can put a shot below her waterline,' Mr Tully claimed.

'No,' Captain Quintrell argued. 'That will sink her and the prisoners who are aboard do not deserve to die. I intend to take her. Free the prisoners. Then you can consider blowing her to Kingdom come.'

'Aye, aye, Captain.'

Drifting alongside, *Perpetual* unleashed a full broadside into van Zetten's sails and rigging, ripping the main and mizzen to shreds. With the remnants of his canvas aback, the pirate's ship made no headway.

'Spray the deck,' the captain called. 'Knock out the swivel guns. Bring her in close enough to board.'

Aboard *San Nicola*, van Zetten was yelling commands and his men were firing wildly when a direct hit on the hull jolted the frigate.

'Send the carpenter below to assess the damage. Helmsman—bring me closer.' The boarding party had already gathered in the waist and was waiting for the call to come up.

'Marines to the rigging,' Oliver yelled, 'Prepare to board.'

With the cracking sound of timbers splintering, the bow of the frigate ground along the side of the old ship. A dozen grapnels were tossed through the smoke to the opposing rail bridging the gap between the two hulls.

'Perpetuals with me!' Captain Quintrell called. At the command, sailors streamed up from the waist, rushed across the deck and reached for the lines hanging from the fallen rigging to haul themselves aboard the enemy ship.

Surrounded by a mob of his men, Oliver clambered aboard and jumped down on to the deck. But, when the smoke cleared, the scene that met him was not what had been expected. Swaying to the motion of the sea, a line of men faced him, their wrists bound with rope, their arms held out in front of them. The line ran along the length of the ship. Behind it were the faces of men holding knives to the prisoners' throats. The Portuguese sailors formed a human shield protecting the pirate and his crew.

'Don't fire!' Oliver ordered.'

Fredrik van Zetten's voice boomed out triumphantly. 'You will drop your weapons or every one of these men will be killed.'

No one moved.

'Don't listen to him!' The words shouted in English came from a man in the line. He was not wearing his dress uniform, but Oliver recognized Captain Espada of the Portuguese Navy.

'Death to this Devil!' he cried.

No sooner had he spoken than a cutlass was raised over Captain Espada's head and brought down with Almighty force, splitting his skull and slicing his face down to his nose.

The frightened seamen, who had served him, froze.

'Van Zetten,' Oliver yelled, 'you are a coward. You hide behind defenceless men. You do not frighten me. I am here to take you and your ship. And, this time, you will not escape.'

'Never,' van Zetten screamed, leaping onto the fife rail at the base of the mainmast. 'Death to the English dogs!' he cried, raising his sword above his head.

At their captain's sign, knives sliced across the pale throats of the defenceless prisoners and blood spurted across the deck. Immediately, the boarding party leapt forward deliberately knocking aside the Portuguese sailors, who were still standing, aiming their weapons at the brigands hiding behind them. Armed with cutlasses and pistols, the first shots brought down more than a dozen of the rebels. The fight was brutal. The marauders' deadly mode of fighting was to slash wildly at arms and legs to cut their opponent down.

Unlike the previous fight where capstan bars, boathooks and belying pins has been the crews' only weapons, this time they were armed with pistols, knives, boarding pikes and cutlasses. Cold steel cut and clanged as Quintrell's men battled van Zetten's crew.

With wrists still tied, the Portuguese sailors who had survived the massacre, dived under the boats for cover or tried to escape from *San Nicola* by clambering over the fallen spars and taking refuge on the frigate. Those lucky enough to pick up a discarded blade cut their bonds and screamed revenge for the death of their shipmates. Skulls were broken, eyes gouged, necks snapped, bellies sliced open. Entangled around one man's feet were the slippery entrails from one victim. They were dragged across the deck. Blood, escaping along the seams, decorated the deck with red stripes.

With his naval sword glinting in the burst of sunlight, Oliver Quintrell thrust forward edging his way through the *mêlée* in search of the one opponent he wanted to confront. But there was no sign of van Zetten. *Was he dead already?* he wondered.

Then a swivel gun, fired from the poop, showered small shot across the deck. A dozen men from both sides fell to the grape, either dead or mortally wounded. Standing defiantly beside the gun, waiting for it to be reloaded, was Captain van Zetten.

Oliver roared as he headed forward directly into the muzzle. Lifting his weapon, he slashed the arm holding the slow-match, the power of his blow almost severing the hand from the gunner's wrist.

The pirate glowered at him from the far side of the gun. 'Ha,' he taunted, 'you will never take me.'

The challenge sent a thrill spiralling down Oliver's spine. 'We shall see,' he replied.

At that moment, Ben Tully leapt up beside him, the cocked pistol in his hand pointing directly at the pirate's head.

'Not this time,' Oliver yelled, knocking the barrel aside. 'The rat is mine.'

The coward leapt back from the swivel gun and drew his sword. Oliver noticed the bandage around his arm, the legacy from their previous encounter. But his own hand still bore the scratch from that fight, and with only half a hand to grip the hilt of his sword, he had no sympathy for the pirate's injury.

Despite flashes of action in the corners of his eyes, Oliver's attention was on the man a few yards away from him.

Slashing his curved blade in great sweeps from left to right, van Zetten paid no heed to the men fighting alongside him and never flinched when he sliced the cheek of one of Oliver's men and the thigh of one of his own.

Thrusting forward, Oliver advanced inch by inch. The swords rang when they met. The razor-sharp blades flashed in the sun. A breath of wind kissed the captain's face as van Zetten's blade sliced even closer. Oliver parried, then pushed the renegade back with lightning quick thrusts until his adversary bumped up against a man fighting behind him. He was unable to retreat any further. In that instant, Oliver darted his blade forward and thrust the point deep in van Zetten's chest.

When he withdrew his sword, a *whoosh* of air escaped before blood spurted from the gaping wound. The pirate's eyes blazed and his jaw dropped open but no sound came out. Before his hand reached to his chest to stop the flow, his legs buckled beneath him and he crumpled to the deck.

Sanding over him, Oliver turned to face his men, 'The dog is dead,' he yelled.

Within seconds, the fighting stopped. Men moaned or cried as they clutched their wounds. Others dropped to the scuppers and sat in silence while their blood flowed over the ship's side. The realization of victory struck the Perpetuals and a cheer rang out. It was echoed from the deck of the British frigate.

'What do you want me to do with the body?' Mr Tully asked.

'Get this pig's carcass off the deck and over the side. I refuse to give him a Christian burial. Damn him!' Oliver cursed. 'The blackguard even denied me the pleasure of seeing him hang from the yard.'

His second lieutenant was standing beside him. 'Why not string him up anyway?' Mr Tully suggested. 'That's what they did with pirates in the old days.'

The captain shook his head, then pondered for a moment. 'Make me a noose from a short length of rope. Then drag this rogue's carcass to the mizzen and lash him to it. I will decide what to do with him later.'

'Captain,' William Ethridge called urgently. 'The ship is listing. I think she's going down.'

'Go below and check the damage. See how much water she's taken in. Tell me how long we have before we lose her.'

'Aye, aye, Captain.'

'Mr Nightingale, go with him and be smart about it.'

The pair hurried away, scrambling over fallen rigging and the bodies of sailors, both dead and living. There was no option for the victims but to throw them over the side. For those that had survived the fight, the difficulty was in determining on whose side each sailor had served. The blood-splattered naval issue worn by the crew of *Pomba Branca* was one indication, and the ugly faces of some of the rogue crew were also recognized. Sorting the remaining Portuguese sailors who had stood bravely on deck beside Captain Espada, from the cut-throats who followed van Zetten was not easy.

'Line the scoundrels up along the rail and shackle them,' Captain Quintrell called, as a weird feeling of *déjà vu* flashed through his head. *Was it worth the trouble of taking these men to Rio? Would the Portuguese authorities listen to him this time and take heed of their participation in the atrocities? Or would they do nothing? Was he wasting his time and putting his men at risk yet again?*

This time, however, van Zetten and his crew had not merely stolen a merchant ship and murdered a few insignificant villagers, they had attacked and sunk a Portuguese naval frigate, killed its captain and murdered many of its crew. This time, they must pay for their crimes.

'Bosun,' the captain yelled. 'Rig up a gangway between the two ships. We must get everyone off. I want the prisoners transferred to *Perpetual*'s hold. Make sure you have enough men with you and stand no nonsense. Shoot the first man who tries to escape. Then batten the hatches securely and have a dozen men stand guard.'

As the bosun hurried away, Mr Tully returned. In his blood-stained hands he held a well-formed noose, neatly tied, made from a length of salt-hardened line. 'Is this what you want?' he asked.

Oliver Quintrell looked at his second lieutenant, a man who had entered the service through the hawse hole. Perhaps he would understand. Striding aft to the mizzen, the captain considered the lifeless body of Fredrik van Zetten. Having lifted the corpse to a seated position on the rail, Mr Tully had rested the rogue's back against the mast and lashed him to it.

Without any sign of emotion, Oliver placed the noose over the pirate's head and, after tightening the knot around his neck, allowed the remaining line to drop to the deck.

'So be it,' he said. 'This is the least I can do.' His gesture and words were not meant as an expression of victory or an apology, but as an offering to the numerous souls who had perished at the hand of the pirate, and to the villagers to whom he had given his promise.

The voice of the young carpenter distracted him. 'Five feet and rising, sir. She won't stay afloat much longer.'

The captain turned to his lieutenant. 'Get everyone back on board the frigate, then make sure *Perpetual* is well clear before this ship goes down. I don't want her taking us with her.'

Half an hour later, with *Perpetual* hove to only fifty yards from the stricken ship, British and Portuguese seamen stood shoulder to shoulder along the rail to witness *San Nicola*'s final moments. Her hull, already riddled with holes drilled by the sharp beaks of the Teredo worm, had finally succumbed to the bite of a nine-pound iron shot.

Her dive to the deep was slow and graceful, the sea first licking her bow and fo'c'sle, before washing along the deck and lapping the poop. With her head down, the ship's stern heaved up slightly and the water rushed aft towards the mizzen. The pirate, lashed to the mast with a noose fixed around his neck, was the last thing to be seen as the ship sank.

There were no cheers or tears as the sea swallowed him up. Fredrik van Zetten had finally met the fate he deserved.

Chapter 20

EPILOGUE

As the British frigate headed south, with over two hundred and fifty souls aboard, Captain Quintrell prayed for following winds and calm seas. On arrival in Rio de Janeiro, his priority was to speak with the authorities and despatch his prisoners—for the second time. They now numbered only twenty-five. While several had been killed in the fight, the remainder of van Zetten's men had escaped on the schooner that had slipped away in the storm. It was unlikely those men would ever be caught.

On reaching Rio, the badly wounded sailors, being cared for in the cockpit and on deck, would be transferred to the hospital. Once that business was attended to, Oliver intended to visit the victualling store and replenish the supplies that had been used. It had been a short, but tumultuous, Atlantic crossing beset by a series of unexpected eventualities, but he was confident he would make Rio without encountering any further problems.

The surviving officers and sailors off the *Pomba Branca* looked forward to reaching Portuguese waters where they would be ferried ashore and, no doubt, be signed on another naval vessel. Oliver also expected five of the six Irishmen who had joined the ship in Ponta Delgada to leave the ship, but with no money and little due to them when they were paid off, they, too, would need to sign on another ship if they hoped to sail to North America.

Michael O'Connor, however, had proved to be an efficient scribe and it was Oliver's intention to speak with him before they dropped anchor and suggest he remain on board. If so, his name would be entered in the muster book as captain's secretary.

As for the two females, he would again ask Mr Crosby if his wife and Mrs Pilkington wished to return home, although he doubted they would do so. This time, he had no intention of raising objections. Both women had proved useful in the cockpit and displayed no more fear than the rest of the crew when they were engaged in the fight.

During the last week, he had observed an improvement in the health and confidence of Consuela Pilkington and noted that, when called on, she had adopted the role of matronly confidante to the ship's boys. While this sort of relationship was not to be encouraged on a naval vessel, he could find no real reason to object to it. He had also noted that Mr Whipple showed a particular interest in the young Spanish-born widow's welfare. It was the expression in the doctor's eyes, when he looked at her, which gave that impression.

Thanks to Providence and the care afforded to him by Dr Whipple and Mr Crosby, Bungs' condition was continuing to improve. Without the need for surgery, the swelling on the side of the cooper's head had resolved. The bruising had also gone and he was able to stand for short periods of time. Being able to recognise people meant Bungs looked forward to the visits from his friends, though the surgeon insisted they did not talk to him for long periods or share jokes with him. He was anxious his patient's brain should not be over-stimulated. It was a relief for Will, Eku and young Tommy Wainwright to see their mate improving. His banter was missed at the mess table.

Though it would be some time before Bungs regained his full mental capacity and was capable of resuming regular duties, having been on death's doorstep for so long, Mr Whipple regarded his recovery as something of a miracle.

Being preoccupied with the problems confronting his crew, the captain had been delinquent in attending to his own affairs. He had not written to his wife, Victoria, since they had left Gibraltar. He could blame that on many things, including the injury to his hand, but he knew it was merely an excuse. It was something he intended to rectify very shortly.

Despite the events of the previous weeks, *Perpetual* was in surprisingly sound condition. It had weathered the storms with little more than a few scratches. New sails had been bent, lines spliced and the damage to the hull repaired. Now he was looking forward to heading south to gain the Roaring Forties—the most dependable winds travelling around the globe.

Accompanied by a flock of black frigate birds gliding gracefully overhead, the British frigate sailed silently past the impressive Sugar Loaf peak and drifted onto the broad waters of Guanabara Bay. Its safe delivery was marked by a cheer from the men on deck. It was an acknowledgement of relief rather than celebration.

The sight of the missing Portuguese frigate swinging from its anchor in the bay was met with mixed reactions, and little was said about it. Oliver Quintrell's immediate attention was drawn to a British 74-gun man-of-war anchored a cable's length away. It warmed his heart to see it.

Once the most pressing necessities of the port had been attended to, Oliver Quintrell accepted an invitation from the captain of the third-rate to pay him a visit. William Liversedge was an old friend who he had encountered on a previous mission.

Stepping on deck, Oliver was particularly delighted to be reacquainted with two officers who had served with him in the past—Lieutenant Hazzlewood and young Midshipman Smith. Having despatched the pair to Kingston in charge of a prize vessel, he hoped to speak with them both at length while they were in port.

'You came in well laden,' Captain Liversedge said, when the pair was alone in the cabin. 'That probably explains why your arrival was later than expected.'

'We do what we have to do,' Oliver said, 'and sometimes it takes a little longer than expected.'

'I am sure you will tell me all about your cruise in due course. But, first, I have something for you.'

Oliver was puzzled. 'This meeting is not by chance then?'

'Not entirely,' his old friend replied.

'I was instructed to meet with you and personally deliver your Admiralty orders.'

'But I have my orders,' Oliver said.

'I fear those are a little out of date. These were sealed in Whitehall only two days after Spain declared its allegiance to Napoleon. I sailed from England two days later. As I am sure you can imagine, many things have changed since you left England, indeed, since you left Gibraltar.'

'So I am discovering.'

'—Britain's relationship with Spain. The Emperor. The war. The lack of money in the Treasury.'

'The usual,' Oliver added, looking down at the envelope his friend handed to him. On the reverse side it carried the Admiralty's red wax seal and on the face, his name, his command, and the word

SECRET stamped across the top. He turned it over in his hands, but did not open it.

'There have been several policy changes since Spain joined forces with Napoleon. Britain now faces a bigger enemy. The cost of war is escalating daily and England needs all the ships it can muster. Tension is mounting, both at Whitehall and on the water, and it is considered that within the coming months there will be a major confrontation with the combined Franco/Spanish navies.'

'I would not want to miss that,' Oliver said.

'I hear you had a privateer snapping at your heels,' William Liversedge said.

'Hardly a privateer,' Oliver replied, with a glint in his eye. 'This demon had me so preoccupied, I gave little thought to the coins I was carrying. Ironically, the brigand was blissfully unaware I had cases of Spanish treasure hidden in my hold.' He relaxed and smiled. 'I don't doubt my orders relate to that cache of treasure.'

'I cannot say,' Captain Liversedge said. 'I am not privy to the contents. However, I intend to go on deck and leave you in private for a few moments to read them. Then, if you are at liberty to do so, we shall share a glass of wine and speak about your sailing orders.'

Oliver acknowledged his friend's courtesy and waited until he had left the cabin before breaking the seal.

* * *

Made in the USA
San Bernardino, CA
05 February 2017